Communitas:
Light at the End of the World

Brennan Silver

ISBN: 0692891277
ISBN-13: 978-0692891278

To American warriors of every conflict: past, present, future...
May you find places of belonging and rest for your souls.

CONTENTS

PROLOGUE

When Man is detached from his fellow man, when he is cut off from his heart, no longer aware of his own thoughts, when he buries his soul in refuse and denies the very existence of his spirit, hell has come...and everything Man touches will wither and turn to ash.

✳ ✳ ✳ ✳ ✳

In the not too distant future:

Fueled by human ego and a narcissism of the nations, massive war broke out on a scale not seen since the first half of the twentieth century. Those most involved included old-world names of: Russia, Western Europe, North America, East Asia, Australia, and a theocratic caliphate which arose in the Middle East. For eight horrific years, the planet descended into chilling, pandemic warfare and the Earth itself seemed to groan in agony until the final shots echoed to an eerie silence. During these years, nations within Europe, Africa, South America, and Southeast Asia were utterly decimated and absorbed into the larger powers.

Battles were waged with the most advanced weaponry. Endless rocket barrages rained down from the heavens like hailstorms. Cities were completely obliterated, along with entire tank and infantry regiments. Eight nuclear devices were detonated across the globe in major cities, and chemical attacks were employed against small, impoverished nations.

In previous conflicts of the early twenty first century, individual battles had rarely yielded death counts higher than 3,000 on either side. During this "Last War," as it came to be called, significant clashes between the superpowers regularly resulted in tens of thousands killed in a single day of fighting or major assault.

Initially, citizens and soldiers of most superpowers felt they were fighting in defense of their homelands, for stability, peace, and the preservation of life. As time wore on, however, it became increasingly difficult to distinguish which nation was good and which was evil—who had drawn first blood and what territory belonged to which people. Physical survival grew to be the sole motivation of many soldiers, and "evil" became merely whoever posed the greatest threat in any given moment.

As genocide ravaged South American and African nations, warriors with conscience became the enemies of their own souls. Too many were confronted by the anguished wails of women, the screams of orphaned children, elders crushed under rubble, and black smoke rising from burning villages. By the end of the war, more than half of the Earth's population lay dead, buried, or rotting in the sun. When the world's leaders convened under a truce to assert new, territorial boundaries, only five superpowers remained to rise in rebirth. Although these possessed other, more formal names, the layperson and commoner of the Earth came to refer to these five by the following: Imperial State, Winter Steel, Submission, Mech-Tech, and Unity.

Imperial State was reborn out of the ashes of East Asian powers. Its territory spanned southeast across the continent and also laid claim to old-world Australia and all islands in the Pacific Ocean. Imperial State operated as a brutal communist regime. All religions were banned under penalty of death in its lands. And it was infamous for its labor camps where so-called "Enemies of the State" could be beaten to death by guards or executed without cause before having their organs harvested for the transplant surgery of a ruling czar or to be sold on the black market.

Winter Steel, which arose from the ashes of old-world Russia, claimed all of Europe by the end of the war. Within its iron grasp, it also commanded the entire, conquered continent of Africa as slave and mining colonies. Winter Steel functioned as a radically nationalistic oligarchy. Its people enjoyed more freedoms than the citizens of Imperial State; however, if anyone was ever rumored to have spoken a word of sedition against the government, they were arrested by night, hooded, and never heard from again.

At times, the secret police would also commence raids on society's "undesirables." This typically consisted of rounding up homosexuals, vagrants, the mentally ill, and physically handicapped for extermination or illegal, medical research. Anyone taken by agents of the northern power vanished without a trace. And worried family members learned to not even bother inquiring as to the whereabouts of their missing loved one.

Submission, was born from a massive Wahhabi uprising, which overthrew Middle Eastern monarchies, dictatorships, and democracies alike. Its borders spanned east to old-world India and west to the Nile River. Submission established itself as a theocratic caliphate ruled by a class of fanatically religious clerics and imams.

Within Submission's borders, the clerics demanded

strict adherence to their literal interpretations of sacred texts. Poetic and literary interpretations of the Koran were forbidden and branded as heresies. Sufi-mystics were hunted to extinction. Art was burned and ancient monuments defaced or outright demolished.

In Submission, women were forced to cover themselves from head to toe. Female genital mutilation, child marriage, and honor killings were commonly practiced, as was the stoning of any woman accused of adultery. Jews and Christians were persecuted mercilessly and forced to live as second-class citizens or could be sold as slaves. And any who practiced non-Abrahamic faiths were hunted like dogs and exterminated as subhuman pests.

Mech-Tech, the most technologically advanced of all the superpowers, metastasized out of twenty-first-century, capitalist America. Its lands included the eastern half of the old world's United States, Canada, Alaska, Greenland, and all of the Caribbean islands. It also absorbed the entirety of decimated Central and South Americas for mining and resource harvesting.

During the Last War Mech-Tech had forged its claim to supremacy by creating massive battle machines, complete with artificial intelligence. Amid the years of fighting, it produced vast arsenals of unmanned aircraft, automated defense turrets, and satellite super-lasers. These unleashed awesome devastation upon the Earth, eventually turning the tide of the war in its favor. But the pinnacle of Mech-Tech's war machines arrived late in the bloodbath; it came to be called the "World Reaper." This massive, mechanized unit stood over fifty feet tall and the diameter of its hydraulic legs spanned that of a large sedan. World Reapers wielded enormous energy-weapons, flamethrowers, and machine guns; they were equipped with ground-to-air missiles and hardened against EMP strikes. They could also be airlifted onto the battlefield and even repair themselves mid-combat if damaged.

Mech-Tech was as much an industry giant as it was a political government. Thus, after the war, it turned to operating less like a military superpower and more like an enormous, corporate conglomerate.

Everything and every place that Mech-Tech touched-died. Scorched earth, smoking craters, and oozing sinkholes marred its landscape. The Earth writhed and languished under Mech-Tech's reign. And within its dominion, logging, oil drilling, fracking, and industrial mining never ceased. Day and night the Earth was ravaged for profit and power. The atmosphere thinned above its lands and solar radiation burnt down on its inhabitants with greater intensity than ever before.

Because of the superpower's endless layers of automated defense turrets, Mech-Tech's postwar borders were militarily unassailable. Even so, its citizenry began to die young from poisoning, organ failure, and various cancers. Alternatively, executive elites lived isolated existences in luxurious, air-locked command towers overlooking their mining fields. Insulated from any of the poisons and wreck they had brought about outside, the ruling barons were safeguarded from consequences by wealth and medical advances in cellular regeneration.

At one time, Mech-Tech began experimental mining and drilling endeavors on the Earth's moon. Unfortunately, a catastrophic explosion occurred which resulted in a sizable chunk of the lunar crust being blown off into space. The massive divot scattered across the heavens for all eternity, leaving the moon's spherical shape marred with a gaping hole in its flank.

Tragically for Earth's inhabitants, the fallout was not merely aesthetic. In the wake of the disaster, for several days every month, when the moon was fullest, humans were henceforward seized by fits of uncontrollable nausea, vertigo, hallucinations, headaches, and epilepsy. Animals became dangerous and behaved erratically during full moons; large numbers of fish would die, and entire flocks of birds simply fell out of the sky.

Doomed by the miserable plight of their environs, the people of Mech-Tech fell addicted to pseudo-lives. A breathtaking series of virtual enviro-chambers had been birthed and made available to the common citizen. It did not take long for most residing in Mech-Tech to choose dream worlds over the grim realities of what surrounded them.

In their dream lives, people could do and be anything they wanted. No fantasy or experience was ever denied them or beyond their reach. And so, like a sand timer, people's lives just slipped away...second after precious second. These dreamers forgot their divine and human dignity. They no longer confronted any unwanted challenges; they cared for no one and ceased to interact with the real Earth. They created nothing of beauty, raised no real children, and made no efforts to cultivate true love. These humans existed, undisturbed and uninterrupted, waiting to die, lost and asleep in their own dream-world fantasies.

The fifth and final domain to rise after the Last War was called Unity. It established its borders over the western half of the old world's North America, to the west of the Rocky Mountains. The antithesis of Mech-Tech, it was environmentally conscious on a fanatic level, and its cultural roots were born from the socialist ideals of a politically progressive tide.

Unity prided itself on being tolerant and embracing all peoples, faiths, and lifestyles. Unlike Winter Steel and Submission, Unity welcomed with open arms all gay, lesbian, and transgendered individuals and couples. In odd fashion, it was also true that if Unity citizens wished to identify themselves as a cat, tree, or octopus, it was required that everyone respect this. Communities were expected to interact with all individuals on whatever terms they so desired, without judgment or ridicule.

The shadow side of Unity was that in order to maintain its freedoms, it had to impose endless laws to restrain individuals from ever criticizing or offending one another. As a government, it was also forever mired in gross bureaucracy.

To ensure that no one was ever oppressed, there were laws preventing anyone from speaking ill of another's beliefs. Debate forums were closely monitored and censored. Comparing one's religious faith to another's with the slightest intonation of superiority was a criminal act known as "vilification," and it was branded as a hate crime. Depending on the severity of the offence, vilification could be disciplined by a two-year stay in one of the state's Reeducation Centers. The offender's children would then be removed from the home under the charge that they had suffered "psychological abuse" under the toxic ideologies of their hate mongering parents. All this-to instill greater sensitivity, respectfulness, and consideration for the common good.

Plant life was wildly overgrown in Unity because the jungle-thick flora was protected against pruning.

Naturally, this made infrastructure and ground transportation very difficult to maintain. There were also laws forbidding the killing of or interference with any animal. All animals were to be afforded equal rights of any human citizen. Thus, doors were outlawed in Unity because they might impede a creature's roaming.

As a result, it was difficult to be productive in Unity. Rodent, pest, and cat populations existed at out-of-control levels. A black bear or family of skunks might wander into someone's home or office at any time, and citizens were forbidden to remove or disturb them. If an animal became aggressive or prevented humans from performing their daily tasks, Unity Pacification Forces were called in to *guide* the creature to a mutually satisfactory location. However, the use of tranquilizer darts was forbidden in such instances because it could be considered too harsh or punitive.

Citizens of Unity could adopt animals as legal dependents or even marry them. If the adoptive mother of a chimpanzee wanted to send her chimp child to primary school with human children, it was illegal for anyone to suggest this was in any way strange or inappropriate. And teachers were then forced to accommodate for the animal's learning in the classroom.

Unity citizens did not own their homes; they were provided housing, a living allowance, healthcare, education, and employment-all by the state. Even so,

Unity citizens were continuously scheming new and more elaborate ways to explain why they were incapable of completing an honest day's work. People were rewarded for their complaints rather than their industriousness, and the notion of gratitude was short lived, if ever considered. In this way, Unity kept its citizens loyal through dependence and a culture of entitlement and perpetual victimhood.

There was a price for these luxuries provided by the state, though. Unity citizens were guaranteed "Provision Rights" if they received the chips. In actuality, one could not be a legal citizen of Unity without receiving the chips. There were two: the first chip was implanted deep in the forearm tissue, nestled against the Ulnar Artery. This chip was used for commerce, identification, tracking, and could monitor a citizen's health vitals.

The second chip was implanted in the right temple behind the eye socket. It had direct contact with the brain and could emit electrical signals to pacify the amygdala and prefrontal regions. These chips could neutralize anxiety and inhibition, making a citizen extremely pliable to Unity directives. The chip had a blue light that would blink periodically or glow steadily if a citizen was being pacified. The blue light would illuminate softly behind the right eye socket, making it appear as though the eye itself were glowing.

Most Unity citizens did not hold full-time careers;

they were provided for by the state. Thus, if something in a city needed to be built, repaired, or cleaned, Unity used a computer-based lottery system to randomly select citizens for service. The Blue Chips of those chosen would be activated, and they were then instructed to report to construction sites, food plants, road crews, or Pacification units for service.

There was no civil unrest within recognized settlements of Unity. From its beginning, the Presiding Council had banned all private ownership of weapons. Only Pacification Enforcers were permitted to possess or use firearms. In addition, Reeducation Centers were employed to eradicate "undesirable behaviors" from society. These functioned as brainwashing and conditioning facilities for non-conformers. They also served as stations for chip implantation. Although no one was ever *forced* to take the chips, they might be bludgeoned to death in a Reeducation Center for extended refusal.

After the Last War, Unity's Pacification Forces occasionally stumbled upon bands of peaceful wanderers, loners, or marauding gangs out in the untamed wildlands. Enforcer units were given clear instructions to arrest such outsiders and bring them in for reeducation and citizenship processing or to exterminate them down to the last one. The unpleasant reality was that Unity was friendly only towards those who went along with its ideals. Behind the locked doors and electrified fences of Reeducation Centers, all resistance was cruelly punished.

For all its talk of peace, tolerance, and loving-kindness, no one in Unity ever forgave a wrong. The deeply wounded and embittered Guides of her Presiding Council railed against the most obscure traces of perceived racial, sexist, or homophobic micro-aggression. They preached endlessly of equality and justice but then visited the basement of a Reeducation Camp to witness the execution of an enemy for hate speech. Secret, subtle, masked behind polished politeness, educated eloquence, and restrained tones, Unity's dark side was perhaps the most sinister of all. Its high-minded ends *always* justified its means...

Though starkly contrasted, the five superpowers of the Earth were strangely and deeply alike, especially in their taste for violent retribution towards dissenters. All balance to life had been lost. The world had grown very full of darkness, and it seemed as though it could hold no more. Yet even in the midst of all this darkness, there existed very small lights. This is the record of one such light.

CHAPTER ONE

The buzz of rotor blades was deafening as the helicopter roared across the smoldering city. He could feel the heat radiating against his face from the blaze below.

"One minute!" the female pilot called over their closed-channel radios.

Seated on the edge of the helicopter's open bay, the warrior glanced back at his battle-hardened companions. They were all solid, rugged, and strong men; they had gone to hell and back with him. Still, today they looked nervous. A few stared in silence at the deck of the helicopter or out the bay door at the burning city around them. Others just spaced out, hugging rifles close to their chests.

In a rapid approach, the aircraft dove towards a clearing in the cityscape. The once pristine Baltimore skyline blurred past, gutted and jagged-edged shells of towers jutting upwards like broken knife blades. Pillars of black smoke poured out of gaping holes from hot spots burning deep below.

"Thirty seconds!" the pilot called back.

"Copy," the warrior responded, into his earpiece. He had spotted them—the group of survivors desperately awaiting salvation beside a manmade lake in the park. Some huddled in the water as a final defense against the blazing inferno around them. The warrior knew this city had become a deathtrap; if one of the charred towers that loomed over them fell, they would all perish, survivors and rescuers alike. He unclipped his rifle and passed it off to one of his subordinates. There were no longer any hostile forces on the ground. These refugees were probably the last souls left alive in the city, and he needed his hands free to help them climb aboard.

Then he spotted her in the crowd.

Instinctively, he turned away; he did not want to look, didn't want to see this again. He saw it every night, relived the heat, the pain, the fear in her eyes, over and over and over again. He knew what happened next, how it all ended, and it never ended well... He wished he could escape the scene. He shut his eyes and squeezed them tight.

Then, all at once, he blinked. The images had vanished as quickly as they had seized him. He was back in the woods, sitting on the soft, earthen floor. He felt the cool, dark soil and the underbrush beneath him. His back pressed against the trunk of an oak. He blinked again, surrounded by the lush, green forest, the birds chirping in the canopy above, the gentle breeze that rustled the foliage.

"Daniel," someone whispered his name. "Dan!" The voice held greater urgency this time.

Daniel Weston glanced up, seeing his friend.

Jonas nodded to the left, and Daniel saw it too: a four-point buck grazing in the thicket less than 100 meters away. Lying beside him, Daniel's black Labrador, Sadie, emitted a soft whine and pointed her wet nose towards the deer.

Dan ignored her. She knew better than to make a noise.

He flexed his gloved fingers and felt the grip of his scoped assault-rifle. Slowly, silently, he flicked the safety off and slid his index finger through the trigger guard. He raised the weapon and snugly pressed its butt against his shoulder. The deer looked up, its ears perked, its eyes large and alert. It scanned for movement and any signs of potential danger. Maybe it had heard Sadie or caught their scent. Cautiously, it looked to the right, then back to center. It stared, listening carefully.

Daniel breathed deeply, slowly, calmly… He took up the slack in the trigger, and at the base of an exhale, he squeezed… BOOM! The blast of the gunshot echoed through the woods, reverberating off of trees. The startled deer lurched at the deafening noise, but it was too late. The bullet had struck it in the lower abdomen, piercing it through the gut. Shock from the round's impact knocked the buck over, but jolted with adrenaline, it sprang to its feet and fled, bounding and crashing through brush as he went.

Daniel gave a short whistle, and Sadie took off in hot pursuit. She had been waiting in anticipation for this. Daniel and Jonas were both capable hunters, able to track a blood-trail, but Sadie dramatically lessened their work. She caught the buck's scent from where it had been browsing and sprinted after it into the thicket.

It did not take long—three minutes and Sadie had started to bark. Jonas and Daniel took their time moving in her direction; there was plenty of brush and brambles to navigate between them and the deer. The buck wasn't going anywhere. The two men trudged through the forest in their boots over fallen logs, marshy ground, and a gurgling stream.

At last, they located the fallen deer halfway up a clear-cut hillside. Sadie awaited them, tail wagging, presiding over the mortally wounded creature. She gave a final bark for good measure, glorying in her find.

"Good girl," Dan praised as they approached. He stroked the dog's silky coat.

"Looks like he ran out of steam trying to make the ridgeline," Jonas observed.

Daniel shot him an amused smirk. "I'd like to see you sprint up this hill with a bullet through your gut."

"No thanks." Jonas grinned. "You'd know more about that than me, man." Jonas was referring to the two occasions during the Last War when Daniel had been shot. One bullet had pierced his left shoulder during a fight in a dense Columbian jungle; the second had passed through the side of his left calf as he'd helped evacuate refugees in old-world Pakistan. Daniel had taken a third bullet square in the chest while fighting in Egypt, but the plates in his flak jacket had served their purpose and saved his life. The bruising had been very real, though.

Daniel did not respond to Jonas' remark; he knelt in the grass and felt the deer's warm body. The clear, morning sun warmed the creature's gray, brown pelt, but Daniel could also feel the final breaths leaving the buck. He lowered his gaze and murmured a quiet prayer. "We thank You for the life of Your creation, so that we may eat and be nourished. May the days we receive from Your creature's life be shown to honor You with our treatment of others and this land. All life flows from You, may all life and beauty return to You."

"Amen," Jonas concluded after a moment of silence. Daniel handed his rifle off to him and unsheathed a black steel hunting knife. "Who taught you to pray like that?" Jonas probed, watching Daniel slice down the deer's abdomen to exhume the gut bag.

Daniel did not slow his work to answer. "Raoul." He grunted a little, pulling for the intestines. "Are you surprised?" He grinned slightly.

Jonas smiled. "Nah, man, if anybody has respect for all life, it'd be him. It's good to hear you talk like that. Feels like you're comin' back to the world a bit, ya know?"

Daniel did not reply at all this time, but continued his knife work. Gerald Raoul Stormcloud was a Lakota-Sioux man in their community. He was in his early fifties and widely respected by all of the people in the camp. Stormcloud generally went by Raoul, although when Jonas was in a playful mood, which was often, he called him Gerry. Raoul usually just stared back stone-faced in these moments, or ignored Jonas altogether.

Raoul frequently appeared stoic and aloof; he was wise as a panther and observant as a hawk. He had come from reservation lands in Wyoming and was journeying alone when he'd crossed paths with the community. He claimed to be the last of his people, perhaps the last of all American Indians. He never spoke of what he had witnessed during and after the Last War, but he'd once confided in Daniel that his name had not always been Stormcloud. It had once been Lightfoot, back when his people had considered him the swiftest and most silent hunter among the tribe. Somewhere between the war and his thousand-mile journey by foot, though, his name had changed.

Daniel did not know the specific reasons. In fact, he knew little more about Raoul than the others knew—just that he had once had a family, a wife, grown children, a vast network of relatives, and even a first grandbaby.

As far as Daniel knew, they were all dead now.

Raoul had arrived to the community like a ghost, haunted, hollow, full of many griefs and mourning. Yet he displayed little emotion, remaining like a pillar of rock to the outside world. Raoul trusted Daniel and spoke to him only because they had both been warriors for their peoples. The respect was mutual.

Sometimes Raoul would say things that left Daniel *knowing* the Sioux elder could see inside his soul. Though his long, dark hair had grayed, and his face showed lines and cracked wrinkles, the older hunter had lost none of his perceptiveness and intuitive power. He knew the dark places Daniel had been without having to hear a word of his story.

From his first day in the community, Raoul had watched the Marine interact with others. When he looked into Daniel's eyes, he saw all that was hidden within. He knew warriors; knew their burdens and secrets, their fears and sorrows. He knew all of the regrets they labored to conceal from the rest of the world. Thus he knew the demons lurking behind Daniel's carefully-guarded exterior.

Sometimes in the evenings the two men would sit together for hours. Daniel would ask about the legends of the Lakota, or they would talk about hunting and tracking. And Raoul would ask Daniel where he had come from, what he had done before the war, and where he had served during the long years of fighting.

Both men were initially wary of each other. Raoul did not share about the traditions of his people lightly with outsiders, especially a white man. Neither did Daniel easily reveal great details about his combat experiences in the Last War. So neither man ever shared more than he wanted or chose from his past, and neither ever felt pressured or coerced to. Sometimes they simply sat in silence, gazing on an open fire or up at the starlit heavens. Though neither ever expressed it directly, they both held deep appreciation for these hours soaking in the canopy of the night sky. And each felt gratitude for the simple comfort of quiet companionship along a weary road of life.

When the deer was gutted, Daniel hoisted its limp carcass over his shoulders and turned to Jonas who still carried both of their rifles. Without a word spoken, they began to traverse their way back into the gully and across the stream; dead twigs and branches snapped and crunched under Daniel's boots. It was not yet noon, but the air was growing hot on the open hillside. Tall, yellow grass glinted gold in the morning sun, swaying back and forth in the warm summer breeze. Sadie sniffed and trotted along close by, merrily wagging her tail and enjoying the array of intriguing scents that wafted around her.

Jonas and Daniel trudged through the woods, retracing a path back to camp. They traded off between carrying the buck or rifles every mile when their shoulders grew sore. They spoke little as they walked; the depth of their friendship had instilled a natural ease around the other. They had become friends the first night they met in the community. Jonas had a winning personality, bright smile, and brilliant whit; he loved to joke and laugh loudly, but when he was with Daniel, neither felt a need to fill silences with empty chatter.

Jonas Wells was similar in height and age to Daniel, six foot give or take, and both were close to thirty years in age. Jonas was built thicker and more muscular, his chest, shoulders, and biceps broad and toned, boasting the power and strength of his body. His skin was the color of rich earth after an autumn rainfall, and his eyes matched in darkness. Jonas had arrived in the community two years earlier with his beautiful wife, Janae, and their charming daughter, Ellie. Janae was a strong woman, also black. Her complexion was lighter than Jonas', though, and her eyes were vividly green.

Jonas hailed from Baton Rouge, Louisiana originally—where he had once belonged to a large family. He was well liked wherever he went; he had become a U.S. Army Ranger in the old world, and like Daniel, had served in the Last War. Jonas tended not to take himself too seriously in his daily interactions with folks. He had an easy-going nature, yet people respected him and never mistook his kindness for weakness. He was tough as nails under pressure and had proven himself a skilled warrior, survivor, leader, and protector, both during the war and since.

Daniel had served in MARSOC, the Special Operations wing of the U.S. Marine Corps. This fact bonded him with Jonas immensely. There was a good-natured rivalry between the two, but at the end of the day, they had both dived out the back of airplanes and fought on foreign soil for the same country and causes. They had both watched their worlds burn and crumble around them. Though neither spoke of it openly, they had both lost family. And they had both taken lives, been shot at, lost close friends in combat, and stared down death too many times to count.

They were both cunning, adaptable, intuitive, lethally-trained, and protectors. These qualities made them natural leaders wherever they went. It also gave

them a code of honor to live by in a world that had
ceased giving any direction to loners. Looking out for
the weak and powerless, hunting down and slaying the
"wolves" who preyed on the innocent—this had become
the compass for their lives, their higher calling.

Less was known of Daniel's background than Jonas',
at least by the general assembly of the community.
Before the Last War, Daniel had come from the Pacific
Northwest. This was where he was from—where he had
grown up before enlisting. Little was known of what
had transpired after this, and this small amount only by
Jonas, Raoul, and Father Paolo.

Daniel was kind and spoke respectfully to everyone in
the community. He offered help where he could, and
was generally regarded as the person in charge of the
camp's security. Still, beyond this, he was quiet; he
shared little about his personal history and with only a
few.

In conversations, Daniel focused on the present, his
life in the community since he had stumbled upon the
camp. If asked about the war, his family, where he had
come from, the five superpowers, or his own ideological
sentiments, he usually responded in vague generalities
and quoted some philosopher or poet. He never shared
concrete experiences from his life before the community.
No one really knew where he had been prior to his
arrival, though most knew he had returned to the

wooded hills of this coastal range because it had once been his home. By the end of the war, he had had nothing else to return to.

After a few miles of trading off the loads, Jonas and Daniel climbed a final, wooded slope. They found themselves standing atop a knoll looking down on a clearing where the community lay. Smoke rose from a few cook fires; a few horses and cows plodded around in fenced pasture, and people were going about their daily chores or tending vegetable gardens. It was more of a village than a camp and boasted a population of seventy-nine, including the children.

Couples and families lived in their own small cabins, and the community worked to pair unmarried individuals with house mates of the same sex. It was not practical for every person to have their own cabin, but exceptions were made from time to time. And no one was ever impeded from building his or her own home if they possessed the skills and will for the undertaking.

The cabins were built of pine or cedar lumber, which left a pleasant aroma for guests who entered. A few had cement floors but most had floors made of wooden planks just to keep the homes from becoming mud pits during the wet, winter months. Each home had a single lightbulb mounted to the ceiling, and some had sinks with running water. Several solar panels and gas generators had been acquired to pump water from the well system.

The glade lay hidden in the densely forested coastal hills of Unity, yet no one in this community bore a chip and they were intent on keeping it that way. The people lived freely, and for the most part peacefully with their neighbors. The scout parties sent out to forage supplies from abandoned towns of the old world were urged to never engage Pacification patrols if they encountered one. This small settlement could not risk its existence being discovered nor its members followed home. Secrecy kept these free folk safe and thriving.

Unity patrols were sparse this far from the main cities. Because of the plant and animal protection laws, most chipped citizens of Unity had no incentive to populate more remote areas like the coastal foothills. Unfortunately, the community's survivors were not the only people who lived out in these wilds. Bands of marauders and lawless men also roamed the free country.

There was a small cemetery plot on the community grounds where more than twenty people had been buried in the past two years. Periodically, a scouting party was ambushed by motorcycle gangs, or a band of killers would try to raid the modest settlement. People inevitably died during the ensuing gunfights of such incursions. It was an accepted reality of living outside the protection of Unity's Pacification Forces. This also meant that any community members discovered by a Pacification patrol were attacked on-sight or arrested immediately. Unity did not differentiate the between outlaws who were violent and those who sought peace. Any who roved the wild country not within its fold were deemed criminals in need of correction.

Occasionally, another, outside party of peaceful wanderers would seek refuge in the wild country. Sadly, Unity's patrols usually swept down on these weary travelers quickly. And if they evaded the power's grasp, they were usually set upon by the bands of lawless men who robbed, murdered, or took them as sex slaves. For the innocent and unprotected, the world had become a cruelly unjust place.

The community had survived in no small part due to the providential arrival of men and women like Daniel and Jonas. Soldiers, warriors, former police officers, people who had been capable and savvy enough to survive the war yet still possessed a conscience. These helped arm and train the people to defend themselves. They emplaced defenses along the community's borders, set rotations of armed sentries and lookouts, and drilled the residents for the day an alarm would be raised.

There was an agreed-upon light curfew. No fires were permitted to burn past 10 PM, nor could external lights be shone except by the night's sentries and watchmen. The inhabitants of the quiet glade lived forever under the threat of Unity's shadow, for her eyes ever scoured the wildlands in search of wayward sojourners. She stalked this hill country like a beast of the night, seeking any goodness which she did not already control. Her appetite for dominion over all peoples was ravenous and she would exterminate any in these lands who resisted.

The fear of being discovered by patrolling aircraft or a passing satellite kept everyone in the community uniformly cautious and compliant to the light curfew. There were special occasions, such as weddings or the annual Harvest Celebration, when lights and fires were permitted to burn later into the night. These instances were rare, however, happening just once or twice per year.

The community was shepherded by a council of seven elders. There was an odd number so that a vote could never be gridlocked in a tie. Elections were held every other summer by way of a silent vote. Community members each wrote down seven names on small pieces of paper. The votes were tallied and the individuals most-selected would then serve the community as council elders for two years. No elder was permitted to serve more than two consecutive terms without taking a minimum of two years off. This helped to ensure individuals did not become too attached to power or the authority of influence.

It was required that at least three of the elder seats be

filled by women on every council. Father Paolo instituted another rule that two of the elders also be under the age of thirty-five. Both of these mandates served to safeguard the council from growing blind or lopsided in its thinking. The perspectives of women and more youthful minds were to be honored and valued by the council and by extension, the community.

The elders were not rulers. They had no authority over their fellow community members in day-to-day affairs. They merely existed as a council to mediate disputes between people, manage the defense and security of the community, and to monitor the reserves of food and other supplies. The council's sole purpose was to serve the people by facilitating peace and establishing plans to circumvent avoidable disasters.

This community was governed by a code of three virtues: honesty, respect, and gratitude. So long as a person could live by these principles, at peace with their neighbor, they were welcome. No allegiance to a particular religious faith was required. There were several agnostics, one resolute atheist, a Jordanian Muslim family, a few Catholics, a range of protestant Christians from Baptist to Presbyterian, and there was Raoul who practiced the spirituality of his tribe, which connected him to the Earth and all living things.

In regards to the three virtues, honesty was considered the foundation for membership in the community and all interactions. Given the close proximity of people living together from diverse backgrounds, misunderstanding and miscommunication were inevitable. Without honesty, trust was impossible; however honesty did not mean total and immediate transparency.

Although newcomers remained on a probationary trial during their first six months, people were not forced to reveal their darkest or most intimate secrets to the council on the first day of their arrival. They were, however, expected to speak truthfully to all community members. If a newcomer was uncomfortable answering a barrage of questions about his or her personal history, to say so was credited as honesty.

Respect was much more than cordial speech and behavior towards one's neighbors. It meant respect for the unique gifts, abilities, and perspectives that each person brought to the community as a whole. Respect required a profound reverence for the experiences of one's past-all those things which had shaped a person into who they were.

Life was to be beautified, cultivated, and celebrated in the community. If someone slandered his neighbor, it revealed the presence of arrogant contempt within. It eroded trust when one presumed to pass judgment on another hastily. If someone stole from their neighbor, it was seen as both disrespectful and dishonest. Such a person had failed to communicate a physical need they had and deprived their neighbors of the opportunity to care for them. There was absolutely no excuse to steal for the sake of covetousness.

Respect was also to be extended to all living things. Animals were seen as God's creation and therefore marked by inherent worth and beauty by their Maker. Animals were to be raised, cared for, hunted, and even butchered humanely and with respect. They were only to be killed for food, in self-defense, or in defense of livestock. No unnecessary suffering or deliberate cruelty was tolerated. Neither were trees to be cut down needlessly. These were only to be felled for the sake of firewood or constructing homes, and in rare occasions, cleared to plant fields for growing food.

If a man beat his wife, it was impossible to hide this from his neighbors. He would be called before the elders, instructed to give account of himself, and make amends to his wife before them. In the days that followed, he would be required to carry out his daily work or chores alongside one or two older men for several months, as a sort of restorative mentoring. The man and his wife would be invited to dinner with older couples and exposed to healthy interactions of both assertive and vulnerable communication.

If a man struck his wife again he was sternly warned that a third offense would result in his expulsion from the community. Meanwhile, his wife and children would be moved into a separate house away from the abusive man while the council continued to work with him towards restoration. Often, he was required to attend regular, individual meetings with Father Paolo or another trusted elder to seek inner healing and direction.

If the man could not change, as a last resort, he would finally be expelled from the community; however his wife and children were welcomed to remain in the camp as long as they chose. Depending on the seriousness of the offense, the expelled individual could not to return to communal living for a minimum of six months.

Expulsion from the community was an almost guaranteed death-sentence by starvation, exposure to the elements, or abduction by Unity forces or violent outlaws. Faced with these realities, a troubled man usually humbled himself and learned a new way of relating with his spouse and children. And as a result of true change, such individuals often found a joy, intimacy, remorse, gratitude, and connection with others, they had never before experienced.

The third pillar of the community, gratitude, was not something which could be enforced, but it was encouraged as often as possible. At the weekly contemplative hour, Father Paolo spoke regularly against the cancers of greed, jealousy, entitlement, and pride.

Like some blight, the priest knew these could spring up with ease, and quickly rot the heart of a man, woman, or the entire community.

Father Paolo came from a Franciscan order. Syrian by birth, he had spent forty years in a Middle Eastern commune with his desert brothers. There he had cared for the impoverished and sick of nearby towns and villages, be they Muslim, Jew, or Christian. He was close to eighty years old, a respected, grandfatherly figure to all. His thin frame, hunched shoulders, and fading eyesight spoke of the many years of toil he had given on behalf of his fellow man, with few comforts.

Father Paolo walked slowly yet with purpose and grace wherever he went. His old head was nearly bald, his face grizzled, and he spoke in a quiet, sometimes raspy voice. He had a gentle manner and lived by himself in a cabin that was more of a shack. His home was barely large enough to house his bed and two wooden chairs. Each night he knelt beside his cot on the wooden-plank floor and prayed for every member of the community by name. Each night, he also prayed for the safety and deliverance of any still wandering out in the wilds—those who had not yet arrived to find sanctuary in the community.

The priest was the North Star of the community, its guiding light and moral compass whenever confusion, conflict, or mistrust took root. He gave thanks for whatever he had each day, even when meals were meager or plain. He spoke blessing to every person in the camp whether they shared his faith or not. And he tolerated no prejudice, not for race, gender, or religion.

Father Paolo facilitated a contemplative hour on most Sunday mornings. Those who gathered usually sang a few hymns together, and he would serve Eucharist each week to any who believed in the divinity and resurrection of Jesus Christ. Sometimes he read or taught from the Scriptures; at other times he simply instructed people to sit quietly and reflect on the blessings in their lives or the beauty around them. This latter task was never difficult given the parishioners sat on finished wood benches in the outdoors, surrounded by lushly forested hills and gentle songbirds in the trees.

Father Paolo did not take confessions on Sunday mornings. People were free to seek him out for private confession throughout the week. Yet he always encouraged them to confess directly to the person they had wronged, if the offended party resided in the community.

Father Paolo refused to call the contemplative hour a worship gathering. He kindly reminded people that worship was what a person did the other six days of the week. Worship was how one treated their neighbor and loved their spouse. Worship was how a man tended his chores, tilled the soil, or built a roof. Finally, the priest refrained from ever calling the contemplative hour "spiritual." He viewed all of life as spiritual, every act and interaction, and he trained the people to see in this way too—to recognize God's holy presence in all things.

Father Paolo, though, was not the only clergyman in the community; there was also Brother Fernando Martinez. Before the Last War, Brother Martinez had lived as a member of a Benedictine monastery in New Mexico. He possessed a friendly and upbeat personality; he was warmhearted, optimistic, and a hard worker. And he was always eager to lend a hand in tasks around the glade, even seemingly mundane ones such as pulling weeds from a garden or scrubbing pots and pans.

Brother Martinez was much younger than the Syrian abbe, only thirty four. He was not as gifted a teacher as the older priest either, but he was well loved by the community. The older priest treated him as a son and considered him his apprentice. He instructed Fernando in the spiritual disciplines of servant leadership, silence and solitude, contemplative prayer, and fasting, all the while knowing that the younger man would one day replace him. Brother Martinez was already helping to shape the breadth and texture of today's community; one day when Paolo passed on to meet his Maker, Fernando would be left to guide its fate and future.

Whenever there was a dispute or grievance between neighbors which could not be resolved privately, a

Restoration Circle was convened. A large circle of stones had been erected and the ground cleared to bare earth in its center. Witnesses and effected family members were welcome to be present, but only two individuals were permitted to enter the circle at a time. Relationships were always to be mended in dyads first. This was done in the hopes that if the two most-affected parties could find reconciliation or mutual understanding, any secondary friends or family members could respect the outcome as well.

For a Restoration Circle to be convened, a minimum of four of the seven elders had to be present. They would take seats in a semicircle around the ring of stones and listen intently to each party's grievance or perspective. Witnesses, neighbors, and family members stood in a second semicircle behind the two in conflict. Before a Restoration Circle could be requested, the offended parties had to initially seek out at least one elder for mediation. If the mediation was unsuccessful, then a Restoration Circle could be called for-in order to receive the full measure of the council's combined wisdom.

To enter a Restoration Circle, each party had to commit to respect the adjudication of the elders and whatever conclusions they reached. At the end, parties involved were required to make mutual confession of any wrongdoing for their part. Sometimes a man would confess to having an arrogant heart and being spiteful as a result. Other times a woman might confess she had built a grudge and slandered her friend's spouse out of jealousy, insecurity, and an unfulfilled desire to feel loved.

Selfishness, envy, pride, fear, and prejudice—all of these were confessed in a Restoration Circle before elders and neighbors. It taught people to perceive the heart's intentions, not simply surface behaviors. Gossip, theft, deceit, intimidation, or wounding remarks—all these were seen as merely the symptoms of a deeper sickness. Restoration Circles kept a healthy monitor on the pulse of the community as a whole. Friends and family who witnessed these times were challenged to take stock of their own hearts and interactions with others. A Restoration Circle also modeled skills of being emotionally vulnerable, trusting, and verbally communicative.

It was never desired that someone should leave a Restoration Circle feeling shamed. Feelings of guilt, sorrow, and remorse were appropriate, but the elders facilitated these gatherings in such a way as to help individuals make amends, not deepen wounds or resentments. It was the wish of the elders that community members leave feeling freer and more committed to sincere living. Tears were welcome, and involved parties often embraced or shook hands by the end of the council's ruling, but most left in peace and with renewed serenity.

For newcomers to the community, the first time they found themselves in the Restoration Circle, which generally did not take very long, they were scared and overwhelmed. Angry-outbursts rooted in fear, confusion, or frustration were common. Many had never been held accountable in positive ways by people who genuinely cared about them. Others had never learned how to resolve conflicts by any way besides shouting or raised fists. Still others had lost their way and sense of humanity in the chaos following the Last War.

It was hard for newcomers to trust. They couldn't believe they weren't about to be punished severely, shamed, humiliated, or expelled outright from their newfound home. They were frightened and disoriented the first time they found themselves at the center of a conflict, standing in that circle of stones. Yet with weeks and months of gentle encouragement, friendliness, compassion, and neighborly generosity, men and women each found their way to a deeper faith in their fellow humans.

Their defenses lowered as they gradually realized that no one in the community was trying to take advantage of them, and all they wanted was a reciprocated, genial decency. Slowly at first, the miracle of miracles would begin to take shape; they started to trust again, or in some cases, for the first time in their lives. They learned to contribute with their hands and work hard. They learned to consider and give back to others if they had forgotten how.

After a year or so, it was not uncommon for a newcomer to start looking forward to a Restoration Circle. It meant burdens would be lifted, relationships would deepen, and the community as a whole would grow. People learned to believe they would not be cast out at the first offense nor abandoned for legitimate need. They learned to receive love and eventually how to give it as well.

From their first day in the community, each resident was encouraged to bring whatever they had for the good of all. As most people arrived in the camp with barely the clothes on their backs and maybe a weapon, often fleeing pursuers for their very lives, to bring what one had rarely referred to worldly possessions. It meant that all of a person's knowledge, skills, abilities, insight, and experiences were considered vital to the thriving and vibrancy of the community. *Everyone* had something valuable to offer and contribute.

If a person possessed medical training or a military background, these were needed and welcomed. If a person had skills in construction, carpentry, farming, gardening, plumbing, automotive repair, or electrical work, they were prized and greatly appreciated. If someone was a member of the clergy, a spiritual director, counselor, teacher, or experienced in caring for children, they were honored and considered useful.

Each was encouraged to cultivate his or her passions and maximize their own talents for the good all, yet no one was ever discouraged from learning a new skill or craft. No woman was ever told she was somehow unfit to learn how to hunt. No man was ever put off from learning to garden or mend his torn garments with a sewing needle. And with danger ever on their doorstep, every community member was urged to learn how to handle a weapon and defend themselves. Neither Unity forces nor lawless gangs showed mercy to the defenseless or passive.

In the old world, Dr. Jane Ellenson had been an M.D. and medical researcher at a prestigious university in California. She was a sound atheist and an outspoken advocate for women's equality. When she had stumbled into the community's camp during its early days, she had been surprised to be welcomed with such grace. She had arrived fleeing for her life after escaping the horrors of one of Unity's Reeducation Centers. Two weeks after her arrival, she approached the elders with a proposal to build a much-needed infirmary in the community, one with surgical capabilities.

The council had supported her plans whole heartedly and rallied the people to assist in its construction.

Today, the infirmary stood as the only cement building on the compound. Constructed of cinder blocks and a concrete floor, it stood at the northwest edge of the community's glade and nestled against the base of a steep, wooded incline. It was long and rectangular in shape, a simple, single-room building with two glass-paned windows that provided light and ventilation. Through supply and salvage patrols, medical supplies and beds had slowly been acquired from abandoned hospitals and care facilities. Of all the buildings in the glade, the infirmary always took precedence for power.

It was open six days a week as a clinic for triage and routine primary care. Even on her day off or during the night, though, Dr. Ellenson could be roused in the event of an emergency. Her passion for the people was too great to not respond to a critical need. Jane also had help in operating the clinic from one former nursing student and an ex-Army medic.

In addition to these, Dr. Ellenson grew close with an Indian man named Sumir Khurma. Sumir was a biochemist, and together they were developing a surgical procedure to remove Unity's chip implants. The hope was that one day, for those who desired it, Jane and Sumir would be able to the liberate minds of any rescued Unity citizen or soldier.

Dr. Ellenson never attended the Sunday morning contemplative hour; she possessed a general distaste for most organized religion. At an early age, she had become painfully acquainted with some of its sharper edges and wanted nothing to do with it in her adult life. No one in the community ever criticized her absence from such gatherings, though; to them she remained a cherished partner in rebuilding a new and hopeful life. Father Paolo was always friendly and respectful to her. He spoke endless words of affirmation and appreciation for her work and presence. Although Jane had once resented and condescended most religious people, she could not deny there was something unique and beautiful being played out in this community.

The day-to-day faith and spirituality, which Paolo taught, was practical and beneficial. It did not require people to switch off their brains. Just the opposite, in fact; it required them to think critically and take inventory of their own intentions. What was lived out in the community seemed to enhance life and freedom, not hinder it. This *faith* was beautiful and even healing, though not necessarily easy. Within the community, sharing life with others was nuanced and rarely simple; it was ever in flux and flow, even as individuals themselves changed through seasons of growth, mourning, or personal victory.

A deep affection grew in Jane towards Father Paolo. He was a father she had never had. He often visited the clinic merely to say hello and check in. He was always polite and humble; he treated the infirmary as her space. Sometimes he would make jokes about his own health issues associated with aging. He never left Jane's clinic without clasping her hand gently and thanking her for all her hard work and devotion on behalf of her neighbors.

The infirmary had come as a result of the elders supporting Dr. Ellenson's passion, education, and commitment toward others. It was now one of the most cherished features of the community, as was Jane herself. Another example of this phenomenon was found in an introverted, middle-aged man named John. He was a mechanical engineer by trade and by his own accord had untaken the task of constructing a dam in the nearby creek. The hope was to harvest some hydroelectric power via a series of small turbines, which John had also devised and was in the process of fabricating.

So each person learned to contribute in his or her own way. People learned to care for their neighbors, and all were challenged to find grace and humility towards one another.

If Unity's Guides had known of its existence, they would have protested that this "community" was unnecessary and a cheap imitation of their own utopia. Though some subtle and others overt, the differences were very real. The doors of the community were never shut to anyone, so long as they could abide in peace with their neighbor. By extension, the doors were always open for someone to leave, if they could not.

Meanwhile Unity and its leaders wanted *no one* to leave. They desired absolute power and influence with no accountability for themselves. The Presiding Council hungered for total and unchecked control of their fellow humans. Unity might have declared its aims to be peace, tolerance, and justice, but its methods were coercion, cruelty, concealed violence, and the domination of wills, all in the name of so-called harmony.

In the community, people were invited to humble themselves, learn, grow, mourn, forgive, and heal. In Unity, everyone was bitter, resentful, and eternally jealous of one another; they were also ultimately all controlled by the Blue Chip. In the community, people were invited to receive love and learn how to give it, including to themselves. In Unity, there could be no love, for all love requires a choice, and all choice requires freedom of will. And Unity granted *no one* the freedom of their own will.

In the community, love meant extending oneself for the nurturing growth, care, or betterment of another, even if it came with difficult words of challenge. In Unity, love just meant never causing another person to feel emotionally offended. In the community, God had gifted humans with the dignity of independent thought and the autonomy to make a choice-for better or for worse. In Unity, the Guides and their Blue Chip *were* God.

CHAPTER TWO

As Daniel and Jonas surveyed the clearing below, the buck still draped across Jonas' shoulders, all was peaceful and tranquil. People of the community were going about their daily work, talking, laughing, and enjoying life alongside one another. Sadie emitted a short whine and sat; she knew she was home and the children would want to play with her. She waited obediently for her master to free her from service for the evening.

"What's going on over there?" Daniel pointed to a small gathering of people near the rows of finished, contemplative-benches. Three individuals were kneeling before an old man; beside them lay packs loaded for a journey.

"You didn't hear?" Jonas responded. "Your boy,

Paolo, is sending off some missionaries today."

"What?" Daniel demanded. "Sending them where? To their deaths?!"

"I don't know, man. It didn't make sense to me either, but you know ol' Paolo, always going on about people's dignity and the value of all life. He must've figured we can't keep all this goodness to ourselves."

Daniel snorted derisively. "You've gotta be kidding me!" The two men watched for another minute; it appeared the priest was blessing each of the travelers before their departure, speaking benediction over them.

"Can you take the buck and hang it in the freezer?" Daniel asked. "I want to see what this is all about."

"Oh! I see how it is." Jonas feigned insult. "White man stickin' me with all the work! Guess it's business as usual then, huh? White power?"

"I'm glad you understand this." Daniel grinned, slapping his friend on the shoulder.

"Man, get your little rat claws off of me! You know you'd be gettin' your ass beat right now, if we was back in the old neighborhood?"

Daniel had already turned to leave. He raised a hand in farewell. "Love you too, Jonas!"

"Mmhmm, keep walkin', white boy."

Daniel halted, and turned back. "Actually, Jonas, this is really because you Army bubbas just aren't cut out to handle the really important business like us Marines."

Jonas sputtered. "Not cut out to? Man, whatever! We Rangers are just too smart for you jarheads. We didn't sign up to be brainwashed, crazy-ass cannon-fodder! All y'all Marines got your brains sucked out during indoc. That's why they call y'all jarheads, see? Empty space!" Jonas was pointing to his right temple now. "Room for rent!" He grinned proudly. "And good ol' Uncle Sam just went and took up that whole space!"

Daniel's face had turned to a pretend-serious expression. "You done yet?" he asked. "Keep talkin' shit about my Corps, Jonas; see what happens."

"I will!" the Ranger declared. "And I could own your ass any day of the week, white boy! Y'all Marines got them stupid-ass, screamin'-eagle, high-and-tight haircuts too!"

Daniel took a step closer and squared off with his friend; their rifles still dangling from his shoulder. "Knives or hand-to-hand, buddy; just name the time and place."

"Oh, don't you worry, Dan, I got you covered." This time Jonas' patted Daniel on the arm. He side-stepped his friend and headed down the slope in the direction of the cool-locker. "Janae wants you to come by for dinner tonight," he called back. "I'm not so sure that's such a good idea, though, seein' as you got all these racist ideas about the black man serving your ass."

Daniel shook his head, grinning again as he watched

his friend go. There was not an ounce of bad blood between the two. Racial joking was part of their banter; something life in the military had fueled. When you knew you'd die for the man next to you, regardless of his color or religion, and you knew he'd do the same for you, it indwelt a profound loyalty. Humor about stereotypes and cultural differences served to diffuse the crushing tension of life in a combat zone.

Sadie whined and looked up with pitiful eyes. "Yeah?" Daniel said, looking down at her. She flapped her ebony tail against the dirt and nuzzled his leg. A throaty attempt to speak emerged from the canine. She was adamantly anticipating her released for the day.

"You're such a softy!" he chided. "We're gonna have to do something about that, toughen you up a bit." Dog and master stared at each other for another moment. Then Daniel knelt down and caressed her head and ears; tenderly stroking her silky coat. Sadie waited patiently, soaking up the affection.

"All right," Daniel said at last. She was sniffing his face with her wet nose; he didn't want any of her licks. "All right!" he exclaimed. "Free!" Before the syllable was fully out of his mouth, the Lab was on her feet and making a mad dash down into the clearing.

Daniel watched his four-legged companion go, ecstatically bounding and sprinting across the glade, tongue hanging out the side of her mouth without shame. He heard children in the camp calling her to come play with them. They sprang from vegetable gardens and cabin doorways, chasing her down to stroke her coat. It was a dog's paradise.

The Marine re-shouldered the two rifles and took his turn to traverse down the slope into glade. He moved purposefully, yet unhurriedly towards the gathered crowd where Father Paolo was speaking an invocation. Daniel's boots quietly pressed the short, dry grass underfoot; the morning's dew had already been evaporated by the summer sun. As he drew near to the back of the throng, he strained to hear. There were at least thirty people in front of him, all present to witness this sendoff of their neighbors. Raoul was there, standing near the back like Daniel. He nodded solemnly in acknowledgement of his friend's arrival. Daniel returned the nod; Father Paolo was speaking.

"May the Lord bless you and keep you safe. May He cause His face to shine upon you and grant you peace along your journey and in any trials you may face."

"Amen," the three missionaries responded. There were two men and one woman, all young, all under the age of thirty. They were physically fit and ready for whatever road lay ahead. The taller male bore the commanding demeanor of a natural leader; the other two would look to him for strength and guidance in the coming days.

"To where will you go?" the grizzled abbé inquired. This was for ritual sake and for the bystanders. He had spent the past few months training and preparing them for this moment.

"We will go to Imperial State," the tall, strong one announced. "To the poor and oppressed there or to their leaders if God so directs us."

When the young man named the eastern power, Daniel closed his eyes and slowly shook his head in disgust. His jaw tightened without him even realizing it; he shot a glance over at Raoul. The Lakota man met his gaze but neither said a word. No gesture of any kind was made, but a great, almost palpable tension settled over the two.

"Are you ready then?" Father Paolo asked.

"Yes," the young woman responded. She was pretty with brown hair and a slender frame, but determination and resolve shone in her eyes. "We have spent time learning the language of the people we are leaving to serve. We are supplied for the journey and will use our hands to work once we arrive there; so we will not be a burden to anyone."

"Very good," Father Paolo commended "And which gospel do you go to preach?"

The second young man spoke now. "This is the gospel: that God made humankind in His own likeness with independent thought and the power to imagine, build, and create, for good or for evil. He marked us with the deep imprint of His Divine Image. So we are true, blessed, and loved sons and daughters of Heaven; the keepers and caretakers of this Earth. To be human is to be divine. Nothing of value can be added to this true identity nor can it ever be taken away. The choice is simply to believe or not believe it.

"Our Father offers forgiveness to anyone who asks for it, no matter their crime, no matter the vastness of their sins. He invites each person to new life, to remember their true identity as His loved child. He calls to anyone who will listen; He seeks partners in healing the Creation, no matter where they have been or what has been done to them.

"God took on physical form in the person of Jesus, to walk among us and experience our sufferings. He became human to show His compassion for our brokenness, misery, and pain, and to heal the wounds which have sprung up from mankind's fear, ignorance, arrogance, jealousy, and greed. He came to unveil our eyes, to reveal the fleeting things which we have tried to cover our naked shame with, to unmask the feeble identities behind which we have tried to hide our imperfections in order to feel some semblance of worth.

"Jesus showed there is a better way to be human. In a world that rules through brutality, He cares for the poor, the sick, the weak, the infirmed, and the outcast.

In his death he declared for all eternity: *If you wound me, I will not strike back. If you wrong me, I will forgive you and pray for you. There is nothing to be afraid of.* Finally, He rose from the dead to show that even death has no power over Him. So neither will death have power over us in the end; there is no reason to live in fear. Death is merely the final curtain between this life and the renewal of all things; a door that we all must pass through. The final "*Yes*" to a call from our loving Father to come home and be whole.

"The Father, Son, and Spirit sit together, each inclined toward the other, all equals in perfect relationship. And there is an open chair waiting, an invitation for any of us, to come and join them, in friendship and conversation, in the breaking of bread together and the sharing of life, joy, beauty, laughter, desire, and healing. Jesus told His followers, 'Now you go and do likewise.' And so we will. What the Master did, He calls us to do also; to walk His path, release prisoners from darkness, heal the sick, care for the brokenhearted, forgive sinners, and proclaim Abba's favor and love for all mankind. But as Jesus suffered rejection, loneliness, and pain by those who could not understand, we also must be ready to suffer for the sake of His message, even unto bodily death."

A silence fell over those gathered. There was a simultaneous stirring of hope and sober reality of what these young three were undertaking and what it might cost them.

"Then you are truly ready," Father Paolo affirmed. "Be on your guard. Remember the words of our Lord Jesus: *Because of me, you will be dragged before kings, rulers, and courts to give account. When this happens do not be afraid or worry about what to say, for the Spirit of my Father will speak through you. You will be given what to say at that time.* Stay with whoever welcomes you for as long as they will have you. If you are not welcomed in one town, simply move to the next. The Lord will go before you, for He knows the hearts that have been crying out for hope and deliverance from oppression, the ones who are ready to hear His invitation of love.

"Finally, do not involve yourselves in political affairs or revolutions. You do not go to start or fight wars. Those in power will fear and hate you, for the true gospel brings life and freedom wherever it travels. Still, any change must come from within-by those people who claim their own freedom. Because the gospel liberates people, your message will be seen as a threat by those who wish to rule over their fellow man. To live from one's true identity, as a beloved son and daughter of the Father, challenges systems of greed, power, and oppression. It awakens sleeping hearts and reveals petty egos for what they are: ragged garments draped over a trembling inner child, hiding from all of its fear, sorrow, and shame."

Paolo paused here and looked at each of the young travelers before him. He felt a swell of warmth, compassion, and love for them. "None of you has taken any oath or vow to this work, and you journey under no compulsion. Take care of each other, my brothers and sister. Look out for one another. I bless you in the name of our Lord Jesus Christ. You are all strong, brave, and courageous. Be whole and well on your road. Be honest and true in your dealings with each other, and be noble towards a violent and broken world that will not understand you. Farewell, my dear friends. God grant you peace and safety in all your travels."

And as quickly as it had begun, it was finished. There was no profound response; if Daniel had arrived a few minutes later, he would have missed the entire sendoff. The three thanked the priest and hoisted packs over their shoulders. The crowd parted so they could all say their final goodbyes, embrace, and give the travelers farewell gifts of food and provisions. Each traveler carried a rifle and a staff for walking. They intended to discard the weapons once they stowed aboard a ship in the Pacific harbor. In the meantime, it was foolhardy and dangerous to pass through the wild country without at least the *appearance* that they could defend themselves against attack.

In that moment, Daniel resembled an out-of-place mercenary. One rifle still hung across his shoulder, the other he cradled in the crook of his arm. He shook each of the travelers' hands and asked if they had everything they needed: food, water, ammunition? The three said that they did and thanked him for his care, training, and protection during their stay in the community.

"We're all more ready for this thanks to you," said the girl; Daniel remembered her name was Stacey.

"Well, be safe out there," he said, trying to be positive and supportive for their sakes. He gave a curt smile. "You can always come back if you decide, no matter what."

"We know," said the tall one. "Thanks again for everything."

Daniel shook the young man's hand firmly and said, "Take care of them." Then the three were walking away. Some people waved; a few shed tears. Daniel just stood stiffly, watching them go, his shoulders tense and a dark grimace setting his jaw. His eyes locked on the three shrinking figures in the distance. They grew smaller with each passing second, until they reached the border of the woods; then they turned back to offer one final wave.

Raoul stood beside him. "It is a beautiful day, is it not?" He looked heavenward as a pair of swallows darted past.

Daniel blinked in the sunny rays and glanced up at

the clear, blue sky. "Yeah, I guess," he admitted reluctantly, his face softening for just a second when he noticed all the natural serenity of the glade and wooded hills around them.

"A beautiful day, even for farewells?" Raoul tested.

The Marine scowled. "I can't believe Paolo is sending them off to their deaths." His voice was quiet; sadness, disbelief, and even some anger tinged his eyes. "Three people, three young, healthy, able-bodied people with good hearts. We need them here, not walking off to an early doom. This is not the time for us to be sending people away-when there are dangers all around us; I can't understand it, Raoul. They were good people, and Paolo encouraged them to just walk off into the horizon!"

"You feel it is a waste?"

"You're damn right I do; I can't understand it! Not only do we lose three good, healthy people, but you know what the world has become out there, what it will do to them."

"You cannot understand? Or you do not like what you cannot control?" the Sioux man questioned. He paused for a moment, inhaling so deeply that he closed his eyes as well. "There are many mysteries in life, Daniel. Why does the otter play while the beaver builds? Why does the eagle choose one cliff for a nest and not another? Why do good men perish while the evil live on to commit more violence? Perhaps the priest knows something we do not."

"What's that?" Daniel asked, unenthusiastically. He had resumed his frowning at the tree-line, the last sighted location of their departed missionaries.

"That we all have a part to play and that some could no more refuse a journey to offer hope to others than a fish could choose to live on land. It simply isn't done. And perhaps it is not our place to concern ourselves with such matters—the path of another. We do not know what lies ahead for them."

There was another long silence, then the warrior inquired, "Do you think we'll ever see them again?"

Another moment of quiet, and then Raoul answered, "I do not know. Life has a strange way about it; this world has seen many unexpected things." He gave a short smirk. "We may yet; we may yet. Do *you* think we will see them again?"

"No," Daniel said flatly, still staring at the woods. "I don't, not in this lifetime."

"You have a sad countenance, my friend," Raoul pointed out. "I wish you could have more hope. I wish you could believe in the possibility of good, though perhaps unforeseen, things." He clapped Daniel on the shoulder and began to saunter away, hands clasped behind his back. He wandered deeper out into the glade, drinking in the trees around him, the warm sun above.

The beauty of it all seemed to break over him like a wave. He was fully enraptured, captivated by the present moment; his soul taken in by everything that surrounded him, the rocks, the trees, the dark earth and animals, the hills above.

Given all the Lakota man had lost and mourned, Daniel knew Raoul was not the slightest bit naïve. Yet he also clearly refused to allow bitter cynicism to consume his heart. Raoul believed the lives of those three young travelers were not his to worry about, nor were they in his power or right to command. They had a path of their own to walk, and no matter where it led, it belonged to them, and them alone.

Or perhaps he simply welcomed a good day when he found one.

The crowd had dispersed behind Daniel; all the people had returned to their work and business for the day. He was left to stand alone, basking in the warm rays of sunlight and the tranquil meadow. The warrior closed his eyes and inhaled deeply, drawing in the serenity and sweet aromas of blossoming wildflowers. He made up his mind to not seek out and confront the priest at this time. He was in no frame of mind to rationally discuss what had just taken place. He knew himself and he knew his temper; he would not be able to speak respectfully right now. He was angry and saw the send-off as being reckless with people's lives. It smacked of poor leadership. And there was *nothing* Daniel loathed more than a would-be leader who failed to protect those under his influence and care.

Feeling a rejuvenated swell of purpose, the warrior gathered up his and Jonas' rifles and proceeded on across the clearing towards his cabin. There was a deer to skin and clean and portions of meat to carve for the families of the community. He mentally resolved that he would have the cuts of the venison divvied among their shelves in the cooler by dinnertime.

No one in the community owned a refrigerator; there wasn't enough power to go around for such luxuries. Instead, they had obtained a commercial-sized, walk-in freezer from an abandoned restaurant and hauled it back to the glade on a flatbed trailer. Besides the infirmary, much of the generator fuel was devoted to this. All meats and perishable foods were stored in the shared ice-closet. People knew their neighbors and shared what they could when it was known someone had a need. No one lived grandiosely over their neighbors; part of being admitted to the community was an understanding that a newcomer would look out for the cares of their neighbor, not simply their own.

On his right, Daniel strode past the camp's lookout-tower, which was built from fresh timber. It stood at the center of the clearing, forty-feet-tall with a ladder to reach the top and a heavy, copper bell which hung in its rafters. The bell was rung only to raise the alarm in case of an attack. It was not the only sentry post in the community, but it was the only watchtower. It stood tall enough to see over all of the grounds. It also lent a vantage point of the nearby country highway beyond the span of woods to the southeast. Regardless of the hour, day or night, there was always a watchman posted in the tower. The community had to remain vigilant; villains and marauders preyed on the unprepared without mercy.

Daniel was passing by a larger, family-sized cabin when Muhsen Ali suddenly stood up from behind a row of corn stalks. He had been tending his garden, kneeling in the rich, turned earth. The Jordanian man was in his late forties; he had a wife, beautiful twelve-year-old twin daughters, and a younger son, Amir, who was the apple of his eye. Muhsen's tanned face appeared tawny in the summer light. He grinned and greeted Daniel. "*As-salamu-alaykum*" (Peace be unto you). He reached out two hands still covered in fresh soil and clasped the Marine's; dirt was buried under his fingernails and stained the knees of his trousers.

Daniel slowed and replied, "*Salamu-alaykum.* Peace to you as well, Muhsen. How are you?" He felt an urge to keep moving. He wanted to conclude his own work on the deer, but he suppressed the impulse to be brief or impatient. Muhsen was a friend, and he would not treat him brusquely.

Muhsen nodded. "I am well, I am well, my friend. I hear you have brought us a deer? Is this right?"

Daniel laughed a little at how quickly news had spread. "Yes, yes, I guess it doesn't take long for word to get around."

Muhsen gestured with a hand. "I saw your brother, Jonas, walking by with the buck on his shoulders." He grinned enthusiastically. "Wonderful! We will have meat tonight then. God be praised!"

"If I get my work done." Daniel smiled back, "Yes, God be praised. Jonas could have taken that shot; he let me have it."

Muhsen nodded and clasped his hands together in a dignified manner. "Of course, of course, brother. You are both appreciated, thank you."

Daniel smiled politely. "Sure, well, I don't mean to rush off, but I've got to get to the freezer or we'll be eating rice, beans, and vegetables again tonight."

"Of course, of course, my friend. You must go. Go! I will not keep you any longer." The neighbors bid each other farewell, the Arab bowing slightly as they parted ways.

Muhsen was a reverent and kindly man, very well educated. Before the Last War, he held two PhDs and worked as a professor of history and humanities at a prestigious university in old-world Amman. Always warm and gracious, he was a devout Muslim and raised his family in the traditions of their ancestors. He was hard-working and treated his wife well, though their culture caused her to be more private and withdrawn in the community. Muhsen delighted in his twin daughters, Quintessa and Jasmeen; he loved to tease and play with them and to tell them stories of their homeland.

Muhsen and his family had fled to the old-world United States when Jordan fell to the fanatical armies of Submission. They had barely escaped with their lives, smuggled out of the country in the back of a cargo truck under the cover of darkness. Before making it out, Muhsen had watched violence and genocide explode within his own city and neighborhood.

Hordes of Submission militants poured into Amman, burning homes and raping girls. Muhsen personally witnessed several of his neighbors dragged into the streets and shot or beheaded. Fellow countrymen were stoned to death or hanged in the public square for acts considered indecent: adultery, blasphemy, or apostasy. Anyone who had been a part of the Jordanian government was killed, including Muhsen's brother. People of other faiths were tortured and brutally executed or taken as slaves. And similar treatment was given to any Muslims who did not adhere to Submission's particular ideals.

The America Muhsen had arrived to was no dreamland either, rather more of a nightmare.

Bankrupted by years of global fighting and instability, the U.S. had languished to the point of economic collapse. There was anarchy and starvation in the streets; Winter Steel had seized several East Coast cities and was pounding the interior with bombs, rocket strikes, and artillery barrages. Meanwhile, Imperial State had invaded America's western shores and pushed all the way inland to New Mexico. Even after Mech-Tech assumed total control of the military and started to beat back Winter Steel's forces, the country remained in a state of complete ruin and utter chaos.

A long and perilous road eventually led Muhsen and his family to sanctuary in the community. No matter what faith, the circumstances surrounding their survival could only be considered miraculous. Something greater than human will had been watching out for the Jordanian family. Some higher power had guided them to this safe haven. Muhsen and Father Paolo often had long conversations about this matter and the purpose God, or "Allah" in Muhsen's language, might have for these peace-loving folk.

Muhsen and his family rarely attended the contemplative hour on Sunday mornings. Instead, he, his wife, and children laid out their prayer mats to kneel or prostrate themselves towards the east and Mecca. His daughters were not forced to wear burkas, though they did wear hijab veils as a sign of modesty and virtue and as a protection of their feminine beauty from wandering eyes.

When his children would ask why they did not join their neighbors in the singing and Sunday gatherings, Muhsen would calmly explain, "The Christians must worship God in the way they have been taught, true to their culture and understanding. We are Arabs and Muslim so we must worship Allah in the way He instructed us to by His Holy Prophet."

Sometimes his children could not understand why there was a difference. To their young minds, it seemed the world ought to be black and white. "But who is right?" they would say, demanding a straight answer. "Are the Christians and Jews unbelievers? Do they not know the true way?"

Muhsen would kindly but firmly respond, "Hush! Enough of this talk; enough of this *who is right and who is wrong*. This sort of talk led to the war and the destruction of our homeland. It is because of such thinking that we were forced to flee our home, why millions of Allah's children were needlessly slain. God calls us to be good and generous to our neighbors in this life, whether they are Muslim or not! *He* will judge who is right and who was wrong on the final day when all stand before Him to give account for their deeds.

"Listen now to my answer: every person in this world is a brother or sister to you. If they are Christian or Jew, they are a brother to you in faith, for we all believe in one Maker, and we share the same Fathers, Adam and Abraham, the Prophet Moses, and the Ten Commandments. If someone is Buddhist or does not believe in God, they may not yet know Allah, but He knows them. They are still a brother or sister to you by nature of their humanity. Allah has made us all, and we are *all* His children. If someone tells you differently, you must not listen to them for they do not have God's peace or love in their hearts. We say, 'Allah is most gracious and merciful.' These words should never be spoken lightly! We, His children, must also be gracious and merciful."

Sadly, because he was Arab and Muslim, it took longer for some in the community to trust Muhsen and his family. There had been mistrust in many hearts when the family first arrived. Everyone knew of the monstrous atrocities committed across the globe by Submission's armies. For those who had no previous nor positive relations with Muslims, it proved a challenge not to suspect them of subversive motives.

Father Paolo did not stand for any of this racism however; he vocally denounced all prejudice lurking in the hearts of the community against Muhsen. "Did you judge me because I was born Syrian?" the priest demanded at one gathering. "Or do you simply judge this man because he calls God by another name? Search your hearts and repent! And do not let the seeds of fear fill you with bigotry!"

It was difficult to admit, but even Daniel found himself on-guard around Muhsen at first. It was absurd and irrational of course, and he knew it. Muhsen had been a highly respected member of academic and higher-education circles, not to mention he was a loving father and devoted husband. His wife and children were *certainly* incapable of causing anyone harm! War had a way of instilling racism and mistrust. Though the open fighting had ended, people still feared a knife in the back if they risked lowering their guard.

When a soldier went to war with combatants of a certain ethnicity or creed, if the enemy claimed a specific deity in its propaganda, this was difficult to forget. There was no mental off-switch which a warrior could simply flip in his mind, especially when such enemies had dealt savagely with local populations and unarmed civilians.

Such fears and racial mistrust served the purpose of protecting the warrior's life during the fighting-when attack could come from any woman, child, or shopkeeper. In the aftermath, however, these instincts only hindered both warrior and society alike. Traumatic memories and deep emotional wounds could not be mended overnight, nor simply by means of rational thought. If these injuries were to be soothed, new and positive encounters with the people group in question would be necessary.

There was hope for the community though; Muhsen and his family were fully settled into a peaceful, cooperative life with their neighbors. During the most recent council election, votes had begun to appear for Muhsen to serve as an elder. This filled Paolo's heart with joy and pride. Another year and Muhsen would surely receive a seat on the council, and then he would be regarded as the leader and guide he already was. With love and true friendship, the wounds and hatred from the Last War would slowly be healed in this humble community.

Muhsen and Father Paolo already enjoyed a close friendship, thanks in no small part to their cultural kinship and ethnic backgrounds. Comparatively, they came from a more similar part of the world than the rest. Jordanians and Syrians had their own political, religious, and ethnic histories of strife and racism, but neither of these two men bore the slightest interest in such things.

Muhsen respected Father Paolo for his fair and prudent counsel to the community; he also appreciated the abbé for how hard he had fought for decent treatment of Muhsen's family. Inwardly, the Jordanian felt a slight sadness that Paolo was not Muslim. He secretly wished the Syrian might one day convert to

Islam, the *true* faith of Arabs, in Muhsen's view. For now though, they shared peace and friendship, with a deep and abiding care between them.

Daniel nudged the door to his cabin open with his boot. It was quiet inside. Sadie was off running through tall grass with squealing children in hot pursuit. Dust danced and floated in the still air as sunlight poured through the window. The Marine's clothes were folded neatly under his cot beside several guns and boxes of ammunition. There was a cheap bookcase in the corner with a few classics and books of poetry on the shelves.

Daniel had the cabin to himself-a gift for his honored role in protecting the camp. But he had also built most of it himself. The single room was smaller than Jonas' and Janae's home and it bore no sink. Early each morning, Daniel would lace up his boots and walk to the well's spigot to pump what water he needed for the day.

The warrior stepped past the potbelly stove near the door-where he sat reading by firelight most evenings. He pulled the magazines out of the rifles and cleared both chambers of any rounds. He laid the weapons down atop the grey siesta blanket draped over his cot. He would give Jonas his rifle back later.

Because Daniel lived alone, his neighbors regularly invited him to join them at their tables for dinner. And he often accepted their generosity gratefully, always careful to ask what he could contribute to the meal. He was well-liked and respected by the families of the community. Children regarded him as a sort of immortal, mythic hero because he had fought in the Last War. Parents frequently had to remind their children that it was not polite to pepper the former Marine captain with prying questions about the intimate details of his combat experiences.

Daniel was always calm and courteous in these instances, but they did wear on him. They resurrected floods of flashing images and memories, which he spent most of his days trying to bury and forget-the sights, sounds, and smells leftover from the war. Thus, some nights he declined all neighborly invitations to share in a meal. He would fix a simple stew of potatoes, carrots, celery, and venison or rabbit if it was available. Then he would dine alone, in peace and quiet with only Sadie lying beside him on the floor for company.

Daniel stepped out from his cabin doorway and for the first time that morning he truly slowed internally-mind, spirit, and body. He breathed deeply, and his shoulders eased a little; Raoul was right, it was a beautiful day. He reflected on the prayer of respect and gratitude he had offered for the deer earlier. Such things were intended to slow people, to help them honor the sacred in each moment. A terrible storm had been raging inside him for the better part of the morning, a swelling and surging torrent of motion and urgency. Turbulent waters, this was how Father Paolo described the soul of a person who could not slow down or come to stillness.

"Uncle Dan!" an unbridled voice yelled, interrupting his contemplation.

Daniel's gaze rose from the earth and he smiled. Without turning his head, he knew the small child this near-shrill holler belonged to. He pivoted to face his assailant. She was nine years old, with caramel-brown skin, and dark hair. She stood just over four feet tall, had her daddy's smile, and weighed fifty pounds soaking wet.

Daniel bowed slightly as if she were royalty. "Yes, Miss Ellie, how may I serve you today?"

Jonas' and Janae's daughter ran up to him out of breath, almost panting for air. Her palms were clasped together concealing something. "I caught a tree frog!" she announced, still trying to catch her breath. "Wanna see?"

"Absolutely!" Daniel winked and leaned over.

The child moved her top hand cautiously. "He might try to jump out" she explained earnestly. But the small amphibian did not try to escape or even move. There he was, just resting peacefully in the girl's gentle palm. His moist skin was a brilliant light-shade of green.

"Where did you find him?" Daniel asked.

"Over there." Ellie pointed to a fenced garden. "On

one of the post thingies that keeps the grapes up." The tall wire fence had been erected to keep deer out, not people.

"He's a neat little guy. Very calm, he must trust you." Daniel said looking up. "What are you going to call him?"

"Patrick," she stated matter-of-factly.

Dan stood back up and grinned. "Pat the tree frog; sounds pretty good. You'll have to catch some bugs to feed him."

"Yeah," Ellie agreed. "Mom said she'd give me a jar to build a—what's the word? It's a home for animals."

"A habitat?" Daniel guessed.

"Yeah! That's the word! Um, I was gonna ask you something, but I just forgot the question." Ellie looked around, the frog still resting in her hand. "Oh yeah! Where's Sadie?"

"Off playing with the other kids," Daniel replied calmly.

"Oh, where's my dad?"

A third voice suddenly cut in, "The hell are you doing hangin' around my daughter?" Daniel turned slowly and grinned at his friend, who was coming down the hill from the cooler. "Ellie, I don't want you hanging around this white devil anymore, you hear? He's a bad influence." Jonas warned her.

"Daddy, Uncle Dan is not a white devil!" the girl

protested, covering her new pet again.

"Oooooh!" Jonas exclaimed, as if surprised. "You sure about that?"

"Yes, Daddy, he's a very nice man!" Ellie nodded firmly for emphasis.

"It seems your daughter likes me," Daniel goaded.

"Yeah? Well, that makes one of us." Jonas winked back; he was drying his hands with a cloth rag.

"You finished with the deer already?" Daniel asked, genuinely surprised. "I was just coming up to help you."

"Yeah? I bet you were." Jonas smirked sarcastically. "Don't worry, I left you plenty to do. I just skinned it; I left it for you to carve up and divvy out portions. You didn't think I'd do *all* the work did you?"

"Not a chance," Daniel retorted dryly. "Thanks for that."

"Well," said Jonas, tossing his head in the direction of the ice-locker. "Them bones ain't gonna clean themselves. I want to see some meat on my plate tonight so-better get a move on!"

Daniel shook his head. "You're incredible."

"I know!"

"Daddy, wanna see my tree frog?" Ellie asked, interrupting the banter.

"In a minute, baby, let's head down to the cabin and see what your mom's up to. You can show me there."

Janae Wells abruptly spoke up, "I'm right here,

Jonas." She was standing thirty feet away with a basket of freshly picked, unwashed vegetables on her hip. She was slender and very attractive. "You haven't been swearing in front of our daughter again, have you?"

Jonas gave a wide smile and laughed a little. "No ma'am! Course not! Come on, baby, it's me! What kind of father do you think I am?!"

Janae stared skeptically. "Mmhmm."

"Good to see you mind your woman so well, Jonas," Daniel jabbed smugly.

"Man, shut your mouth," Jonas hissed. "*I* run my house! She knows who calls the shots in this family."

"How 'bout you say that a little louder then?" Daniel prodded.

"I don't have to, I'm the boss around here. Boss ain't gotta say nothi-"

"Uncle Dan," Ellie cut-in loudly. "Daddy says he can kick your ass!"

Daniel absorbed this with an amused nod. "Is that a fact, Ellie?"

"Yeah, that's a damn fact," Jonas muttered, under his breath.

"Really, Jonas?!" Janae snapped. "Oh, that's great! See what you've done, now she knows A.S.S.!"

"Baby, it's not a big deal! Look, Daddy's a hardcore warrior, and the world's a rough place. I'm just tryin' to raise Ellie up to be like her ol' man: a tough Ranger!"

Jonas grinned proudly, one hand resting on his daughter's shoulder.

Janae did not look convinced. She adored her husband, but she sometimes held serious reservations about his 'parenting' philosophies...

"Actually, Daddy," Ellie said looking up. "I've been thinking I might want to be a Marine when I grow up- like Uncle Dan!"

"What?!" Jonas demanded.

Daniel nearly fell over laughing. "Buuuurn! In your face, brother! Your own daughter just sold you out!"

Jonas glowered down at Ellie's innocent face. "We're gonna talk about this, you hear me? I don't know where you get these ideas, girl. 'Be a Marine like Uncle Dan.' Are you even my child?!"

"Yes, Daddy!" Ellie giggled and wrapped herself around his side in a hug.

"We're gonna talk about this, girl; you've gone and lost your damn mind," Jonas exclaimed, walking her towards Janae. "Marine, my ass!" He grumbled.

He reached his wife, leaned over and kissed her. "Love you, can you believe this girl?"

"Love you too, baby." Janae kissed him back. "She's gotta make up her own mind. She's stubborn like her daddy."

"Oh, like me?"

"That's right." Janae grinned, kissing him again.

"So not like her mama, then?" Jonas questioned. "I'm just checkin' cause when you said 'stubborn', I thought you was about to name somebody *else* in this family, not me."

"Nope," Janae responded; she set the basket down and wrapped her arms around his neck. "Just like you." She laughed, looking up at her man's dark eyes and handsome features.

Jonas squeezed his wife's behind.

She let out a gasp and smacked his hand. "Jonas!"

"What? You got a nice butt! My hand just had a muscle spasm. Seems to happen around girls with nice butts." He swatted her playfully for good measure. "See? It just happened again! I can't control it! I don't know what happened."

"Mmhmm, well, mine had better be the *only* butt you're touching!"

"Of course! Nicest one around," Jonas buttered. "I only go for the best."

"Oh, is that a fact?" Janae rolled her eyes but smiled inwardly at his flattery.

"Eww!" Ellie exclaimed. "You guys are so weird! It's gross to talk about butts!"

Jonas looked down at his daughter. "That's right, Ellie, we are weird. Weird stuff happens when you start hanging around with boys, so you better not hang around any 'til you're at least forty-five. Got that? Take a good look and remember, it's gross, isn't it?"

Ellie nodded with sincere disgust.

Still laughing, with her arm around Jonas, Janae called out, "Daniel, are you coming to dinner with us tonight?"

"That depends," he answered. "Are you making that corn bread I love?"

"You know it!"

"Then I'll be there." He grinned.

"We'll see you later, man." Jonas waved. He and his family turned to walk back to their humble cabin.

Daniel watched them go, Jonas and Janae with arms around each other's waists and Ellie frolicking beside them in her own world, the frog still in her hands. There was much love and joy in that household. Daniel always looked forward to an evening together with them—the warm glow of light in the cabin as they sat around the dinner table, the roars of laughter when he and Jonas got carried away, Janae's folded arms and eye-rolls when they did. And there were good, quiet conversations the three adults had when the night grew late and Ellie was tucked into bed.

Daniel loved these friends he had been blessed with, and he knew they loved him. It stirred old feelings in him, familiar but forgotten desires from another lifetime. He felt a surge of powerful emotions rise from his stomach until they welled up in his chest. He stiffened a little and tried to ignore them, forcing them back down. He turned and began walking back up the sloping earth towards the cooler. There was work to finish.

He knew he would never have a family of his own.

CHAPTER THREE

Janae Wells awoke from a deep dream. It was dark outside; the cabin was pitch black around her, and the air was warm and still within. Slowly, her awareness gathered and she began to recognize the faint sounds of a disturbing ruckus out in the night. Beyond the cabin door, it echoed across the sleepy glade—a violent commotion of incoherent bellows gaining momentum.

"Jonas, Jonas, wake up!" She shook her husband. "Jonas, you need to wake up now."

"What, baby? What's wrong?" Jonas snorted groggily. He wanted to keep his eyes shut and go back to sleep, but the worry in her tone made him pause. He rolled over and propped himself up on one arm, yawning in the darkness and straining to listen.

"It's Dan, baby," Janae said, concern growing in her

voice. "You need to go help him."

Jonas heard it now too—the distant sounds of a man's distressed cries and intermittent rage. They were muffled by the cabin walls but distinct. Daniel's cabin lay roughly a hundred yards up the gently sloped terrain from Jonas' and Janae's.

"What's going on?" a small voice called out in the darkness. It was Ellie; her parents' voices had woken her. "Is Uncle Dan all right?"

"He's fine, Ellie, go back to sleep," Jonas ordered. He didn't want her getting worked up with fear. "Uncle Dan just has bad dreams, sweety, kind of like you sometimes. I'll go over and check on him."

Jonas arose and fumbled for his pants in the dark; the angry shouts and hollering continued in the distance. "How long has he been going like this?" Jonas snapped in frustration. He was worried about his friend; he also didn't want the whole camp woken up by this frenzy.

"I don't know," Janae confessed, tossing him a shirt. "I woke you up as soon as I heard it."

"Can I come with you, Daddy?"

"No," Jonas replied flatly.

"Daddy, take Patrick to Uncle Dan; it'll cheer him up!" Ellie held up the tree frog housed in a glass jar with holes drilled in the lid for air.

Jonas ignored his daughter. He knew she was just trying to be helpful, but he didn't have time for childish antics right now. He pulled on his boots and laced them hastily; then he strode for the door and threw it open. As he stomped out, he overheard his wife softly consoling, "Ellie, come over here and snuggle with mama, baby; just 'til daddy gets back. Don't worry about Uncle Dan, he'll be all right. He's just having a bad dream; Daddy's gonna go wake him up."

The night air was cool and refreshing on Jonas' face; he filled his lungs with cold oxygen to further rouse himself. The cabins had the tendency to grow stuffy at night with multiple people sheltering in them. The Ranger gave a momentary shiver; the night's chill was invigorating, and slowly his mind became more alert. He trudged up the sloping earth towards the upheaval of Daniel's shouts and thrashing. Jonas knew his friend had nightmares almost every night, but they were not always so intense. The worst ones seemed to come about once every two weeks.

Celestial lights twinkled down gently from the deep, blue heavens above. The glittering sky was clear and starry tonight, and Jonas began to discern the vague outline of Daniel's cabin ahead. As he drew closer, he suddenly distinguished the dark silhouettes of two other individuals. Their shrouded shapes startled Jonas at first. He had not expected to find anyone else out here already; he begrudgingly wondered why they hadn't already roused the tormented Marine. One of the figures was squatted with his back to the side wall of the cabin; the other stood a few feet from the front door, arms outstretched.

"The hell are you two doing just standing out here?" Jonas demanded. "Why haven't you woken him up?" The two individuals looked up. When the starlight reflected off their faces the Ranger grew even more indignant. "Wow," he mused bitterly. "And y'all call yourselves his friends...some friends!"

The one sitting with his back to the cabin was Raoul; the one standing with arms outstretched turned out to be Father Paolo. The latter was murmuring quiet prayers for the tortured soul inside the cabin.

Disgusted by their inaction, Jonas reached out for the door handle to tear it open. A few thuds from flying objects crashed against the walls and floor within as Daniel's unconscious, agitated ranting continued unabated.

"Do not do it, Jonas," a solemn voice called out; it was Raoul.

"And why the hell not?!" the darker man shot back.

"His spirit has not been able find its way home from the war; this is why he still fights battles by night. He must face the spirits of those who haunt him—the ghosts of enemies slain by his hand and the brothers he could not save. Only then will he find any hope for peace. Your friend is a warrior, and he must walk this path though it be filled with many griefs and mourning. If you wake him now, you will rob him of his dignity and honor. A warrior must fight his own battles. And his soul must find forgiveness and cleansing before it can ever return home."

"Well that's really interesting, Raoul," Jonas retorted in irritation. "Maybe that's how your people do it back where you come from, but where I come from, we don't leave a man behind! We don't *abandon* our fellow warriors in a fight! And this—" Jonas pointed to the cabin "—is leaving a man behind!" He turned to Paolo. "And you, Father, what are you doing?! Can you really just stand there praying while the man suffers a few feet away?!"

The priest quieted his prayers and looked up at the Ranger. Paolo's frail, knobby figure appeared ghostlike in the moonlight. Age had weathered his frame and vigor, but it had not taken his resolve. "Daniel sleeps with a loaded pistol under his pillow most nights. I thought it best to wait for extra support—for someone such as yourself—in case we need to subdue him for everyone's safety."

Jonas felt a twinge of embarrassment for his impetuous wrath. He was humbled by Paolo's response; it was practical and seasoned with the wise patience characteristic of the old priest. "Well," he replied quietly. "That's the smartest thing I've heard since I woke up. My apologies, Father."

There was an anguished cry from the dark cabin, and everyone turned towards the door. Inside, Sadie had begun to bark. Her master's distress had finally elevated the dog's anxiety to a point of doing more than cowering in the corner. She cautiously ventured to Daniel's side and licked his exposed palm nervously.

Daniel jerked awake with a final bellow of rage and aggression. He sat staunchly upright, panting for his breath as Sadie nuzzled and licked his hand again. She looked up at her master with concerned, mournful eyes.

"It's okay, girl," he reassured her, gently stroking the Labrador. He rubbed his forehead and eyes then lay back down. He blew out a long exhale. "That was a pretty bad one, huh?" he said to Sadie.

Sadie did not respond. She just sat quietly and stared up at him. Daniel glanced around the dark cabin. His blankets and pillows were knotted and strewn everywhere. The loaded pistol Paolo had referenced dug into the back of his neck, its hard, pointed edges stabbing his flesh and leaving indents. The warrior grunted in annoyance and pulled the cold, metal object from behind his head. He let out another sigh and stared up at the ceiling, exasperated.

Was this it? Was this his life? Was this all he was fated to do for the rest of his days? Sleep alone on a cot? Have flashback night-terrors with a loaded pistol at arm's reach because the community lived under the veil of unending threat?

There was a knock at the door. "Come in," Daniel beckoned. The door was already cracked open before he finished speaking.

Jonas poked his head inside. "You doing all right in here?"

"Yeah. Yeah, man, thanks for checking." Daniel replied, embarrassed. This wasn't the first time he had woken people in the camp, and it was getting old.

Jonas stepped across the threshold and closed the door behind him. He grabbed the empty chair resting near the potbelly stove and set it down next to Daniel's cot. Then he plopped down and began petting Sadie. He said nothing.

Daniel sat up again and glanced at his friend, who met his gaze. "There's nothing to say, man. It...is. It just...is."

"I know, brother," Jonas responded, his eyes revealing a deep well of emotion. The look communicated more than words ever could—a bottomless chasm of feeling. He fought to hold it all back. It was a silent understanding and promise: *I know. I know and I'm with you to the end, no matter what. I'm here, and I won't ever quit on you or leave you in this fight.*

The great torrent in Jonas was for more than just Daniel's suffering; it was for every comrade he had ever lost, every Ranger he had ever laid to rest, every soldier who had ever slept on the cold, hard ground a thousand miles from home and family, every grime-covered Marine who had shivered through the night in frozen mud or held a dying friend's hand during a firefight in their final moments before passing.

It was for every warrior he had ever buried, and the soul's anguish over every hole he'd ever blown through the chest or head of another human. For the pain of every warrior: all they had seen, done, or failed to prevent-only to come home and be haunted by it in their dreams. It was for all they had sacrificed for in the name of peace and freedom or God, family, and country.

Daniel extended a sturdy hand, his gaze unwavering. Jonas clapped the open palm firmly with his own. "I know, man," he repeated. "I know."

✵ ✵ ✵ ✵ ✵

CRACK! The sharpened blade of the ax split through the end of the log and sent its two halves tumbling wildly. The morning was still cool, but Daniel had worked up a sweat. He wiped his brow; the long summer had tanned his torso and back. Shirtless, he kicked away a stray piece of firewood and reset with a new log. He swung the ax. CRACK! The end of cedar fractured down its core. He leveraged his ax free and swung again. The second strike finished off the log, splintering the fibrous sinew still holding it together.

It was a Sunday morning; besides several birds chirping and singing, Daniel could hear the chorus of a closing hymn being sung in the distance. Another contemplative hour was concluding, and Father Paolo was no doubt speaking a benediction over those gathered. Soon the faithful parishioners would pass by, returning to their day's business or rest.

Daniel rarely attended the contemplative hour. He did not fancy himself a canary and inwardly disliked the singing parts; more than this, he simply wasn't very religious. He tried to respect all life as Raoul and Father Paolo taught him to, and he believed there was a God. Unfortunately, because of all the violence and cruelty Daniel had witnessed in his life, he had come to believe that God abandoned mankind to its ends long ago. This, or the Maker had never cared much for the human race.

Father Paolo's preaching challenged this sort of thinking, and sometimes Daniel genuinely longed to believe in the God the priest spoke of. This God who rescued people and restored justice, order, and peace. It was simply too good to believe though—a fairytale, wishful thinking. Most Sunday mornings, Daniel assigned himself to sentry duty at one of the tree-stand lookout posts along the wooded border of the community.

The former MARSOC captain would sit in a tree's branches with his back pressed to its trunk, surrounded by lush foliage and chirping songbirds. He would listen to Paolo teach and the congregants sing, all from a safe distance. He never spoke a word of criticism against their beliefs or practices, and he appreciated the peace it helped to maintain in the community, but it wasn't for him.

Daniel swung the ax again. *CRACK!* A piece of wood flew off the stump being used for a stand and ricocheted violently off his right shin. He winced in instantaneous pain and tried not to scream profanities. His eyes watered for a moment, but he didn't make a sound. He kicked the piece of wood away with all his might and reset.

Once in a while when he was working outside, young women in the community would pass by. Sometimes they would smile at him and then look down quickly or giggle and whisper to a friend. He knew he was attractive to them; he took care of his body and they saw the leader he was—his strength, courage, and honor. Today he doubted any women would be so interested in him. He imagined them avoiding eye contact and moving past quickly.

In a community of fewer than a hundred, it was not hard to figure out who was waking everyone up in the middle of the night. Daniel felt certain he scared them all to some degree. They cared about him of course, appreciated all he did for them, but they had no idea what to do with his demons. None of them knew how to respond to whatever haunted him at night.

CRACK! Daniel split another log. He leaned over to grab the piece of wood and toss it aside when he heard a voice behind him: "You swing that ax like a man who needs to confess something."

Daniel turned around; it was Father Paolo.

The old man smiled warmly. "The community sees all you do for us, but you and I know the truth."

"Yeah? And what truth is that?" Daniel asked with an amused grin. "I didn't hear you come up, Father— didn't figure you for the sort to sneak up on people."

"Perhaps you underestimate me, Daniel," the old priest said, a glint of mischief in his eye. "*Or* perhaps today you have much on your mind and would not have heard anyone come up on you." There was a long pause. Paolo waited, watching Daniel mentally process this as he set up another log. "You are full of anger, Daniel, and much pain and sorrow too." The priest lamented, letting the words hang in the air.

Daniel did not meet his gaze nor even look at the older man. He split another log and muttered, "What do you know of it, Father?"

"I don't!" the priest fired back. "But I would *like* to.

Come and see me at my home later today."

Daniel glanced up, maybe to check if the old Syrian abbé was serious or not.

"If you wouldn't mind," Paolo concluded courteously, "I'd like to speak with you further, in confidence of course."

Daniel's eyes met the priest's. He hesitated, unsure if this was a good idea. "All right," he acquiesced quietly. He wasn't sure what he was getting himself into. Would the priest try to head-shrink him or invoke some weird, mystic ritual upon him? Maybe a strange combination of both! In his former life, Daniel had found little use for "shrinks" and again, did not consider himself particularly religious. Nevertheless, he knew Paolo to be trustworthy. In truth, the warrior had never met another human as genuine or sincere as the priest. He lived solely to care for the physical and spiritual needs of others.

Daniel knew this kind of meeting would likely mean softening his outer defenses and lowering his guard some. He also knew he probably needed whatever help Paolo could offer him. Besides, what would be the harm in talking to the old abbé a little? If he didn't like it, the Marine could march out of there and never lower his guard again. "I'll come by later," Daniel said quietly. He gave a curt nod of acknowledgement and then returned his attention to splitting firewood.

Father Paolo was not the least bit offended by Daniel's impertinence and obvious reservations. The priest had learned long ago to check his ego when interacting with people. However individuals behaved revealed more about their own issues than his respectability. He turned to leave, lingering just for a moment to pet Sadie. The weathered Syrian bent down and stroked the faithful creature's head. Sadie was lying in the dirt safely out of range from Daniel's swinging ax and the flying log fragments. Paolo showered the ebony dog with affection, and then he, too, went on with his day.

✵ ✵ ✵ ✵ ✵

The afternoon was bright and warm when Daniel arrived at the priest's quarters. It was a very modest cabin, almost a shack, but it was cleanly constructed. Daniel did not waste any time hanging around the outside of it. He rapped on the wooden door loudly, and Father Paolo opened it shortly, graciously welcoming the warrior inside.

"May I offer you some tea?" his host asked.

Daniel accepted his clergyman's hospitality and took a seat on one of the simple, wooden chairs in the small space. Father Paolo ground some mint leaves and dropped them into a mug. Then he poured hot water from a kettle on the stove before offering the cup to his guest.

A short laugh escaped Daniel when he saw an old, familiar cartoon dog on the otherwise plain, white mug.

"Ah." Paolo smiled, easing himself into the other wooden chair. "Memories from another time. The old world lives on in our hearts and imaginations. They were simpler times, in a way. Some had far more than they ever needed. Many lived in luxury."

Daniel took a sip of the hot tea and stared at the mug for another moment as he reminisced about happier and more peaceful times. The black and white dog was frozen in motion, dancing jubilantly across the ceramic cup. Daniel let a final smirk go and then looked up at Paolo. "Well," he said, "I'm here, Father; what would you like to talk about?"

"Is there anything *you* would like to talk about?" the old priest inquired patiently.

"Not particularly," Daniel answered. "It was you who invited me up here."

"That is true." Paolo conceded with a smile. He waited another second. "How are you feeling about your place here in the community these days? You've been here what—two years now?"

"Something like that," Daniel agreed. He browsed around the small quarters. Father Paolo was tidy and a minimalist. His worldly possessions could be stuffed into a single bag if needed: a Bible, a half-dozen other books, a lantern, a few candles, a crucifix on the wall, a beautifully decorated chalice for serving Eucharist, and a few neatly-folded, simple garments.

"It's a good place to be," Daniel replied. "Certainly better than anything else out there at this point."

"Comparisons are fine, but how do *you* feel being here?" Paolo asked.

"It's a good place," Daniel repeated. "I try to contribute where I can and keep people safe, but sometimes I wonder if there's any place for men like me." He paused and leaned forward. "These are peaceful folks, Father; I went to hell and survived to come back. There is no place on Earth for men like me. I'm not a butcher or a tyrant like the bands of animals out there." Daniel tossed his head. "Those savages...but I don't I really fit here either. Most people went through tough, ugly things to find this place, but they never had to embrace their darker side. That's why I've had to teach them how to fight and defend themselves. It doesn't come naturally to them. They never saw the truly heinous side of other humans."

"You assume much about your brothers and sisters here," the priest observed. "Do you judge their experiences without truly knowing where each of them came from?"

"Yeah, maybe," the warrior replied. "But I know

they're not on my level and hopefully will never have to be. All I have to do is watch them, look in their eyes. Most of them are sheep, Father, they'd do just about anything to avoid a fight and maintain peace—even if it meant surrender or living on their knees. They can be trained to defend themselves, but most of them aren't real fighters."

"Not like you."

"No."

"So where does that leave you?" Paolo asked, genuinely curious.

"I'm a wolf without a pack."

"Ah, a loner," the priest reflected. "Even here, surrounded by all these good people, you feel you are an outcast, an outsider?"

"I'll never truly be one of them, but that's what makes me a leader. I'm something different that they need, something vital to their survival."

"The sheepdog metaphor."

Daniel nodded.

"You feel you have no identity apart from being a warrior." The priest observed.

Daniel grew quiet and just stared at the old man. He felt like this was some sort of a trap, and he could feel his jaw tightening. He did not intend to scowl, but his face certainly did not exude joy, ease, or trust.

Father Paolo chuckled slightly and changed the

subject for a moment. "I heard a circulating rumor that you did not approve of my sending off our three young neighbors yesterday."

"No," Daniel answered flatly. "I did not."

"Tell me why?"

The former Marine captain leaned back in his seat and exhaled. He looked away. "I know you didn't push any of them to go, but you encouraged them to—with a bunch of idealistic fairytales." Daniel did not mean for such obvious contempt to slip out, but it did, so he just kept going. "We sent those people to their deaths, Father. You have to know that, and that's on us. . . ."

The old priest's countenance was saddened, but his presence remained resolute. "Daniel." He sighed. "You don't really believe in the things I preach, do you? You don't believe that we are all loved children of one holy and benevolent Father and that the evils of this world have come as a result of mankind's endless self-loathing, fear, shame, and the false identities we attempt to hide behind. That it is the great lie-that we could never be loved as we are: unvarnished and imperfect, fearful and naked, scarred and flawed. That we are totally, completely, and perfectly loved in spite of this, yet paradoxically and simultaneously because of who we are?"

Daniel grimaced skeptically. "It sounds nice, Father, it just doesn't work for me—not when it comes to violent, evil individuals who prey on children or the weak."

Paolo let this pass. He would avoid an intellectual debate; there were greater things at stake in the moment. "If you could believe," the priest continued, "all that Christ came to reveal and communicate to the human race, then you would understand that I could not *possibly* have discouraged those three from leaving. Even if they do meet death, even a painful death, they have already found true life. They have stopped clinging to a world of temporal wealth accumulation, comforts, and pride. For them, the notion of keeping to themselves what they have finally discovered and truly embraced as their own-would be a kind of slow, living death.

"And what exactly do you think they realized?" Daniel asked.

"That God is not far away and all of this..." Paolo motioned around the room and to his own flesh "...is both good yet temporary. There is so much more and people must be ready. Most are not ready to enjoy real life in unfettered connection, in love, joy, and peace with God, their neighbors, and themselves."

"If you say so, Father," Daniel replied, unconvincingly. He glanced around the room again. The former combat leader had no desire to disrespect the old priest's sacred beliefs. In truth, he respected Paolo deeply, but there were mountains of life's filth and refuse blocking him from the kind of social and spiritual vision the priest was trying to articulate. Some great, mental barrier impeded all faith and transcendence in the warrior—some massive block fueled by years of anger, pain, outrage, and injustice.

The priest smiled warmly. "Perhaps we should talk about something else." He waited, but Daniel did not volunteer anything. Finally, the Syrian abbé asked, "Can you tell me about your dreams?"

Daniel's eyebrows shot up in surprise. Father Paolo's demeanor was gentle and non-demanding; Daniel had even expected this question at some point, just perhaps not so directly. He shifted uncomfortably and looked away. He took another drag of his tea to delay the inevitable revelation a few more seconds. Finally, the former MARSOC leader lowered the mug and leaned forward. He stared at the wooden plank floor for several moments, questioning his decision to come here, to tell the story. He rubbed his forehead and facial scruff; then it began...

He heard the helicopter blades start to hum around him, heard the haunting shouts from his Marines. He felt the heat against his face—that terrible blast and concussive shock-wave.

The warrior closed his eyes and inhaled deeply, filling his lungs. He relaxed his body and waited—waited for it all to begin once more—that loud buzz of static that jolted through his ear canals. It always felt like it came from the core of his brain and startled him every time like jolts of electricity, deafening and intrusive.

With the cuts of static, images began to flicker and race. They played like a film he'd been forced to watch over and over until he knew every part. But it was no film; it was his life, his story, and it had all really happened, all of it...

"Most nights," he began, "I dream the same thing."

"Tell me," the priest encouraged.

"I'm riding on a helicopter with my team; it's a rescue operation. We're flying through the city of Baltimore, and the place is a burning wreck, falling apart all around us. We'd been sent in to pick up a final group of survivors after Winter Steel had stopped pounding the city with artillery and rockets." Daniel paused here and swallowed. "We had just located the survivors; they were in a park next to a lake. We dropped altitude and started our descent to land and pick them up." Daniel's voice trailed off, and he looked away again, this time as if he were seeing through the walls of the cabin and out towards something in the distance.

Paolo waited. He was keenly aware they were treading on sacred territory—the hallowed ground of a warrior's suffering.

"We were coming in fast," Daniel continued, "and I

could see them clearly. We were only a few hundred meters out. That's when there was a sound like clapping thunder. We looked up and saw two dozen rockets break the skyline and descend on the city. A few struck burning business towers already on the verge of collapse, several slammed right into the park and the survivors..."

There was another long pause, "In a second, the park was completely engulfed in a giant fireball. The blast rocked us hard, nearly knocking us out of the sky. One of my team almost fell out the side door of the helicopter, but we caught him by his flak jacket, and the pilot got control of the bird."

The flitting images abruptly overrode Daniel's vision and suddenly he was there again:

Captain Weston heard the familiar roar and looked up. Three Russian jets cut across the city in front of him and began dropping ordinance payloads to finish off anything left alive below.

"They're firebombing the city!" one of his sergeants barked to the pilots. "Get us the hell out of here!"

The sounds echoed in the captain's ears—the blaring alarms from the cockpit. His sergeant reached out and grabbed him by shoulder, shouting over the noise: "Sir, we have gotta get out of here now or we are all going to die! They're gone, sir! They're all dead down there, there's nobody left alive!"

The images faded. Daniel had returned to the small shack. His face was stoic, but his eyes revealed a bottomless chasm of grief, regrets, and sorrow.

"Is that the end of the dream?" Paolo asked gently.

"No," he admitted, trying to gain greater control of his inner world. "After the blasts and firebombing, when the memories have played out, I see a woman. She was in that crowd of survivors. I saw her just before those Winter Steel rockets blew them all to hell."

"Did you know this woman?"

"No, I just saw her that day, standing there, waiting to be rescued. After the city fades away, I always see her, up close. She's about twenty feet away, and we're standing in that park alone. There's a shroud of smoke and flame around us, but I can see her, as clearly as I see you now. She's very beautiful and pregnant. I can see her belly and the love in her eyes for her unborn child. I see the sadness in her eyes—the fear; I think she knows she's about to die. She speaks to me—I can see her lips moving, but I can't hear what she's saying. I call out to her and try to get closer, but as soon as I take a step towards her, the rockets hit. And then she's gone, engulfed in the blast and flames. The explosion blows me back, sends me sailing away from her. And then that's the end, that's when I usually wake up."

"And you feel responsible for her death? You feel guilty?" Father Paolo asked.

"Guilty doesn't even come close to what I feel, Father. Yes, I've thought of it a million times over: if we had lifted off the airfield even fifteen minutes earlier, if we had pushed our speed a little harder we could have saved her. We could have saved all of them. But we didn't...and now they're dead, along with millions just like them."

Daniel's expression was morose and his voice grim. "It's not the dead we should grieve for, Father, it's the living. I'd like to think the dead have found some peace at last, even if only by a lack of consciousness, but the living? *We're* the damned ones—left to struggle on, left to this world of evil and darkness, loneliness, injustice, and sword..."

"And guilt!" Paolo interjected. "You carry such a heavy burden of pain and guilt, Daniel. You carry many things not yours to bear. You did not commit the acts of murder against those you tried to save."

"*Tried*, Father, that's the key word: tried and failed. Their blood and pain hangs on me, too. If I had been faster, stronger, more prepared...if I had trained and equipped my men better, we might have—"

"What?" the priest cut in. "You might have saved the whole world?"

Daniel remained stoic; he refused to take the free pass his friend was offering him. "Believe me, Father," he said woefully. "That day I dream about was not even close to my worst mission. It's frankly kind of ironic that *that* is what my unconscious has chosen to fixate on. There were countless others I wasn't able to save: South America, Egypt, Pakistan...Marines, friends, unarmed civilians. The list goes on and on. Maybe Baltimore was just a tipping point..."

"How about family?" Father Paolo inquired.

Daniel's face transformed into a scowl, but he did not respond.

"Tell me, Daniel, where did you come from before the war?"

"Here," the warrior admitted with disdain, making evident these were not pleasant memories. "Not here in this exact place, but *here* as in sixty miles from here, give-or-take, back before it was Unity, back when it was the good old U.S.A."

"Please." Father Paolo gestured. "Tell me."

"Not much to tell. When I was real young my parents had a farm, but that didn't last. There's never been a lot of money in farming, and my old man was a drinker so that made things even more difficult. After we lost the farm, we lived in the Portland area. The old man got a job at a paint factory; when there was any money that didn't go to his drinking, he liked to gamble. He got us all evicted and homeless more than once." Daniel paused here long enough for an ironic smirk to cross his lips. "He was a mean bastard from the beginning, but he turned out to be an evil son-of-a-bitch. Pardon my French, Father."

The priest dismissed the apology. He cared far more about Daniel's capacity to share than a few profanities.

"Whenever he came home drunk, we all tried to stay out of his path. Mom took the worst of it; he'd beat her senseless, sometimes with a belt. Sometimes it was bad enough to send her to the emergency room, but she never told on him. I think she was afraid he'd kill us kids if the police got involved. I always tried to hide my little sister or piss him off enough to turn his wrath on me instead of her."

"Sounds like you were a protector from the beginning," Paolo reflected. "Always trying to take care of people."

"*Trying* is right," Daniel lamented ruefully. His face periodically twitched with pain and grief, but he would try to hide it by looking away. "My little sister, Rainey, was a sweet girl—innocent. She deserved a safe childhood and parents who cared for her. That piece-of-shit didn't just beat her though," Daniel snarled with bristling hatred. "Sometimes he'd lock himself in the bedroom and touch her. As she got older, I know he raped her. And there wasn't a damn thing I could do to stop him. Sometimes I'd beat on the bedroom door and make enough racket to piss him off, just to distract him from her. He'd come flying out in a rage ready to throttle me. I'd yell for Rainey to run and hide. Then he'd catch me and bash my head against the wall or just take the belt to me."

"Where was your mother during all of this?"

"Like I said, she always got the worst of the beatings. Sometimes she was recovering from his abuse. I don't think she ever knew what he did with Rainey until near the end. The old man never let her leave the house without him, and none of us were allowed to have our own phones. Once in a while he would send mom to the store, *usually to pick up more beer.* That's when he would..."

"Abuse your sister?"

Daniel nodded; his ghostly expression spoke how deeply the traumas had burrowed into his mind and soul.

"How did it end?" Father Paolo asked. "Did you run away?"

"No, I joined the military. I knew the Marines were tough, but I figured nothing could be worse than living under the old man's reign of terror for sixteen years. Back then you could enlist at seventeen if your parents were willing to sign off. I started meeting with a recruiter secretly after school and waited until after my seventeenth birthday. One night when the old man was drunk and in a decent mood—I think he'd been winning at poker with his junkie friends—I pulled out the papers and asked him to sign them.

"In his stupor he slurred, 'So you gonna make something of yourself, huh? Helen, you hear that? The boy's gonna be a Marine! A killer, just like his old man!' I remember his creep- friends grinning and clapping for me; I think they were all tweaked out. Totally drunk and unaware, he signed the papers. My mom didn't want me to go; I think she was afraid I'd get killed in some far-off war. But she knew the old man might kill me himself soon if I stepped out of line on the wrong day.

"I shipped off to boot camp two weeks after they both signed. We never told the old man that I was leaving until after I was safely aboard a flight to San Diego. The night before I left, I begged my mom and sister to run away and stay with my aunt until I could come back for them. We all cried and they promised to try."

"What happened?"

"I went to hell for three months. The Marine drill instructors didn't mess around. That first night I arrived, they shaved my head and stripped me of every possession. I was no longer allowed to speak, move, or even piss without permission. If you failed to obey a command you got socked in the gut or thrown against a wall. At least in Basic it was all to make us disciplined so we'd survive when they dropped us into a combat zone. At home the old man did all that stuff and worse just 'cause he was in a foul mood or felt like it!

"Our drill instructors did everything they could to destroy people psychologically. Their goal was to weed out the weak and break the belligerent or guys with egos, and they succeeded. They knew how to make a grown man cry. They pushed us physically until we'd collapse in puddles of our own sweat, unable lift ourselves off the ground, all the while berating and screaming at us. They'd cut our chowtimes short so we couldn't eat or force us to dump our meals in the trash. You learned to be fierce and effective even when exhausted, hungry, and sleep deprived. If you couldn't adapt, you broke or washed out.

"They'd curse you out so intensely that your face would be covered in their spit by the time they finished screaming. They taught us to shoot—to nail someone between the eyes at five hundred meters with only iron sights on your rifle. We learned hand-to-hand combat and riot control, how to fight and kill quickly and effectively. On two hours of sleep, we climbed mountains and covered sixty miles on foot in three days with a hundred pounds on our backs, plus your weapon! Then they'd tear-gas us as a reward." Daniel laughed.

"After boot camp I went to infantry school. Our Instructors pushed us even harder physically, but by then we were Marines so they didn't treat us like the lowest form of dog shit under their boots anymore.

They taught us to kill with anything you can imagine: knives, grenades, machine guns, the butt of your rifle, a rock or metal pipe...even your bare hands. We learned how to move tactically as a unit, in the dark, through cities, and over mountains. They *drown-proofed* us. In full fatigues and combat gear, we'd jump off forty foot towers into freezing water; then we had to tread water, fight off aggressors, and drag our buddies and all our gear to land.

"We learned to rappel off buildings and out of helicopters, how to scale cliffs and survive in the wilderness with nothing but a knife and canteen. At seventeen, I learned how to close with and destroy my enemies, how to clear buildings block by block with my squad. I could go on, but this was all just the beginning. I hadn't even hit my first unit in the fleet yet, let alone applied to MARSOC or officer's school; that all came later."

"What happened to your family?" Paolo asked, trying to redirect the conversation.

There was a momentary pause as Daniel refocused. "When I completed all my initial trainings, I was assigned to my first unit. After I reported in, I spoke with my corporal about my home life and how I wanted to get a place off base for my mom and sister. By this time, I hadn't been home in six months. It was generally unheard of for a new, unmarried Marine to live off base, but I had good N.C.O.s who really looked out for me.

"Once they heard about my family's situation, they took my case up the chain of command, and I was approved to rent an apartment off base providing I personally stayed in the barracks for my first year. I wasn't making much money as a private first class, but it was enough to get a small place. That's all mom and Rainey would need to start with, just something to get them away from him...

"One weekend, a buddy in the unit loaned me his car, and I drove home from Camp Pendleton, California, to get them. It was not a peaceful ordeal."

"I imagine your father did not let them go easily," the priest mused.

"Hell no," Daniel retorted. "It had been six months since he'd seen my face or even heard from me, so it was a shock when I walked through the front door that Saturday morning. He was sitting at the kitchen table, still hung over from the night before but already starting to drink for the day. His red eyes about fell out of his head when he saw me." Daniel laughed, remembering the moment. "I had put on a lot of muscle since he'd last seen me; I had the jarhead haircut, and I stood a lot taller too, like nothing could touch me."

"Like a Marine." Paolo smiled.

"Yeah, I guess. I was still brand new to it all though—just starting out. If he had been sober that day, things might have gone down different, but he wasn't. He got all proud and affectionate when he saw me, like the previous sixteen years of his shit had never happened. He tried to stand up and give me a hug; he was still bigger than me. You gotta understand, Father, the old man was a big bruiser. Anyway, he started slurring, 'Well, looky here, we got ourselves a big, bad U.S. Marine! Helen, get out here and take a look at your boy! He's all growed up into a man, a chip of off the ol' block!'"

"I'm sure you didn't care for that comparison."

"I ignored him. I wasn't gonna waste another second of my life on him. I called my mom and Rainey out into the living room and told them to grab anything they needed and head outside to my friend's car. We were leaving in three minutes. The old man was caught off guard, but he didn't like that one bit. He got all emotional for a second, started sniveling about how we couldn't just leave him alone and abandon him.

"My mom and sister could hardly believe I was actually standing there. Mom had tears in her eyes; Rainey was just in shock. Honestly, it was hardest for me to see my sister. She had shut down while I was away, closed off to the world. I could tell she was on the edge, her long sleeves hid the cuts on her wrists that day. I could have wrapped them both up in my arms, but none of us had time for that kind of reunion.

"Fortunately, they were cognizant enough to listen that day and go for a few belongings: birth certificates, a jacket, a change of clothes. They knew they were never coming back to that place or him. They looked at me like I was Superman, like I had just torn the roof off the house to destroy him and carry them to safety. The old man was not happy. As soon as he saw Mom and Rainey were listening to me and planned to leave, the self-pity vanished and his old, familiar rage showed up again.

"He told me I was a 'snotty little shit' who never learned to respect my elders. Then he started yelling: 'After all I did to raise you and put a roof over your head, you think you can barge in here and take my family away?! I should have finished you off years ago!' I didn't bother responding, I hated him so much. He had never been a father to any of us, and even if he had been sober, nothing would have gotten through to him. He was like a mad grizzly.

"My mom and sister came back out from their rooms ready to leave and headed for the door. He tried to grab Mom by the arm, and that's when I snapped. I slammed into him and I told him to keep his hands off her. Well, I said a lot of other stuff too... I think he was legitimately shocked for a second or two that someone had dared to physically challenge him under his own roof. The surprise didn't last though; he flared up and came back at me in a rage.

"By then Mom and Rainey had made it to the door, so I leg-swept and choke-slammed him to the floor. I put a knee on his chest and pulled a Kabar knife I had hidden under the tail of my shirt. I pressed the blade against his throat hard; I *wanted* him to feel it against his trachea. I wanted him to know he didn't have power over any of us anymore. One wrong move and I'd have slashed his carotid artery and watched him stumble around gasping while he spewed his blood all over the walls." Daniel's eyes were on fire now; his jaw was so tight Paolo half-expected to hear teeth start cracking. "Believe me, Father, I *wanted* to end that piece of filth!"

The priest maintained his tranquil demeanor. "But you did not, did you?"

"No," Daniel replied, "I knew if I killed him I'd go to prison for it, and there was no way I would throw my life away for that piece of shit."

"You must have realized your mother and sister were also going to need you in the days ahead."

Daniel exhaled. "Yeah, well, I didn't kill him that day. I pressed that knife against his throat as hard as I could without slicing him, then I leaned in and said, 'If you EVER try to find us again or even attempt to make contact, I'll kill you. I swear to God Almighty! I will finish the job I started here today and END YOU! That's a promise, do you understand me?' He couldn't speak or nod his head with my blade to his neck, but he swallowed and his eyes acknowledged my words. I saw something in the old man that day that I had never seen before, Father."

"What was that?" Paolo asked.

"Fear. I'd seen hate, rage, even malevolent glee in those eyes before, but I had never seen him scared. And, Father, that day, with me on his chest and a knife to his throat, he was shittin' his pants."

"And you found great satisfaction in this."

"You better believe I did." Daniel growled, his voice constricted with rage.

"Was that the end?" the priest inquired. "Happily ever after with your mother and sister?"

There was a long pause. "Not exactly," Daniel replied grimly. "Mom and Rainey moved to California with me; they lived off base from Camp Pendleton where I was stationed. Things were good for a while, and we were all happy; there was a lot of celebrating at being free, safe, and reunited. I spent most of my weekends with them. Rainey was still in high school, but mom was able to get a job as a waitress, so after the first year we found them a small house.

"I was rising in rank quickly. Even though I was young, my command saw me as a natural leader. I got things done, never made excuses, performed well under pressure, and took to the warrior's life with ferocity. I was promoted meritoriously to lance corporal and within six months of that I was already being recommended for promotion to corporal. That may not mean much to you, Father, but in the Marine Corps, especially the combat-arms, it was basically unheard of. For someone of my age and experience level to be considered for promotion to an N.C.O. rank."

"N.C.O.?"

"Non-commissioned officer—corporals and sergeants—the backbone of the Corps, the enlisted squad and platoon leaders. Anyway, I was doing very well and mom and Rainey seemed to be adjusting okay, too. About that time I was deployed to the South Pacific; my unit was stationed aboard a naval aircraft carrier as part of the attached Marine element. This was back before the Last War had started.

One night when we were out at sea, I was ordered to report to my company commander's office. The captain, my lieutenant, and platoon sergeant were all waiting for me with a serious phone call. My mother had been diagnosed with stage-four kidney cancer. She hadn't been allowed to see a doctor regularly since before meeting my father, so she had gone in for a routine check-up back in the States, and the next thing she knew, they were rushing her to the hospital for surgery and to start radiation therapy. The news was-they were trying to get control of the cancer, but it was extremely advanced. The doctors recommended that my command allow me to come home immediately."

"And did they send you?"

"Yes, and it was a good thing they did. They dropped me at a naval base in the Philippines, and I caught a military flight back to the States. The cancer was ravenous. It seemed to metastasize by the hour; it was killing her and nothing the doctors were doing even seemed to slow it down. The disease ravaged her body in a matter of weeks. Rainey and I sat with her and slept in that hospital room just to be close to her during those final days and hours. I tried to be strong for Mom and Rainey, but we all cried a lot.

"At the end, she couldn't eat anything, and she lost the ability to speak. I just remember her eyes, those sad eyes. I knew she was sorry; she had so many regrets for staying with the old man, for not going to the police. We told her we forgave her; we remembered how he tried to keep us all in cages of fear. To this day I know he killed her; he put her through so much hell and made her live in terror all those years...that's what made the cancer grow so fast; that's what killed her.

"After the funeral, Rainey started bottoming out. She had done all right when Mom was alive, but as soon as she passed, Rainey started getting high and hanging with a bad crowd. She never drank, alcohol was the old man's vice, but she stopped going to school for days at a time.

She was eighteen and a senior by then. I was a corporal and had a whole squad of Marines to look out for. I had sixteen guys to train, mentor, and discipline; there were times I'd be gone all night or for days at a time.

"Rainey just kept getting worse, and I didn't know what to do. The command let me go live off base to look after her, especially since Mom had just died. Rainey would lie on the couch and watch TV for days at a time. She wouldn't move except to use the bathroom. She stopped taking care of herself and started stealing from me. She barely ate. I tried taking her to shrinks and counselors, but she just skipped her appointments while I was out training during the day.

"Somewhere in there she starting using heroin. How she came in contact with it I still don't know, but apparently she knew somebody who dealt. I yelled, begged, and pleaded with her to get help. I forbade her to leave the house; I even threatened to call the cops on her if she used. More than once I tried to check her into rehab, but she always quit after a couple days, or she'd just refuse to sign the paperwork.

"It was about that time when she revealed something. It wasn't just that the piece of filth who called himself our father who had molested and raped her growing up. One night when she was going through a withdrawal on the couch, she told me he sometimes let his sleazy friends rape her when he needed cash or had a debt to settle…"

Daniel's face had moved beyond any category of rage. For the first time since the start of their conversation, a single tear traced down along his nose and trickled off his face. He sniffed and looked away, wiping his eyes. A long pause ensued; then, slowly and still avoiding eye contact, the warrior spoke: "I came home one night and found her lying on the floor, vomit on her lips. She had overdosed right there in my living room. I held my baby sister that night and cried 'til the ambulance came to take her away. She was good kid, Father, you would have liked her."

"I have no doubt of that," the priest said.

"She was beautiful…she had raven-black hair and a sweet smile. She was kind of shy but had a mischievous streak to her; she always had a lot of joy until…" Daniel's voiced ebbed away. "Anyway, the paramedics came and declared her dead. I had the body removed 'til I could figure out some burial arrangements, and that was it. My family was gone, and I was alone."

"Is this the first time you've ever told someone what happened?" the Syrian abbé asked gently.

"I kept a couple buddies in the loop when it was all going down, but after I buried Rainey, I probably only ever told one other person."

"That is an enormous load to have carried by yourself all these years; so much pain to bear alone."

Daniel did not respond to the priest's affirmation. "You know, Father," he went on, "when I first came here to the community, the only reason I didn't write you off was because you didn't preach about a God who sends people to hell for not believing the right things. My family was never religious, but I've always wanted to believe that if there is a loving God out there, like you talk about, that Rainey's with Him. That she's safe and finally at peace. She had her whole life stolen away from her; she never stood a chance."

Paolo offered a comforting smile. "I am certain God knows your sister by name, Daniel, and that He is intimately acquainted with the agony she was forced to endure. I can only imagine how He wept over her suffering and humiliations. I also want to say, you may have never called yourself religious, but your life exemplifies Christ whether you realize it or not."

Daniel looked stunned by the priest's words. He had been told many things in his life, but nothing like this. He waited for an explanation.

"Over and over again, throughout your life, and often at great personal risk to your own safety, you have sought to intervene on people's behalf. You have devoted your life to protecting and defending the weak, innocent, and powerless. The strength, courage, and compassion of our Lord Jesus reign in you whether you realize it or not. And you have the heart of your Father in Heaven, a heart to see people live in peace, freedom, and restoration."

The Marine did not know how to respond. He felt a bit awkward by all the references to God and Jesus, but he answered quietly, "Thank you, Father; that's very kind of you. No one has ever said anything like that to me before."

"A final question," the priest entreated.

"Sure," Daniel responded.

"What about your earthly father? What do you wish for him, wherever he is?"

Daniel was not confident he understood the question, but the mere mention of the man who had wrought so much pain for Daniel and his family made him stiffen.

"Do you hope God has sent him to some kind of hell?"

Daniel's jaw tightened. "Yes," he managed in a dark tone.

"Interesting."

"What is? That I hope he burns in hell forever if there is one?"

"Yes," Paolo replied. "You want God's mercy and love for your sister, but you hope your father is tormented and tortured forever."

"Rainey was an innocent victim!" Daniel exploded. "She didn't deserve any of the shit that happened to her! And that piece of filth made her live in hell! Why shouldn't he pay for it?!"

"Yes indeed," the priest responded mournfully. "Your father truly made *all* of you live in hell with him. Daniel, I'm going to say one final thing today, and then I will be silent. It may be very difficult to hear, but for the sake of your own heart and healing I ask you to simply consider it."

The warrior was still seething and simmering, but he remained silent and waited.

"You say Rainey was an innocent victim, and I agree. My heart weeps for the endless misery, pain, and fear, she was forced to endure. You also made no attempt to conceal your father's most heinous crimes against all of you. He was to you, a monster, and worthy of hellfire. Here now is my final word to you: I would *never* seek to minimize, condone, nor excuse the unspeakable wrongs your father committed nor the unfathomable damage and pain his actions caused. I loathe the violence and sins he committed. His sickening cruelty leaves me justly angry for you and your family! And yet, I am cautious to hate him. And here is why: at some point, somewhere far back, many years, I wonder if perhaps your father was not an innocent child and the terrorized victim."

A thick silence hung between the two. To his credit, Daniel did not explode again. He just sat and brooded. Finally, through a thinly veiled snarl he offered his objection. "Father, the man who called himself my father did nothing but bring us pain; surely there has to be a punishment for that."

The old priest nodded somberly to the hanging crucifix on the wall. "Yes, I believe there may have been," he lamented. "Still, in ways we may never know, perhaps your father did face the consequences of his egregious crimes. Even so, if he arrived here in our community today without a *serious* change of heart, I expect we would find him incapable of life among us, of peacefully sharing in real love or joy with his fellow man." A faint expression of hope tinged the priest's weathered face. "But Daniel, in ending her life prematurely and leaving you alone, even your beloved sister brought you pain. We are *all* broken sinners in need of God's mercy."

The warrior looked down at his mug with the cartoon dog still dancing carefree across it. The cup was empty now, and the afternoon had begun to turn to evening outside.

"Thanks for the tea, Father."

CHAPTER FOUR

The woods blurred past along the country road. Overcast skies had claimed the day, yet the cool morning air felt soothing and rejuvenating to the soul. Two weeks had passed since Daniel's two-hour *confession* with Father Paolo; they had spoken little since. Both remained cordial in passing, but the warrior was still mulling over things the priest had said. Father Paolo sensed this and gave Daniel all the space he required. He was eternally patient and maintained faith that deeper work was underway regardless of whether they met together or spoke.

Daniel gazed out the side window of the 1980s crew cab pickup truck as it bumped along the uneven road. After years of neglect, with no road crews to clear fallen tree limbs or debris or to repave potholes after the winter freezes, lonely roads like this one had largely fallen into disrepair. Rural highways were generally overgrown by surrounding forest and vegetation. Tree branches littered the asphalt now, and years' worth of leaves and pine needles had buried the once-distinct lines under a blanket of padding. Abandoned vehicles lay idle for years along the shoulder; at least those that had not been plowed off the roadside by military convoys or scavengers.

The green and white truck emitted an odd whine from under the hood. There was no clear cause, but Daniel guessed the belts were worn out. The era of the aged vehicle was another sign of the war's lingering effects, traces of the past world gone by. During Imperial State's invasion of the West Coast, several EMP devices had been detonated over key cities: Seattle, Tacoma, and Portland. The result had been the instantaneous collapse of the region's power grid along with nearly every electronic device with a circuit board being fried. This included all twenty-first-century vehicles and most cars from the late twentieth century.

Overnight, millions of vehicles equipped with electrical ignition or fuel injection systems were rendered useless. Before a single bomb was ever dropped and before the first naval bombardment, much of the West Coast's infrastructure had come to a grinding halt with sweeping blackouts and defunct technology. Chaos, looting, and violence had erupted as police and National Guard units scrambled to contain mass hysteria and restore order. All the while, an invading power hammered the coastline less than a hundred miles away, skirmishing with American military forces and local militias to establish a beachhead.

A few rain drops rolled gently down the window pane. It was a signal of the end of summer; the early days of fall were fast approaching. Daniel had always enjoyed this time of year, the autumn smells and crisp breezes, misty mornings and the first refreshing rainfalls in months. The coastal range was stunningly gorgeous during the changing colors. And the community would soon be having its Harvest Celebrations. Daniel looked forward to it all, even the simple pleasures of peaceful folk.

He sat behind the driver's seat, his assault-rifle resting between his thighs with the muzzle pointed to the floorboard. Jonas sat beside him in the rear passenger seat. Two other veterans of the Last War rode in the front. Ava Martinez sat behind the steering wheel while Jamal Williams rode passenger beside her. On this scout-and-scavenge supply run, they all rode in silence for the most part. Each was enjoying the serenity and chance to reflect, in addition to the change of scenery from the community's grounds. Patrols went out only twice per month or when there was a dire need for something specific. Thus it was considered a privilege to be selected for one of these missions.

Ava was the younger sister of Brother Fernando Martinez. She, too, had grown up in New Mexico but had enlisted in the Army at the age of eighteen. She'd served as a diesel mechanic, repairing and maintaining armored, tactical vehicles. She had been assigned to a motor transport logistics unit; however, when there were no trucks in need of repair, she'd been tasked as security on military convoys during the war.

Ava had logged plenty of hours wearing her flak jacket and Kevlar helmet, getting shot at. When the war's chaos finally reached the home front of American towns and cities, she had witnessed her fair share of it from behind a mounted machinegun on an armored vehicle. It was hard to forget the heat of flames against her face as they burned sprawling, suburban neighborhoods.

It was impossible to forget the pools of blood and civilian bodies lying in the streets. It was impossible to forget the sound of a toddler screaming for his parents who'd been crushed under a collapsed house. It was impossible to forget having a Molotov cocktail thrown at her vehicle, especially when she was the soldier standing exposed in the machinegun turret. And it was impossible to forget the sickly sweet scent of melted flesh and steel the day an enemy fighter jet made a bombing run on her platoon's column of vehicles.

Shortly after Mech-Tech had assumed control of all U.S. forces, Ava had left the Army to find her family. Fernando was her only remaining relative; he had survived because his monastery took a pacifist stance during the war. The brothers had turned their seminary into a hospital and refugee aid station until Imperial forces had commandeered the grounds for a command center. After months of occupation, Imperial State was forced to pull out and withdraw from New Mexico entirely. But before leaving, they shot most of the brothers simply out of spite. It was not long after this that Ava arrived to find her brother, who was one of the last remaining, half-starved survivors of the tattered commune.

During the post-war turf squabbling between Mech-Tech and Unity, the brother and sister pair migrated north until they eventually stumbled upon the community. They were two of its earliest members. Fernando quickly assumed an apprentice role with Father Paolo while Ava provided security and worked to repair vehicles for sustainable transport.

At just twenty-six, Ava was slender in frame but tough in a fight. She was fiercely loyal, sometimes with a temper, but strong in mind, spirit, and body. Daniel had immediately recognized her as an asset from the moment they met. The former MARSOC captain had arrived in the community roughly a year after she and Fernando.

Jamal Williams was another black American who lived in the community. He had grown up in Detroit and at twenty-eight, he was younger than both Daniel and Jonas. He was tall and thin, even a little lanky, but a skilled warrior nonetheless. He'd served in the famed 25th Infantry Division during the war where he gained invaluable experience as a frontline N.C.O. and combat leader. He had fought against Winter Steel in Europe and Submission in northern Africa, back before America had capitulated to Mech-Tech in a last-ditch effort to save itself from total annihilation.

Jamal tended to be somewhat cocky, brash, and aggressive in personality. He was a smooth talker, a comic with the ladies, and always a flirt. In his previous life, he had been a bit of a philanderer, but a few positive influences and life in the community were slowly tempering him.

When it came to patrols, Daniel called Jonas, Ava, and Jamal his "Crack Team." The community had done nothing to attract veterans or ex-military personnel; it just happened that such individuals tended to survive longer than most in the lawless, rugged country. Training and combat experience lent them an edge of endurance on the open road. And their instincts for reading a diverse spectrum of personalities bestowed keen intuition about the intentions of strangers they met in the wildlands.

In some ways, all four of them were loners. In spite of family and the community's desperate need for seasoned warriors and leaders, they stood apart from the general populace—not always by conscious choice. They were simply different, and each inwardly knew it. The things they had seen and done, the fires they'd passed through, all the blood they'd spilt along the way to survive; there was no taking any of it back nor would any of them have chosen to. They were who they were for better or ill. Each was looking for peace and belonging in his or her own way; each secretly longed to stop running and find rest for their souls.

The truck engine whined again. Daniel looked to the front as they passed damp forest, streams, and countryside. He spotted a half-dozen white-tailed deer bounding across an open field to his left. The thought did not even enter his mind to raise his rifle or shoot one. He just watched them go, undisturbed in the land God had given them to roam. He felt a deep appreciation for their elegance and beauty, continuing on with life even after the world had ended. A wave of solace and contentment washed over Daniel. Perhaps this was what mankind had always been intended for— to live simply, find family, and enjoy the Earth.

The team passed an old, abandoned lumber mill on

the right. Shortly after this, Ava turned the truck right at a bridge, and they crossed over a small river. They were more than twenty miles from the community now and drawing near to a small, deserted town. That such rural townships had largely been forsaken was the only reason scout parties could search them for supplies. They never ventured very far inland. The further a team journeyed into the interior, the higher the risk they ran of encountering a Unity populated zone or Pacification patrol.

Traveling inland also meant losing the cover of tree canopies, which hid travelers from the eyes of aerial patrols. Whether one turned north or south, the land to the east sprawled out into mostly open plains for thirty miles. This reality meant that eventually the community would run out of deserted towns, gas stations, and homes to scavenge supplies from. They would eventually have to become totally self-sufficient or they would perish.

In the backseat, Daniel pulled a map of the local area from his tactical vest; he had found it in a gas station's convenience store during an earlier mission. He unfolded it and took in the black Xs denoting the locations they had already scavenged fuel and supplies from. There were red markings with numbers as well; these represented places community scout parties had been ambushed by biker gangs or bands of other nefarious characters. The top number represented how many enemies had engaged them, the bottom number was how many community members had been slain or taken during the fray.

The red marks were painful yet vital reminders of the dangers they risked every time they journeyed away from the glade. There had been many successful patrols which returned without incident; however, some had not been so lucky and still others had unwittingly led enemies back to the home refuge, resulting in bloodshed, chaos, and many killed.

"Up ahead," Daniel spoke calmly to Ava. He pointed to the dilapidated sign for a small grocery store a few blocks up on the left-hand side.

"Stores are big targets," Ava replied quietly. "It's probably already been hit by marauders."

"True," Daniel responded. "But *we* haven't hit it yet, so we may as well cross it off the map."

"Keep your eyes open for trouble," Jamal cautioned, checking his M-4 assault rifle. You know how the outlaw gangs like to set traps at these sorts of places to rob innocent people who don't know no better."

Jonas stretched in the back seat. "Man, I'd just love it if they had some fried chicken left!"

"You want a little watermelon and purple-drink to go with that?" Daniel smirked, still facing forward. His gaze was fixed over Ava's shoulder.

Jonas cocked his head and scowled. "Startin' in a little early this morning aren't we, *captain*? And what if I do? What's it to you?!"

Jamal chimed in, "Man, I don't know 'bout y'all, but I could go for some real backyard barbeque right now, hot off the grill with some potato salad and deviled eggs, just like my mama used to make in the summertime! Sound good, Jonas?"

"Hell yeah it does, brother! I could go for some Louisiana crawfish, too, with a little shrimp gumbo! Mmm! That'd hit the spot!"

"How 'bout you, Martinez?" Jamal grinned. "What's your order?"

"A hot shower and massage," Ava shot back without hesitation. "I want a hot dude to rub my shoulders with oil and bring me cocktails! You boys can keep your food; I just want somebody to pamper me a little, and I wanna sleep on a nice bed, one of those ones with the memory foam!"

Ava cranked the steering wheel hard to the left and pulled the truck into the empty store lot. She shifted the vehicle into park and killed the engine. Everyone grabbed their rifles and climbed out. Jamal stretched and shook off the residual morning fog. Each party member eased their truck door shut quietly. All of them knew better than to create any extra noise out here. They were in "hostile territory" now and did not want to draw any attention to their presence.

Daniel motioned for Jamal and Ava to take cover behind a large fallen tree at the edge of the parking lot. It offered a concealed vantage point of both the store front and the street to their right. He tossed a two-way radio to Ava and held up nine fingers to indicate which channel to monitor. He then motioned to Jonas and the two of them moved quickly away from the truck and their companions. Swiftly and silently, they crossed the vacant stretch between them and the building's entrance, approaching in a low, tactical glide.

A pair of bolt cutters were slung across Jonas' back, but one of the front double doors was smashed in. Shattered glass lay on the floor inside. It was a disheartening sign to Daniel but not completely unexpected. Ava was correct; stores were prime targets for looters and travelers. After eight years of global fighting and four years of post-war neglect, the two warriors were unlikely to be the store's first visitors.

The two men eased themselves carefully through the empty doorframe, attempting not to catch any gear on hanging shards. Crushed bits of glass crunched under their boots on the hard, tile floor. Daniel stood up and surveyed the darkened space. The vacant, unlit aisles appeared mostly bare. A few shopping carts lay strewn about the front, and more than one cash register had clearly been rifled open. The air was still and dank; it reeked of mold and mildew. The store's front windows and floors were caked in black, brown, and green grime.

"Welcome to the Holiday Inn," Jonas said grimly, standing upright in the dim entrance.

"We hope you enjoy your stay," Daniel continued the joke.

They separated and stepped warily down divided aisles. Both warriors flicked on the flashlights mounted to their rifles. They scanned for anything of value left on the empty shelves, and for any booby traps or trip wires. After a minute or two they reunited before a dismal and abandoned deli. Jonas confessed, "This place gives me the creeps, man."

"I'm not really a fan either," Daniel remarked, still surveying the empty darkness.

"You and I both saw Third World ghettos and slums back during the war, but these sorts of places always feel different..."

"All those grotty places we had to operate in overseas weren't a part of us," the MARSOC warrior observed. "It wasn't *our* town or country. Their poverty or political problems weren't ours to solve at the end of the day; we were just there to hunt the bad guys and maintain peace and order. But this..." Daniel paused, glancing around "...this used to be home. You can picture it, people getting on with their lives, buying food for Sunday dinners with family. Somebody owned this place once—was proud to call it their own. Now it's empty, full of ghosts and hollow memories; good people used to shop here and run into their friends. But somebody probably died here during those last days...shot over a can of baked beans or something stupid like that. People kill each other for the most trivial shit now." Daniel spat.

The two men split up again, wandering up and down the remaining aisles. Daniel found a couple boxes of feminine hygiene products and antacid medication. "Never know who might need these," he told himself. Jonas met him in the back corner of the store next to some gutted boxes of crackers.

"Find anything?" Daniel inquired.

The former Army staff sergeant held up the stainless steel meat cleaver he'd plucked from behind the fish counter, along with a few canned-food items. "Peaches and corn." He grinned. "Think they're any good?"

"Doubt it." Daniel smirked. "But it's worth the chance. You did better than me."

"What'd you get?"

"Couple boxes of tampons and some off-brand Tums."

Jonas' grin widened. He choked back some laughter and a tide of witty jabs. Noise discipline was paramount in unsecure locations like this. They never knew when a threat might be close or when someone might be watching them.

"I can tell you're really enjoying yourself right now," Daniel said.

Jonas held up a hand and shook his head, still biting his tongue and trying to get serious again. "Let's check the back," he said, tossing his head.

Daniel unzipped the mouth of his pack for Jonas to dump in the supplies; then he sealed it back up and shouldered it. The two men moved stealthily towards the black double doors leading to the back stockroom. Rifles at the ready, Daniel counted down three fingers and kicked one door open, then both veterans pressed through into the dark void beyond. They shined their lights around; nothing but gutted cardboard boxes and a few stripped pallets.

"Well, that was disappointing," Jonas said glumly. "Wanna see if the forklift still drives?"

"Yeah, pretty anti-climactic," Daniel agreed. "Makes you wonder if people have just gotten too lazy; nobody's willing to put in the work of laying a half-decent trap to rob you anymore. Damn greedy bastards." The Marine grumbled, kicking an empty box across the cement floor. "They just clean a place out and go home to gorge themselves around a campfire. What happened to the real bad guys, man? When we were in Egypt rooting out Submission nutjobs, they used to cut holes in the ceilings and drop grenades down on us when we came into a house! People just lack real motivation like that anymore."

The dark humor faded and silence returned; the companions began rummaging through open boxes and crates for anything of value missed or left behind. "You've been pretty quiet around the camp the last couple weeks," Jonas observed.

Daniel glanced over at his friend, but kept digging through plastic shipping tubs. "Yeah, I guess."

"Anything on your mind?"

Daniel did not look up this time. "I told Father Paolo a lot about my past—where I grew up and about the dreams. He said some things I've been chewing on since; not all of it I liked."

"I see," Jonas said. Another long pause. "Janae heard you again last night. She said it wasn't as bad as some nights, but it was enough to wake her up."

Irritated, Daniel stopped sifting. "Yeah? Well, if I find some earplugs I'll be happy to give them to her."

"Nobody's blaming you, Dan," the Ranger reassured. "Nobody's saying it's your fault. I'm just glad you were willing to spend some time with Paolo. Maybe that could help, ya know? Clear out some of that garbage from your system. People care about you, man; we all just want to see you let go of the past."

Daniel gripped the edges of the box he was working on; he looked over in the direction of Jonas' voice. He could not see his friend through the inky blackness of the stockroom, just a flashlight jostling around about twenty feet away. He drew in a breath and then let it go. "Jonas, sometimes the past won't let go of *you…*"

✡✡✡✡✡

It was quiet outside, tranquil even. A few birds chirped close by in small shrubs or overhead on forgotten power lines. There were no sounds of traffic nor of other people. There were no lawn mowers or crying babies, just a gentle breeze hinting at the near change of seasons.

Jamal stood facing away from the store, visually scanning a row of small houses and fenced yards along the deserted block. There were no signs of human life. This place was truly empty, a great void with only the echoes and traces of people's lives, hopes, and shattered dreams.

"You know you should probably get down and take some cover," Ava reproached. "Never know when there might be some asshole out there with a sniper rifle who wants to rob us."

Jamal made a dismissive noise with his lips. "Man, you worry too much, Martinez. You were what, a specialist in the Army? Did your four years and then got out?"

"It was six, actually," Ava corrected. She leaned into

the buttstock of her rifle and peered through the mounted scope. "What about it?"

"Nothin'," Jamal said. "It's just, I was in eight years and made sergeant in the infantry. Believe me, when you been on as many ops as I have, you get a sense when something is about to go down. And ain't nothing gonna happen today 'cause there ain't nobody out here *in* this piece-of-shit, God-forsaken town."

Ava heard his words, but she didn't care for his ego or complacent attitude. "Well you do you, I guess," she said from her prone position behind the fallen tree. "I prefer to stay alive and down here."

Jamal repeated his dismissive noise. "Suit yourself," he said. Suddenly he felt someone grab his forearm and yank him towards the ground. "Bitch!" he snapped with indignation. "What the—"

"Shhh!" Ava held a finger to her lips and pointed.

"Holy shit!" Jamal marveled in a hiss. "It's been a while since I seen any of them out here."

Up the street just a few blocks, twenty Pacification Enforcers were split in two columns marching straight towards the two veterans. Their white armor and heavy weaponry was unmistakable. These were Unity's police and shock troops tasked with maintaining order and eradicating her enemies, so-called "peacekeepers" with a brutal reputation. Between the two rows of Enforcers marched eight prisoners with hands cuffed behind their necks; two of them were children.

A thunderous rumble came from above; lose rocks and bits of gravel began to tremble on the asphalt of the parking lot. "Oh, shit," was all Jamal could utter. He crouched lower trying to hide himself under a large bough of the fallen tree.

Ava seized the radio. "Get out! Both of you, get out now! And don't go out the back!"

Inside the pitch black stockroom, metal shelves had begun to rattle on the concrete floor; the rumble from above had grown deafening. Daniel and Jonas heard Ava over the radio and looked up at each other through the darkness. Without a word, both bolted simultaneously. Clutching rifles, they rammed through the double doors and sprinted for the front of the store. They charged back up the barren aisles towards the natural light leaking through grime-covered windows.

A growl and hissing whine pierced the air, and the rumbling roar of engines grew even more intense above their heads. What little hearing the two warriors' had left from the war was being threatened by this overpowering din.

From Ava and Jamal's concealed vantage point, they nervously watched Daniel and Jonas escape the storefront, climbing back out through the shattered door. They lingered for a moment under the building's overhang, waiting for directions. From their position, they could not yet see the massive shuttlecraft hovering above the street and parking lot, but they knew they would be spotted for certain if they tried to cross the open expanse and rejoin their comrades now. Ava jerked her head sideways, motioning them to move along the front of the building, away from the street.

Daniel and Jonas moved with purpose and haste. They eased themselves along the store's front then broke from the side of the building in a mad dash for a collection of neighboring houses. They would swing wide and double back to their friends once they were certain they could avoid detection by the aircraft. As they ran, Daniel stole a quick glance over his shoulder. He was dying to catch a glimpse of the hulking beast of a vehicle.

The enormous shuttlecraft lowered itself slowly to the ground, cutting power to the gargantuan twin turbine rotors contained in the hollowed-out portions of its wingspan. The whine and rumble died away as the beast's hydraulic engines discharged a final hiss of steam.

From her hiding place, Martinez scoped in on the craft with her rifle. It was an awesome vessel—a testament to Unity's grip over the masses and by extension all technological advances. Its appearance resembled a massive grey hawk with the cockpit looming and horizontal tail flaps extended out the back.

After a few moments, a long, steel ramp lowered to

the pavement from the underbelly of the beast. A clean-shaven man wearing a crisp, black uniform descended; his dark hair was neatly clipped and his jaw line imposing. The troop of Enforcers arrived as his polished boots touched the asphalt. Their armor and boots pounded the blacktop with menacing clout.

The prisoners were forced down on their knees before the darkly clad officer. Then half the squad took three paces back and formed a firing line behind the weathered travelers. Another half-dozen Enforcers fanned out in a semicircle, facing away from the aircraft to create a security perimeter. They clutched their weapons tightly, scanning for any sign of threat or opposition.

The officer slowly paced down the line of prisoners. With a gloved hand, he lifted the chin of one woman until her eyes met his, then he moved on. He surveyed the pathetic lot with contempt, eyeing their worn and soiled garments with disdain. "Was this all of them?" he inquired of the patrol leader.

One of the armored guards nodded. "We shot two others who refused to surrender. They killed three of ours." The Enforcer's unfeeling voice was muffled behind the mask of his helmet.

"Any weapons?" the officer checked.

Another trooper stepped forward and dumped several firearms onto the ground. His commander glanced down at these with amused condescension: an M-16, a scoped 30.06 hunting rifle, one pistol, and one sad MI Carbine from the 1940s.

"I don't know why you people always insist on resisting." The officer sighed. "Only to delay the inevitable." He clasped his hands behind his back and glanced down at the pitiful lot. One of the children began to cry, and a woman sobbed with her face to the pavement. "Oh, do stop that," the officer chided. He pushed her head up off the ground with his boot. "You all could have led perfectly happy lives had you simply submitted and become lawful citizens of Unity. You could have avoided all of this had you merely surrendered when my men cornered you. But no, you chose a more difficult path, and now what? Am I to feel pity for your losses?

"What's more you shot and killed three of my men! The Presiding Council does not accept insurrection nor take lightly the murders of its soldiers. And for what?" The officer laughed. "So you could live out here in the dirt? Scratching a life off these hills like barbarians, bathing in a river once a month? You'd have all died of starvation your first winter!"

He glowered down at the simple folk, a cruel sneer creeping across his face. "Last opportunity. Who will take the chips and register themselves as lawful citizens of Unity? Who is willing to serve the *true* common good and not simply their own violent, selfish natures?"

Even from two hundred meters, Martinez recognized a soft blue blink behind the officer's right eye. In the daylight, it was almost impossible to detect—so faint that had Ava herself blinked, she would have missed it entirely or thought she imagined it. "Come on, Daniel," she muttered. "We can't let this asshole take these people."

"I say we waste 'em all," Jamal growled "Show 'em they're not the only ones out here who know how to fight."

"We wait for Daniel and Jonas," Ava retorted immovably. She knew two against twenty was not good odds—even worse if the shuttle took off again. She noted the rocket pods and energy turrets under its wings. Additionally, she was certain the pilots could detect human heat signatures from the cockpit. So far they had been lucky and nothing more. Probably the only reason they had not yet been spotted was because the ship had landed to rendezvous with its patrol. Had its mission been to scour the countryside for signs of life, the results might have been very different.

"Put the children aboard the shuttle," the officer ordered. "They are the innocent victims here. A little reeducation and they'll find a better life in Unity." He paused, "Unity cares for misled and *abused* children."

Two Enforcers seized the terrified children and

dragged them toward the ramp. A female prisoner shrieked in panicked anguish and threw herself at the guards. From behind, a third Pacification trooper shot her between the shoulder blades with a pair of stun probes. The leads stuck into her back and an electric charge immediately knocked her face first onto the blacktop. There she convulsed violently under the pulsing current of electroshock.

"Yes?" The officer smirked at the woman. He stooped down and lifted her head by the hair. "Will you take the chips to stay with your children?"

She was still trembling and shaking from fried nerve endings. A single tear streamed down the mother's cheek as she stuttered, unable to form words. Amazingly, she was able to nod her head yes.

"Done!" exclaimed the officer. He snapped a finger and tossed his head towards the cargo hold, motioning for more Enforcers to drag her aboard as well.

A man in his late thirties cried out, "Jannalynn! Please don't! Don't do it! They'll take your soul! You won't even be able to think for yourself once they give you the implants! They're evil, all of them!"

The officer had heard enough. He kicked the man in the stomach with the point of his boot. The prisoner grunted in pain, trying to regain his breath; then an Enforcer struck him in the back of the head with the butt of his weapon. The man fell forward and emitted a moan, unable to move. The officer knelt down in front of him and grabbed a fistful of the man's hair to lift his gaze.

The defeated resister stared into the officer's cold, loveless eyes; he stole a glance toward his family huddled in the ramp entrance of the shuttle. Blood dripped from the man's mouth and tears streamed from his eyes, but he still had some fight and anger left in him. "Your leaders speak of love and tolerance without end." He spat blood. "But they're all a bunch of liars. Look at yourselves! Look at what hypocrites you are! You're monsters!"

The officer drew his pistol and forced the man's mouth open, then stuffed the muzzle of the weapon inside. "Now you listen to me," he instructed with an iron grip. "You are a fool. Your wife and children will live on without you. She will find another man to love—a law-abiding, *honorable* citizen of Unity. You will be forgotten, your corpse will rot out here in the mud. Birds will pick the flesh from your bones, and coyotes and wild dogs will fight over your carcass. That will be your fate. But who knows…" The officer smirked, glancing over his shoulder towards the shuttle ramp. "Maybe I'll take some time to become more intimately acquainted with your wife. She looks like she'll clean up nicely, once she completes her time in a Reeducation Center of course." The officer grinned.

"It's a brave new world, friend. Just unfortunately not for the likes of you."

The captain pulled his pistol out of the man's mouth and nodded to the Enforcer standing behind the prisoner. The guard seized a black hood over the man's bloodied face, while another Enforcer cinched a thin, steel wire around his neck. The prisoner struggled, grunting and gurgling for air. Yet with his hands still in restraints behind his head, he could not even claw at the wire around his throat.

The officer stood up and straightened his uniform, brushing off a few specks of dust. "Think of your family," he said, patting the hooded head. "That's the last time you're ever going to see them again."

"Now?" Jamal snarled.

"Not yet," Ava whispered. She spoke calmly, but she felt a sick anxiety inside.

"You gotta be kidding me," Jamal hissed. "I can't watch anymore of this shit!"

"If we open fire without Daniel and Jonas, we'll all get killed! And we won't do those people an ounce of good," Ava shot back.

The officer was pontificating again. "You have all been found guilty of treason against the people of Unity and against its esteemed Presiding Council! You are trespassers and enemies in this land! The ordinary punishment for these crimes is summary reassignment to a Reeducation Center; however, as you have refused to cooperate, your sentence shall be immediate extermination. Prepare to meet whatever *god* you believe in."

"That's it," Jamal said. "I'm done waiting. I can't make you go with me, but I'm going in! Don't try to stop me from killing these assholes." He raised his rifle and aimed for the officer's head. He planned to move from cover and draw fire away from Ava once he took his first shot. "Here goes nothing," he breathed.

Suddenly a strong hand caught Jamal's arm. He looked back. Daniel and Jonas had arrived. "Hold your fire!" Daniel ordered in a hushed tone.

"Are you insane?!" Jamal protested. "They're gonna kill all those people!"

Daniel yanked the younger man back down towards the ground. "Yes, and if we intervene, we damn the whole community! You take one shot and everyone back at camp will be dead within three days. Even if we take all of them out, what do you think Unity is gonna do when an entire patrol doesn't come back? Do you think they're just gonna forget about it?! No, no, no, they'll come back out here, only next time they'll bring an army! They'll bring out a force a *hundred* times the size of this one! They'll use aerial patrols and satellites to find us. Then they'll wipe us out, burn every home, and butcher every man and woman before finally blasting the entire clearing into a smoking crater!"

Jamal was keyed-up with no place to unleash his rage.

Jonas spoke calmly to him. "He's right, man. We can't stop this."

"So what?" Jamal demanded. "We do nothing?!"

"That's right," Daniel answered, stone-faced. "We do nothing."

"Man, I can't do nothing and live with myself!"

"Then look away," Daniel said. "This isn't your call to make; it's bigger than any of us. You take one shot at any of those Enforcers, and you kill every person in these hills for fifty miles around."

Jamal couldn't speak-he was so angry. He wanted to stand up and kick something. Jonas pulled the younger man close to him. Jamal beat the Ranger's flak jacket repeatedly with a clenched fist.

Daniel eased himself to the ground with his back to the fallen tree trunk. He sniffed and looked over at Martinez. "Ava," he said gently. "You're not gonna want to see it. Look away." Daniel craned his neck to look over the log. At that moment, the commanding officer pointed his pistol at the hooded prisoner and shot him through the face. The man was likely already dead from strangulation, but now the body collapsed onto the blacktop.

The officer replaced the spent round from his pistol's clip and gave a curt nod to the squad leader. In turn, the lead Enforcer motioned with his arm, and the rest of the Pacification unit opened fire. The cacophony of automatic-rifle fire erupted with ferocity and did not let up for a full thirty seconds. Even once the travelers' bodies had fallen, they continued to be riddled with rounds until puddles of blood pooled around them on the pavement.

A few of the troopers laughed or hooted in victory. Some exchanged congratulatory high fives or fist bumps. The officer instructed the squad leader to wrap things up. "Melt down the criminals' weapons and get your men on board. I'm sick of being out here. I want these prisoners turned over for induction and processing by nightfall. They'll have to be interrogated as well for any information about other rebel bands residing in this region."

"Yes, sir," the lead Enforcer responded, then turned to issue orders. "Gents, lock it down. Melt the weapons; we're moving out immediately."

The captain was about to stride back up the ramp and board the shuttlecraft when his eyes abruptly fell on an old pickup truck with the green stripe running along its length. It was parked less than a hundred feet from the ship. He scowled and furrowed his brow; the truck appeared very clean for an abandoned vehicle. There was freshly spattered mud along its base. Someone had driven it recently, possibly that very morning...

He glanced around, looking for any trace of the owners; if they had driven it that day, they could not be far off.

He did not believe the vehicle belonged to the rebels they had just tracked down. He'd been hunting them for the past week. He felt vexation stirring within. If the truck belonged to another band of rogues, it was best to track them down and arrest them today, but he was tired. The report of one successful peacekeeping mission would more than satisfy his superiors for the week. They would be delighted to learn that another gang of outlaws had been rounded up and dealt with.

As an Enforcer ignited his flamethrower to incinerate the contraband weapons, the captain signaled him and pointed to the truck. The Enforcer responded by turning his torch on the pickup and dousing it in a massive deluge of near-liquid flame. He clenched the trigger and blasted the cab with blinding hot fire until the steel began to melt. Under the immense heat, one of the metal doors warped at the hinges and fell off the truck's frame, crashing to the pavement with a jarring clang.

From their concealed position, Daniel and his team scarcely breathed; no one dared to move an inch. The former MARSOC warrior cursed himself for not having instructed Ava to hide their transport better. He had been careless and sloppy; his complacency and lack of foresight would cost them. They had just witnessed the slaughter of a half-dozen innocent people; now he and his team would be forced to traverse their way back to camp, on foot, exposed, and across twenty miles of rugged hill country, most likely in the dark.

The engines of the shuttlecraft suddenly erupted to life, the deafening roar and whine returning as the spinning turbines started to wind up. The last of the Enforcers were boarding the vessel. Two stood guard at the base of the ramp while the final one with the flamethrower torched the pile of bodies and the storefront. Then they, too, embarked onto the aircraft, and the hydraulic ramp raised shut, sealing with a final hiss.

The gargantuan craft lifted off with a powerful thrust, the buzz of its housed rotor blades increasing in volume. Then it roared savagely towards the clouds. Daniel and his team could not physically pin themselves any closer to the fallen tree. They hugged the earth, lying perfectly still, waiting and praying that the craft's scanners would not detect them amid its departure.

At long last the behemoth vessel rocketed away across the horizon and over the hills. The scout party breathed a collective sigh of relief, then began to pick themselves up. As the air transport traced away in the distance, Daniel's *Crack Team* stared gravely at the charred corpses and blazing inferno before them. They took in the black, twisted frame which had once been their vehicle.

Unity had visited its costal ranges, and all it had left in its wake were tears, spilt blood, and flaming wreckage.

CHAPTER FIVE

Daniel and his team retraced their path back towards the safety of home; they followed the roads, yet were deliberate to stay off them and out of sight. On foot their pace was much slower, and dusk overtook them before they reached sanctuary. The small band was forced to spend a fitful night out in wild country. Each team member rotated two-hour watches while the others tried to sleep, huddled together for warmth on the wet ground under a canopy of dripping trees. None of them dared to even think of lighting a fire.

They rose early the next morning, tired, sore, and damp; they stayed quiet most of the trek home. Each had been deeply impacted by the brutality they had witnessed at the hands of Unity's Pacification Forces. Daniel and Jonas were the most adept at brushing off instances like the day before. Too many years of killing and death had produced in them a heightened ability to erect impregnable mental barriers and emotional walls to shield their psyches in the short term.

But Ava was clearly shaken by the ruthless violence of the day before, wrestling with confusion and a deep sense of sorrow. The savagery had triggered flashbacks from her service during the Last War—memories she had worked hard to forget.

Along their long march home, she did her best to keep it all locked down, but Daniel and Jonas could see she was struggling.

Meanwhile, Jamal continued to stew. He had hardly spoken to anyone since a shouting match erupted between him and Daniel. During the course of the blowout, he'd cursed and blamed the former Marine captain for allowing innocent people to die. Daniel, in turn, did not take these accusations lightly. He lambasted the younger man for his arrogance and ignorance, once again pointing to the almost certain fallout which intervening would have wrought. Every man, woman, and child in the community would have paid a heavy price for any brash actions taken, and all to settle a little bloodlust for revenge.

After the explosiveness died down, Jamal said little else, only muttering periodic, irritated remarks to himself as they walked. He refused to acknowledge

Daniel or a single word he said.

Fatigued from a dreary night on muddy ground, the team trudged wearily back towards camp. Jonas was looking forward to seeing his wife and daughter and kissing both his girls. Daniel was thinking about meeting with the council to review emergency plans of evacuation and rendezvous points in case the camp was ever besieged by Unity's forces. Still fuming, Jamal wanted to blow off some steam by blasting ammo through his rifle or beating out his rage on the punching bag that hung from the ceiling in his shared cabin. Ava just wanted to sleep, wash her face, and maybe cry a little once she could get some privacy.

As they ascended a slope and passed between the trunks of soggy birch and cottonwoods, Daniel froze. They were less than a mile from the camp, but he held up his right hand signaling everyone else to stop. He looked to the right and listened carefully. Everything remained still.

Behind him, Jonas strained to hear anything out of place. He leaned forward and whispered, "What is it?"

Daniel held up a finger for silence. "There aren't any birds singing, and I heard something…" He scanned the woods and mess of branches above.

Every team member regripped their weapon, readying themselves for ambush. Daniel gave a series of patterned whistles and cautiously took one step forward. The team followed, their senses heightened and on alert. Daniel gave the whistle again. This time an answer came back in a similar pattern. The response echoed through the canopy of trees so that no one could tell which direction it had emanated from. Daniel carefully took another few steps, passing between two young oaks covered in wet moss.

A stealthed figure emerged from behind a tree, giving Daniel a start.

The Marine's rifle was already raised and trained on the figure before he realized it was a friend. "What are you doing-sneaking around out here?!" he demanded. "I could have shot you!"

"As I could have shot all of you," the Sioux hunter said with a slight smirk. "Did you not hear my response to your signal?"

Daniel scowled.

"You seem on edge," Raoul observed. "We expected you back last night, and I did not hear a truck on the road."

"Yeah," Daniel replied. "We ran into some trouble out there. I'd rather not talk about it here; it'd be better to gather the council."

Raoul nodded; he understood the circumstances must be grave. "It is good you have returned now. There is trouble in the camp. I was hoping I might catch you hiking back from the vehicle stash."

BRENNAN SILVER

"What is it?" Daniel asked.

"We have...guests," Raoul stated with clear reservations. He slid his bow back over his shoulder so that it lay against his full quiver of arrows. A long knife and tomahawk were secured in the Lakota's belt. He was dressed in deerskin trousers, and his long, raven hair fell over his shoulders. Even on this cool morning, he wore his black flannel shirt unbuttoned. "I fear they are not good men." He continued, "Their manners are ill and their eyes are full of darkness. I see greed and malice when I look at them."

Daniel absorbed Raoul's vexing report and disconcerted tone. Then, with no further discussion, he said, "Let's go; lead the way."

✾ ✾ ✾ ✾ ✾

The band of five's reentrance to the glade created an immediate stir. The community was immensely relieved to see the scout party return unharmed. Janae rushed from the family garden to hold her husband tight. Her head rested against his chest as she whispered the overwhelming fears that had haunted her throughout the night. Ellie came racing down the slope from the rows of cornstalks, calling excitedly for her daddy. Jonas scooped her up in his arms and kissed her as well.

Jamal broke off from the pack and vanished from the

156

growing throng of smiles, hand-shakes, and applause.

"I'm gonna put my weapon away and clean up," Ava said quietly to Daniel. "Wake me if you need some backup dealing with our guests."

Daniel nodded appreciatively. The Latina veteran was the kind of person he knew he could always rely on, through thick and thin, whether she was exhausted or not.

Over the jubilant din of the team's safe return, Daniel called to Raoul. "Where is Paolo?"

The Sioux man nodded in the direction of the priest's cabin up the hillside. There was no hesitation; Daniel set out in an aggressive stride up the slope and past the watchtower. Raoul followed in-step not far behind. Daniel glanced off to his left, mentally noting the three unfamiliar figures.

They all sat dining at the community's outdoor tables, which had been crafted from long slabs of finished cedar log halves. From a distance, Daniel sized up the three men, evaluating them for vulnerabilities; they were large and burly. All three had bearded faces and wore multiple, dirty layers of long-sleeved shirts. Their resemblance was not unlike fur trappers or mountain men from the pages of history books.

Undisturbed, they ate their fill of beans, stew, chicken, and homemade bread. Occasionally, one would laugh to his companion or make a brief comment.

Besides this they focused on their food, only raising their heads to nudge each other if an attractive woman passed by. In these moments, they would each eye her with unremitting appetite, like wolves who'd spied a solitary doe. This pattern left the women of the community feeling *deeply* unsettled. Whispers had spread quickly to avoid the strangers until Daniel and his team returned or the council could address these strangers directly.

Daniel and Raoul reached the plateau of the slope and found Father Paolo sitting peacefully outside his cabin door, engaged in meditative silence. "I hear the footsteps of two strong hunters." He smiled with eyes still closed. "Tell me, what business do you bring to an old man today?"

Raoul was the first to speak. "Our visitors have a foul spirit about them. I fear harm will come to the community if we cannot convince them to leave peacefully. I have looked into their eyes; these are the sort of men who broke treaties with my people long ago, the kind of men who lied and murdered, raped our women, and slaughtered the bison herds for sport. These men have no honor nor respect for life. They will bring only sickness and death to our refuge home."

"I thank you, my friend," the priest replied earnestly, opening his eyes. "I take seriously your insights and intuition about these travelers."

"Why were they allowed inside the perimeter?" Daniel asked.

"To my knowledge," Paolo answered, "when the sentries stopped them, they made no attempt to quarrel or resist. All guests should be welcomed as Christ, Daniel."

The former Marine captain dropped his head and sighed in frustration. "Father...they did not resist because our sentries have guns and got the jump on them. Raoul tells me these men only carried hatchets, machetes, and knives?"

"And one pistol," Raoul clarified.

The Syrian had shut his eyes again. "Daniel," he breathed, raising a hand for peace. "*All* are to be welcomed as Christ." He reopened his eyes, and there was a twinkle of humor in them now—a slight smirk of mischief on his lips. "Not all must be invited to stay, though. Speak to these men; if you find them unsavory, escort them back to the edge of the wood. We will give them food for their journey and send them on their way."

Raoul and Daniel were both satisfied with this response. The Sioux man bowed slightly in reverence for the older man, and the priest lifted a hand in a gesture of blessing. Then the warriors turned to leave.

"How long have they been here?" Daniel inquired.

"Only a few hours," the Lakota elder replied with

unrest in his voice. "Our sentries caught them in the forest early this morning, right as dawn was breaking. But they've already caused many to feel...uneasy."

"That didn't take long," Daniel quipped dryly. "Did our watchmen disarm them?"

"Yes, I made sure of that," Raoul replied. "It was a condition of their entrance into the settlement."

"Good work. At least there's that. Let's go have a chat with them."

On their way down the hill, Daniel and Raoul passed Jonas walking with Janae and holding Ellie. Daniel nodded to the Ranger and said, "Keep your rifle on you, we may need some extra persuasion."

Jonas nodded. "I'll be right there." He continued on with his family toward their cabin but planned to double back and rejoin his brothers.

As Marine and Sioux hunter approached the tables, they overheard their burly visitors laughing to one another. Some lewd remarks were exchanged about someone they had recently seen. Daniel came to a halt at the end of the long table and announced his presence in greeting: "Good morning, gentlemen."

One of the bearded travelers glanced up at Daniel and gave him a quick head-to-toe look over, doing his own size-up of the Marine; then he returned to the conversation with his friends. The other two did not even acknowledge the former special operations captain.

Daniel felt an immediate flash of white-hot anger at their blatant disregard. Not even close to being thrown off, though, he remained steady and leaned over the end of the table, rapping on the wood with gloved knuckles. His loaded assault rifle still dangled from a carabiner on his flak-jacket. "Hey, precious," he said to the one who'd eyed him. "I'm talkin' to you."

Without any cue or instruction, Raoul drew an arrow from his quiver and notched it on the string of his bow.

"Well looky here." One of them grinned, his teeth stained brown and yellow. "We got the Lone Ranger and Tonto! Isn't that what it looks like, boys?" He laughed to his companions.

Daniel stared coolly across the table, waiting.

"You take yourself too seriously, don't ya, chief?" the same one opened his mouth again. "What can we do for you? I take it this is your town, lawman?"

Daniel noticed small bits of scrambled egg in the man's beard as he reached for a tin cup of coffee. The MARSOC operator ignored the question and asked his own: "Where you gents coming from and where are you headed?"

The talker was clearly the leader of the three, if not in rank, then by personality. "We were part of a camp further up north. Some stuff went down; I figured it was time to split. My boys here came with me. As for where we're headed, don't know yet. We're making it up as we go. Might head further south to hole-up for winter. This is a nice spot, though; figured maybe we'd stick around for a few days, see how things go."

Daniel glanced over his shoulder. Jonas was ten yards back to his right, rifle at the ready. "I think you gents would be better off back out on the road." Daniel stated calmly but firmly. "You can get a good night's sleep here tonight; you'll be safe within our borders, no one will touch you. In the morning, we'll give you some food for your journey, then I think it'd be best if you moved along."

One of the companions stopped chewing and tried to engender pity. "That priest-man said we was welcome here. How come you're giving us the boot? We ain't done nothin' wrong."

"The priest doesn't speak for the camp, I do. And I say you go," Daniel responded bluntly. He didn't care if his words were inaccurate or harsh. These men did not need to know how the community functioned; they just needed to know they weren't welcome to stay. "There've been negative reports from some of our women saying they don't care for the way you've been looking at them. Care to explain yourselves?"

"Hey, my man." The leader laughed with a shrug. "You can look; you just can't touch, am I right?"

There was a lull. Daniel felt a wave of irritated disgust at the remark and did not even bother to respond.

The roughneck went on. "It sounds to me like what's really goin' on here is you've got the monopoly on all these fine ladies, the pick of litter! Or is it the *whole* litter, boy? You get whatever you want whenever you want it, so you don't like the idea of some bigger, badder, *real* men coming in here to mess things up?"

He leaned back in a hand-crafted wooden chair, grinning. "Looks to me like you got plenty of nice flowers walkin' around here. Why not spread some of that warm, sweet lovin' around a bit, *boy*? Seems like you're just plain greedy! A selfish so'm-bitch who wants all these lovely ladies to himself!" The ringleader and his burly companions all had a short chuckle at this. "What do you think, boys? Ain't that mighty selfish of this jumped-up, faggoty, little prince? And his posse of goons." The stranger lowered his voice and leaned sideways to peer around Daniel at Jonas and Raoul.

The vein on the side of Daniel's neck flinched. He was just about to level this thug when two women approached to help clear some dishes from the table. They were oblivious to the tense exchange underway. They had seen Daniel standing at the table and felt safe enough to approach. One woman was middle-aged with graying, curly hair and named Frieda; the other was a shy, quiet girl named Abby; she was seventeen, blonde, and pretty. Daniel looked down for a moment, regrouping his faculties before he destroyed the fiend across the table.

As Frieda and Abby gathered the empty serving dishes and plates, one of the men thanked them politely. Meanwhile, the ringleader just ogled the two women, watching their bodies work and move. He especially eyed Abby's youthful figure when she leaned over to pick up a fork that had fallen into the dirt. Then he had the audacity to shoot a grinning wink down the table at Daniel.

When the women had finished their voluntary kindness and moved a safe distance away, Daniel finally looked up again. He locked eyes with the brute and strode right for him.

The bigger man began to chuckle, seeing he had gotten to Daniel, but he was uncertain what would happen next.

Still wearing his brown leather combat boots from yesterday's patrol, Daniel kicked the man between his right shoulder and chest.

The bearded leader flew over backwards, crashing to the wet grass with the broken chair. He was still laughing when Daniel stalked over and pressed a heavy combat boot down on his throat. The brute stopped laughing as the weight choked off his windpipe and the muzzle of Daniel's rifle hovered inches above his face.

"You're lucky these are good people here, and I don't

call *all* the shots," Daniel growled. "Or I'd have already blown your fat, stupid head off. You remind me of my old man; the last time I saw him, I told him I'd kill him if I ever saw his face again. Now shut your fat, filthy mouth and listen up. I'm not your *man*, and I haven't been a boy in twenty years, you got that?"

The muzzle of Daniel's rifle was now pressed against the brute's teeth making it very undesirable to move, yet he managed to nod his head. His two companions sat motionless at the table. Raoul had a razor-tipped arrow trained on the eye socket of one. Jonas stood near the other one with his rifle's muzzle pointed at the man's temple. "Make a move," the Ranger taunted. "*Please*, give me a reason to end you!"

"I ain't movin', mister," the burly follower replied, raising his hands slowly. "You got no reason to shoot."

Daniel looked down at the ringleader. "You're an animal, a wolf who preys on the weak and unsuspecting. If there was trouble back at your last camp, I'll wager you were a part of it." He looked up at the other two. "I can tell you two are followers. Whatever wrongs you've done, this asshole probably led you to them, but if you keep running with him, he's going to get you both killed, I guarantee it. That's not an *if*, it's a *when*; so I suggest you lose this guy, and do it quickly."

The two followers at the table nodded silently, more out of compliance and fear than agreement.

Daniel continued, "Your boss' vulgar words and disrespect have earned you an early departure date. Today. Right now. We will gather some provisions for you, then you will be escorted back to the perimeter and go on your way. But we will only give you food for two now." Daniel looked down at the leader. "We don't waste food on *dogs*."

"What about our weapons?!" the brute barked from the ground. "You gonna give us back our weapons or leave us defenseless out there in the wilds?"

Daniel's gaze had not left him, and his boot was still crushing the man's throat. "You'll find your weapons out on the road a few miles east of here. Let me be clear—if ANY of you are ever seen within a mile of this camp again, all of my sentries will know to shoot and kill you on sight. You will never again set foot in this place. If you do, it will be your last day on Earth. Do you understand me?"

The two seated on the bench nodded submissively. The one on the ground grunted, choking a little.

"Mark my words, gentlemen, I do not bluff," the warrior said, glancing around at the three travelers. He motioned to his own companions. "Get them up; we're done here."

* * * * *

The night sky was dark and looming; the moon and stars had been shut up by thick layers of rolling clouds. The light from a mounted torch burned brightly beside Daniel and cast dancing shadows across his face. Jonas observed his friend standing there-alone and watchful-beside the lookout tower; he approached quietly. The Marine heard Jonas' soft footsteps against the grass and glanced over. He smiled at his friend then centered his gaze again. His arms were folded across his chest; the air had grown damp with a slight chill, enough to make anyone outdoors shiver occasionally.

"You don't have to be out here tonight, man," Jonas said. "Why do you put so much on yourself?"

Daniel shifted his stance, bending one knee and then the other. He regripped his weapon firmly with a gloved hand. "You have a family, Jonas—a wife and a child. Your first allegiance will always be to them." He paused briefly, looking his friend in the eye. "Not all of us have that, and it falls to us, to hold back the night so you can get some sleep. It's not a burden." Daniel smiled lightly. "It's just how things turned out. We all have a part to play. Mine will always be lookin' out for people, even if they never asked."

Jonas patted his fellow warrior on the shoulder. "You're a good man, Dan, you know that, don't ya? We appreciate you."

Daniel smiled one more time. "I do know that, Jonas;

thanks. We wouldn't be able to hold things together without you and Janae either."

There was a long spell of quiet between them. With no evening stars to take in, they had only the stillness. Behind them, the torch whipped and gusted as a breeze picked up.

"You remember what it was like *before* the war?" Daniel reminisced.

Jonas grinned nostalgically. "Man, that feels like such a long time ago."

"Kind of was!" Dan laughed. "We're gettin' old, brother...but do you remember what it was like? The rat-race? Everybody always wanting more. A five bedroom house with a three-car garage and a month's vacation somewhere tropical? Remember how people used to stab each other in the back and run each other over, work overtime, and never see their kids, all so they could buy a new Cadillac or B.M.W.?" Daniel let an ironic grin escape his lips. "People were on antidepressants and anti-anxiety meds like the stuff was candy, and for what? Another shiny piece of aluminum to show off or make themselves feel something. I mean, don't get me wrong, there were some good things about the old world! Hot showers, nice-smelling girls—"

"Holiday dinners with family," Jonas cut in with another sentimental grin, "when everybody would gather together at Mom and Pop's. Lots of laughing, people bringing gifts over for the kids."

"Sure!" Daniel agreed. "There were good times. My point is, though, so much of that stuff we used to chase, didn't really matter. And none of it made anybody a better or happier person. I look around here now, and I see how we all look out for each other. Sometimes there's not much extra to go around, but we get by. People are friendlier, calmer, more fulfilled and grateful. They've got more purpose and peace living in shacks, playing *Little House on the Prairie* than all those rich Beverly Hills folks ever did.

"For a second, when I can push aside all the death and killing that got us here, I think maybe, just maybe, we're better off for it. Maybe this is how humans were supposed to live, connected with their neighbors, connected to the earth."

"It was a lot of death, Dan...a *lot* of death that got us here," Jonas lamented. "And most folks on the planet aren't living like us these days..."

"I know," Daniel conceded with a contemplative smirk. "It just gets me thinkin' sometimes. When Paolo preaches, I think that's what he hopes for—more of the world to be able to live like this: contented, thankful, at peace with their neighbors, connected to the Earth and their Maker."

"You're goin' all hippy on me, Dan." Jonas grinned. "How do you think your MARSOC boys would respond if they heard you sayin' all this get-back-to-nature stuff?"

Daniel laughed. "Brother, I was the captain and team leader before the end, *nobody* flicked *me* shit! Well, my master sergeant probably would have ribbed me a little. I guess I've come to believe a warrior can be a poet, philosopher, farmer, and lover too, and none of those have to negate his competence as a fighter."

"Nothing like a little Native or Samurai culture to temper the soul." Jonas chuckled. "Raoul would be proud of you, man."

A long silence returned. Crickets chirped and sang in the trees and underbrush. A pair of bats flitted past, on the prowl for nocturnal bugs. At last Jonas asked the question: "You think those assholes will stay gone?"

Daniel shot him a skeptical look. "They never do," he said, a wariness tinging his voice as he stared back out at the night. "Once they see what we've got here, they always come back. And they usually bring some friends with them..."

* * * * *

The late morning was cool and overcast like the one before it had been, but without the drizzling rain. Two cows lowed as they trod the dew-covered, sloping earth; the bells hanging under their necks clanged as they plodded along. People in the community were returning to their normal routines and daily work tending gardens, chickens, and laundry, milking the cows, and mending a torn shirt or pair of jeans. This day was peaceful, which found Beth Forsythe picking apples from a mid-season tree and placing them in a basket.

Beth was twenty-three and unmarried with no children. She bore a Scandinavian appearance, and she liked to wear her blonde hair in a headband-styled braid. Like many others, she had arrived in the community on her own, half-starved, beleaguered by many losses, and extremely fortunate to still be alive. She had grown up in Connecticut amid the Last War, with parents who tried to keep her in school for as long as possible. The last grade Beth ever completed was her sophomore year of high school; after this, the illusion of normalcy was shattered by the military invasions of Imperial State and Winter Steel on American shores. Beth had lost her entire family in the chaos that ensued. Even her younger sister had not been spared from an unfeeling fate out on the open the road.

Today, Beth was level headed and serene. She had moved beyond her grief. She remembered her old life but accepted that it was long over. She worked hard to be of service in the community, and she was tough, mentally and physically. She bore no inhibitions toward either carrying or using a firearm if need be, and she enjoyed the self-defense trainings that Daniel Weston periodically offered. She was also known for routinely volunteering on the perimeter as a sentry or lookout.

On this day, Beth labored alongside a close friend—a younger girl named Abby Jenson. Abby was sweet and somewhat shy, sheltered even. Unlike Beth, Abby had not the slightest interest in learning how to fight; she preferred to read and help the community in more nurturing ways. She was one of those who had survived purely by the protective graces of others. Without the community finding and watching over her, she would have been killed or snatched by lawless men long ago. Abby reminded Beth of the younger sister she had never been able to see grow up.

Together the young women worked and laughed, picking apples and placing them in wicker baskets. They spoke of the growing anticipations for the approaching Harvest Celebration—the cider pressing, baked pies, and sweet corn. It was a good life here, as good a one as people could find anymore. There were perils outside the borders of the community, but with many good people surrounding them, they rarely felt the dangers threaten them directly.

✱ ✱ ✱ ✱ ✱

The *wolves* lurked inside the eastern tree-line; they

watched the two young women laughing as they carried out their work. The killers eyed them hungrily like prey, captivated by their every move. The leader knelt on the ground wiping the blood of a young sentry off on his pant leg. They had murdered the young man not five minutes earlier; swiftly and silently, the three had crept up and set upon him all at once.

Covering the lookout's mouth with a meaty palm to stifle any noises, the brute had plunged his enormous hunting knife deep into the young man's back several times to prevent him from crying out or firing off a round. The other two had helped lower the body to the ground quietly, then dragged it off into the bushes to hide under some brush and leaves. None of the brutes knew when the sentries changed their posts on the perimeter, so now that they had committed to the act, they had to move quickly.

One of the husky followers huffed to the ringleader, "Hey, Jax, you sure about this? That military-Joe seemed pretty serious, and they've got a lot of guns around here. We might not come out on top with this one."

Jax scowled at the women out under the apple trees, not impressed by his companion's hesitation. He turned his glare on the lackey. "You goin' soft on me, Luther? Shut your mouth and get ready. We just killed a man, they're not gonna let that go. I don't know about you two, but I want some sweet lovin' from one of those gals. I want this whole damn place; I'm tired of livin' in the dirt. I ain't leaving, so we're gonna make this place ours. Ain't my fault that asshole kicked us out. It's time we showed him we mean business. He wants to play rough? We can give him rough."

Jax pulled the pistol from his holster while Luther checked the chamber of the murdered sentry's rifle he had picked up. The third outlaw, Beryl, slowly scraped the blades of a hatchet and machete together. He grinned. "I'm ready to get mine; let's show these peace-lovin' fairies we mean business. The ladies are gonna looooove me!"

"On three," Jax instructed. The outlaws crouched low, ready to kick into gear. It had been a few weeks since they'd killed or raided a camp; they were ready for some action again. Adrenaline pumping, Jax counted down three fingers, and they rushed from the trees, all wearing grins. No one fired a shot; they moved stealthily but quickly across the open field towards the girls. The hunt was on, and they loved it.

As Jax drew near to Abby from her left flank, he reached a hand out to grab hold of her. Beth turned at that exact moment to see the burly stranger with arm extended. Completely caught off guard and stunned, her eyes widened and her mouth fell open, as if to scream, yet no sound escaped.

Jax seized Abby by the hair and yanked her towards

him, pressing the muzzle of his pistol against her temple. In the same moment, Luther grabbed Beth in an enormous bear hug and attempted to toss her up over his shoulder. Abby had frozen in terror with a gun to her head, but Beth would not go quietly. She kicked, screamed, and threw elbows at the back of Luther's huge head.

Beth was creating an enormous commotion of protests and cries: "Let me go! HELP! Daniel! JONAS!!! We're under attack! Ring the bell! Ring THE BELL!!! Somebody, HELP!!!" She knew their cabins were close, and many neighbors were within earshot.

"Shut that bitch up!" Jax snapped.

Beryl stomped towards her menacingly, sharpened machete in hand, ready to slit her throat. But Luther, being less bright and tired of being kicked and elbowed, hurled her to the ground. Beth kept kicking and managed to tuck herself into a guarded fighting position even stunned, bruised, and on her back. What Luther lacked in intelligence, initiative, or finesse, he made up for in brute power. He leaned down and socked Beth hard, square in the face with a huge, closed fist, knocking her unconscious.

"Let's go!" Jax barked. "We can't get caught out in the open like this!" Luther threw Beth's limp body over his shoulder once more and the pack of killers retreated back toward the woods. Down the slope from them, a young, married man emerged from his garden and shouted in protest. Jax swiveled from the waist and shot him in the chest, then kept moving. The man dropped instantly when the .45 slug nicked his heart, piercing a lung and ricocheting off the inside of his ribcage into other vital organs.

Daniel who had been seated outside his cabin, working to tan a deer hide, heard the shouts and cries for help. His heart rate shot up when he heard the woman scream his name. He looked to Sadie who was lying in the dirt close by. He gave a sharp command in German, and she bolted from his presence in the direction of the ruckus. Then he seized his rifle, which was leaning against a nearby stump, and checked the chamber before charging after the dog. He shouted to anyone close enough to assist; he called out for Jonas, Raoul, and Ava-even as he rushed after the assailants. From the corner of his eye, he glimpsed Jonas racing up the hill towards him.

* * * * *

Inside the woods, the three brutes sprinted away from the glade as fast as their legs would carry them. They dodged trees, retracing deer trails and worn paths on the forest floor. Luther, who was fairly out of shape, wheezed to his leader, "Jax, how far are we gonna run?! I can't keep going like this, we ain't gonna be able to enjoy these ladies with the whole camp up our asses!"

"Shut up and move!" Jax shot back, grunting in annoyance at the incompetence of his companion. "Did you not hear a thing I said earlier? We're settin' a trap! When those boys send their fighters in after us, we'll get the jump on 'em and weed off their best men in an ambush. If we're patient, we'll be able to thin the herd; then we can have this whole town! Once we kill off their leaders, the rest will surrender to any demands just to save their own skins. This camp is run by a bunch of weak sheep! We kill off the few strong ones and the rest will give us whatever we want. *That's*, when we'll have our fun…"

CHAPTER SIX

As the three villains pressed harder and faster to put distance between themselves and the community, Luther suddenly heard the sound of racing footsteps gaining on him from behind. He turned just in time to see a black Labrador charging him in a dead-sprint. The dog went for the husky man's legs, snarling and biting down hard.

Luther let out a howl of pain and tried to kick the dog loose, but Sadie dodged his boot narrowly and darted away. She circled him ferociously for a moment, her lip curled and fangs bared; then she lunged again, attacking and mauling his calves and thighs. By now the canine's commotion had brought the hasty retreat to a standstill. She tore flesh, shredded pant-leg, and chewed muscle in her jaws.

"Shoot that mutt!" Jax ordered. "She's gonna bring

them all down on top of us!"

Beryl threw a hatchet at the dog; it did not stick, but the impact of the weighty head injured and knocked her off Luther for a moment. Badly bruised, Sadie leapt back to her feet in an instant, snarling as she prepared for a third attack. At that moment, Jax shot her through the side, and the bullet knocked her into the dirt. She let out a sharp bark and whine followed by low growls; this time she was unable to get back up. Luther adjusted Beth's unconscious body hanging over his shoulders and pointed his stolen rifle at the dog. He fired several shots into her until she gave up and ceased struggling. Blood began to pool on the earth around the faithful creature as the life left her body.

"Let's go!" Jax screamed. "That mutt just cost us our lead!" The autumn reds, yellows, and greens of trees and brush blurred past as all three resumed their flight away from the settlement. Each began to question whether or not they would be able to make their ambush site in lieu of the brief delay. The break in running had allowed them to catch their breaths, but now fear and doubt crouched at the backs of their minds.

Luther planted one hefty boot in front of the other as fast as he could, each step thudding against the earth almost as loudly as his heart now pounded in his chest. He had begun to breathe heavily again and his vision blurred. Then a voice called out to him from behind,

"Hey, asshole!" Luther turned to look back over his shoulder; there was a split second where he saw a black man standing there with a SCAR assault rifle raised. Then a round struck him in the forehead, right between the eyes. The bullet passed through Luther's brain cavity and blew out the back of his skull.

The shot was muted by a silencer on the end of Jonas' weapon. He had called out to make the burly man turn so he could avoid grazing Beth by accident. The heavy man dropped with a tremendous thud, and the young woman's body went rolling off the earthen trail into the undergrowth. Blood streamed from Luther's punctured, meaty head; he was long gone.

Beryl, who had stopped running and turned back, saw his companion hit the ground. In a burst of rage and adrenaline, he charged Jonas with a machete cocked over his head, ready to hack down the Ranger. Simultaneously, Jax raised his pistol and fired several shots at Jonas; one bullet struck him in the left thigh. Jonas' leg buckled under him, and he struggled to right himself and return fire under a hail of bullets.

Beryl was still charging, mere feet away, machete poised to swing. Then three rounds tore through the left side of his torso. He grunted as the wind was knocked out of him; he crumpled to his knees, touching his side lightly. He held his hand out in front of him and saw the fresh blood on his fingertips. Jamal glided down the wooded slope beside him and came to a halt, towering over the bearded killer. Beryl looked up at the former infantry sergeant; their eyes met for a single moment, then Jamal put a final shot through his head and it was lights out.

Jax bellowed in outrage, seeing both his companions had been killed. He fired wildly at Jamal, who dove for cover. The brute leader hollered out, "I've got this girl here! You drop your weapons and back off or I'll put a bullet in her head like you did my friends!"

Jonas and Jamal exchanged glances and stared down the desperate killer. Their rifles were honed on him but neither fired. "Let her go," Jonas commanded. "You brought this on yourself! We let you live before and told you not to come back! We even warned you what would happen if you did, but you chose to come anyway!"

"Shut your mouth, *negro!*" Jax roared, his words dripping with contempt. He thrust the muzzle of his pistol against the side of Abby's head.

Jonas felt the burn of racial hatred from the hillbilly. He wanted to end this villain once and for all—to rid the world of his evil. Beside him, Jamal was bristling as well. Jonas called out: "We've got you outgunned and we're not going anywhere. You've got a prisoner and we want her back!"

"You back off, or she dies!" Jax warned, tossing his

head. An unsettling grin had crawled across his face, and there was a wild look in his eyes.

Suddenly a bullet ripped through Jax's shooting hand. He cried out in pain as the pistol flew over his shoulder. Then two more suppressed shots blew out both of his knees. He buckled to the ground screaming profanities in agony, choking back sobs and whimpers. Then a fourth round pierced his right bicep, tearing through flesh and muscle and shattering bone so that he let out a howl of anguish. In a matter of seconds, the belligerent rabble-rouser had been reduced to a pitiful heap of moans and wails.

Jonas and Jamal glanced at each other again; neither of them had fired a shot at the man, yet there he was-crumpled on the forest floor under a large birch tree. From behind them, Daniel suddenly stormed out of the brush. He did not even acknowledge their presence but surged forward, stomping directly towards the crippled murderer.

Still conscious, Abby was able to slip free from her bloodied captor's grasp. Her face was tear-streaked and ghostly white as she crawled to Beth's side and checked to make sure she was still breathing. She shook her friend, trying to wake her.

For the second time in twenty-four hours, Daniel towered over Jax, yet this time he wasted no words. The warrior's lip quivered and his entire body shook with unfettered rage. He seized the larger man by the shirt collar, lifting him up from the ground and slamming him against the tree trunk. Then he beat Jax's face to a pulp. Highly trained in hand-to-hand combat, Daniel tore Jax apart, beating him to within an inch of his life and unleashing the full fury of his speed and finesse. He struck powerful blows against the outlaw's kidneys and ribs, cracking several for good measure and rupturing his spleen. Then he leveraged and broke both the man's arms at the elbows.

Bloodied and weary, on the verge of passing out, Jax gave the Marine a dazed smile. He coughed and spit up blood, finally managing to get out his last words. "Guess I might have underestimated you..." Then the wandering thug crumpled to the forest floor again.

The former MARSOC captain grabbed a fistful of the brute's scalp. He unsheathed a black titanium knife and jammed the blade deep into the side of Jax's girthy neck. The man's eyes bulged and he made noises like he might vomit. Blood gurgled in the back of his throat and windpipe, and he tried grasping at the foreign object lodged in his neck. In growing alarm, he realized this was impossible; his broken arms simply would not cooperate any longer.

With cold eyes, Daniel glowered down on the bearded fiend. The brute was wheezing his final breaths, blinking, as if trying to focus his vision. Daniel pulled the knife free from his neck, then shanked him three more times in rapid succession in the same spot. The color was drained from Jax's face, and the light had begun to fade from his eyes. Blood spurted from the gaping tear in his neck and a steady flow ran off his shoulder. Daniel knelt down in front of the man and looked him in the eyes. "I don't know if there's a hell or not, but I promise you, no one is going to miss you on this Earth, and I hope whatever God is out there, sends you to the darkest pit forever."

Jax's eyes were full of fear and panicked resistance. He knew he was dying but desperately trying to bargain for life. One of his palms involuntarily grasped at Daniel's shirt, brushing his enemy's hand as it did. Daniel looked down at the fumbling palm; his expression dark. He stood up and kicked the man's body over backwards. Jax fell away, twitching, trembling, and stammering quietly in the shrubs as the last of his life drained away.

The warrior stared down at the bloody dirt. "Are the girls all right?" he asked his companions numbly.

Jonas nodded. "Abby helped Beth back to camp; neither of them looked too badly hurt. I think Abby will have a harder time with all of this; she was pretty shaken up when she left."

Daniel snorted in frustration. "You think? She's just a kid! A seventeen-year-old girl who just got assaulted and kidnapped by three rapist killers who held a gun to her head!" Daniel spat. He shot a glance around at the bodies and stiffened with rage all over again. He was completely covered in Jax's blood and didn't care. He cut loose with a flurry of profanities, feeling a swell of emotion in his chest and behind his eyes. "They killed my dog, man! They killed my dog! Sadie was great! All she ever did was love the kids around here, and those assholes shot her, like, forty times!"

Jamal exhaled. "I think they killed Sean O'Connell too—shot him on their way out of camp..."

Daniel cursed again. "He has a wife and two young kids! And you, Jonas, you're shot!"

Jonas waved his friend off. "I'll be all right, brother; Janae might have your ass for this later, though." He grinned.

"What do you wanna do with them?" Jamal asked, tossing his head in the direction of the three bodies.

Daniel looked down at the corpses again, rolling Luther's heavy body over with his boot. "Bring me some gas."

"What?"

Daniel glared at Jamal. "Bring me a can of gas! NOW!"

Jamal's ego bristled. He was not in the habit of taking orders from Daniel, but he saw the former MARSOC captain was on the edge and might fight anybody who pushed him right now. Jamal threw up his hands and said, "All right, whatever, man." He cradled his M-4 and turned to walk back towards the glade.

Meanwhile, Jonas studied his companion carefully. "What you gonna do, Dan?" he asked warily.

Daniel glanced at his friend, and shoved Beryl's body over to Luther's with a boot. He remained silent as he stalked towards Jax's drained corpse under the tree. He seized a lifeless leg and dragged the limp body through the dirt to the other two. There was now a contorted pile of cadavers heaped together in the middle of the trail. "I'm gonna burn these sons-of-bitches, Jonas. Then I'm gonna leave 'em out here for the coyotes to tear apart and a warning to anyone else who comes by-thinking they might want to cause us some harm."

"That doesn't really sound like you, Dan. You think Paolo, would be a fan of this idea?"

"The priest didn't have to chase down these animals to save Beth and Abby. I don't really give a damn what the father might think about it. I didn't see him out here killing these animals."

Jamal returned presently, clutching a plastic gas jug and a little short of breath. Daniel seized it from him with an empty, "Thanks." Then he commenced to dousing the heap of bodies with the fuel, making sure every inch of them was thoroughly soaked and dripping. He emptied the entire jug on the pile; a notable excess given how precious a commodity fuel was to the community.

Daniel used the final drips to create a trail away from the bodies to avoid being blasted by the flames when he ignited it. He tossed the jug aside and pulled an old zippo lighter from his pocket. He had carried it since the war; on its side was emblazoned the proud crest of the legendary Marine Raiders unit. Daniel knelt in the dirt five feet from the bodies; he flicked the flint wheel twice and produced a small flame. He gently lowered it to the ground and ignited the fuel trail.

Fire shot across the ground and a loud whooshing noise erupted as the oxygen in the air was consumed in a split second; the pile of bodies burst into flames. From his hunkered position, Daniel watched the dancing, hot tongues leap and lap. Slowly, he rose, staring into the blazing inferno-stoic, unblinking, ruminating only on the fact that these brutes had gotten everything they had coming to them. His back was rigid, and his shoulders and muscles taut. All he felt was an engulfing fury in his soul, a fury which could match the towering blaze before him. A mixture of hatred and darkening rage clouded his thoughts.

Jonas and Jamal stood back at a distance, neither having a desire to be scorched by the overwhelming heat. Jamal could not have cared less about three corpses being burned, particularly when they belonged to the likes of these men. Jonas, on the other hand, felt a profound unease as he watched his friend stand unflinching before the blinding heat and reaching flames. Daniel remained transfixed, staring into the fiery abyss with a deep feeling of satisfaction at the sight of his adversaries consumed in immolation.

※ ※ ※ ※ ※

A chill breeze whispered through the cottonwood branches, rustling the changing leaves. A few of the yellows and oranges had already begun drifting to the forest floor. There were fewer birds chirping and singing now. Summer had passed and autumn was beginning to show itself. The usual sparrows, swallows, and robins had departed on their southward flight for the cold months. Their absence left a kind of empty silence in the wooded hills, which only the wind and sound of swaying branches now broke. Occasionally, a squirrel or other woodland creature would scurry through the brush and fallen leaves as well.

It was another tranquil Sunday, the morning after the bloody skirmish with the three nefarious wanderers. The Marine warrior had placed himself on perimeter guard duty once more and assumed his usual tree-stand post. He rested peacefully with his back against the cottonwood's sturdy trunk, rifle nestled in his arms against his chest.

There was little noise coming from the clearing this morning. Father Paolo had directed everyone to enter a time of silence and reflection in lieu of the loss of Sean O'Connell and Jake Sundquist, the two community members killed in cold-blood the day before. Sean left behind a now-widowed wife and two young, uncomprehending children.

Father Paolo did not believe in glossing over great losses nor in taking emotional suffering lightly. He wanted all of the community to lean into this pain, to feel it, wrestle with it, and harness it for good in the days to come by caring for the widow and orphan. The great chasm and jagged peaks of grief lay before them collectively. The sudden, violent deaths of friends also gave pause for each to individually consider how they were living their own days. Were there things they had neglected to say? Did they need to change how they interacted with loved ones? Tomorrow was not guaranteed—the last twenty-four hours had served as a tragic reminder.

As the hour of gathering drew to a close, Father Paolo reminded them that there would be a burial and graveside memorial for both of the fallen men later that afternoon. He also noted grimly that the following night would mark the start of a full moon. The monthly headaches, vomiting, hallucinations, seizures, and vertigo were unlikely to abate. They were still paying the price for the mortal wound Mech-Tech's tampering had dealt the heavenly body.

"Take care of each other," the priest charged them. "You are your brother's keeper! You are your sister's keeper! Now, more than ever, we need each other."

In his tree, Daniel inhaled deeply. He stared out through the branches. Yellow leaves shook in the breeze, and for the first time in the two years he had been there, he wondered if the community was the right place for him anymore. God-knew they needed protection and leadership, but maybe he'd stayed too long. He might be better off back out on the road alone.

This would not be last time the glade was attacked or lost people. Daniel had seen enough death for twenty lifetimes. He knew the blows would just keep coming unless a just government brought order to these lands. He laughed inwardly at the absurdity of such an idea. Those days were long past. No new powers would rise in this hemisphere—not under Unity's restless gaze and Mech-Tech's unquenchable greed.

Daniel had buried Sadie behind his cabin earlier that morning before taking his post. He did not want to admit it, but her death had layered yet another blanket of sadness over his already troubled heart. He mentally chastised himself to remember she was "only a dog;" she didn't merit any *real* grief.

Still, Sadie had gone down fighting to save those girls, and the brutes had killed her for it. That was the kind of dog she was: faithful, companionate, protective. She may have just been a dog, but she had been a *good* dog, and Daniel had sent even her to her death. She would never lick his hand again nor paw at his leg while he stroked her black, shiny coat. He would never chide her for being a beggar again.

The warrior hurled a stick he'd been whittling with his knife. It crashed through the leaves and canopy, landing somewhere down in the underbrush.

"Mr. Weston?" a soft voice called up from below, interrupting his brooding.

"What?" Daniel asked, heaving a sigh. His response came out gruffer than intended, but he lacked the energy for much tact or diplomacy this morning.

"It's Abby, Abby Jenson; I just wanted to say thank you. Thank you for..." the girl's voice trailed off, and she could not finish. Emotion overwhelmed her and she choked.

Daniel looked down from the tree-stand. The girl was trying valiantly to compose herself and speak her piece, but the tide of emotions were growing stronger. The former captain hoisted his legs over the ledge and dropped ten feet to the muddy ground, rifle still cradled in his arms. He stood up and felt the pain in his knees. He wasn't in his early twenties anymore.

Abby sniffed and continued trying to choke back hot tears and sobs, but the wash of fear and anger at what had happened the day before overpowered her. All the imagining of what *might have* happened if Daniel, Jonas, and Jamal had not been there to intervene.

The warrior wrapped the seventeen-year-old up in a strong, enveloping embrace. The girl went limp in his protective arms; then she just cried hard for several long minutes, her head pressed against his tactical vest.

"I'm sorry," she sobbed through broken words.

"It's all right," he said. "It's all right; you're safe. Nobody's gonna touch you here."

"But those men died because of me." She began to cry again. "Mrs. O'Connell's husband! Those kids lost their..." That was all she could get out before another wave of emotion broke over her.

A cloud of furious expletives swirled inside Daniel's mind as he continued to hold the girl. He hated those men for all they had done and tried to do. "That wasn't your fault," he reassured "None of it. Those animals did this; *they* killed our friends, and that had nothing to do with you or Beth. They were evil men. If it hadn't been us, they'd have found another camp of innocent people to prey on."

After a few more minutes of crying and irrational self-blame, Abby finally calmed down and composed herself enough to speak. She backed out of the embrace, brushing stray tears and mussed hairs from her face. "Sorry," she apologized, looking sheepishly at the earth. "I had it all planned out in my head what I wanted to say to you, and none of it came out right."

Dan smiled a little. "How's Beth?" he asked, trying to shift the focus of conversation.

Abby exhaled, continuing to regroup her thoughts. "She's got some bruises and a black eye, but she'll be all right, I think. She's a lot tougher than me."

"You're strong too, Abby," Daniel affirmed. "You went through hell yesterday, but here you are, back on your feet the next day. Give yourself some credit; you didn't let this beat you. You didn't let those animals break you."

Abby blushed a reluctant smile of pride, still avoiding direct eye contact. "Do you think you could, you know, teach me how to fight sometime?" she asked a little nervously. She bit her lower lip and looked away.

"Absolutely," the warrior answered "Come find me anytime; we'll get you squared away on some training."

"Okay." She smiled shyly. "Thank you again. I'll let you get back to your guarding."

"Take care." Daniel bid her farewell. "I'll be seein' you real soon." He saw Paolo standing a few yards behind her. The teen thanked him again and then went on her way.

"A very sweet girl," the priest observed, watching

Abby go.

"What do you want, father?" Daniel asked; he was in no mood to play games.

"Are you angry with me, Daniel? Have I done something to offend you? I was only going to comment that you saved Abby's life."

"Maybe I'm paranoid." Daniel said, narrowing his eyes. "But I've been waiting for some kind of rebuke from you."

"And why might that be? I came here to thank you and commend your swift action and bravery yesterday. Have I said anything that would lead you to believe I'm here for something else?"

The Marine frowned skeptically and waited.

"I also came to tell you that the council has agreed to meet later today to revisit your proposals for emergency evacuation and rendezvous plans. We all feel this is very important, especially in light of events these past few days..."

"And?" Daniel prodded.

There was a long pause before Father Paolo reluctantly concluded, "The council did also ask me to speak with you about the men you killed yesterday."

Daniel shook his head in disgust. "Unbelievable."

"Daniel."

"I knew it! Why did you try to deny it, Father?! Don't come up here trying to be all chummy and coy with me when you've got something to say! How dare you try and make me feel guilty or paranoid! You just say what you've gotta say so we can get on with it like men!"

The priest remained composed. "I was not trying to trick you, Daniel; you are my friend and even like a son to me. I did not want you to feel I was *only* coming here to chastise you. Your defensiveness reveals some inner turmoil though."

"Father, you go right ahead and chastise away! My conscience is clear; I've got nothin' to say for what I did with those bodies. They were evil men and they got everything they had coming to 'em."

"Daniel," the Franciscan said softly.

"I didn't see you out there with a gun, Father! I didn't see you chasing down those animals to save Beth and Abby! Did you get anybody's blood on you yesterday? 'Cause I sure as hell did, covered in it!"

"Daniel."

"If you and the council wanna hold yourselves up high and sit in judgment because I made some evil sons-of-bitches pay and then *burned* their bodies, you go right ahead! But you won't ever hear me apologize or see me shed a tear for any of it!"

"Daniel!" Paolo cut in sharply, finally interrupting the younger man's tirade.

"What?!" the warrior shouted. Then he realized he

was out of breath and felt foolish. The priest had yet to level a single accusation against him. "I mean, what, Father?" Daniel said, softening his tone.

The old Syrian was trying hard to hide his amusement; he was smiling kindly now with no judgment. He held up a frail, knobby hand for peace. "Daniel, I did not come here to condemn you. It is true that word of what you did to those men spread quickly through our small community. Jonas shared with me the intensity of your anger, which was deeply unsettling to him yesterday."

There was a pause before the priest continued. "He also informed me that your intent is to send a message to any future trespassers. He told me that after burning the bodies, you strung all three of them up under a tree limb." Another long pause. "Though it saddens me, and I find your *message* dark and disturbing, I am not here to sit in judgment over you. I am here out of concern, Daniel. I am concerned for your heart, your mind, and your soul...a darkness grows within you."

The Marine stood quietly now, waiting for Paolo to continue.

"At our last, long conversation, we discussed your feelings of love for your sister and hate for your father. I am here to tell you that if you cannot forgive your father for all of his wickedness, you leave yourself at risk of becoming like him."

This final remark cut deeply and Daniel glowered. He resented the very notion. How could the priest even insinuate such a thing?! It stung like a betrayal, and Daniel shot back in a low tone, "I would *never* be like him!"

"And yet you are! Whether you like it or not," Paolo pressed him. "Daniel, you are not simply you. You are a combination of both your father *and* your mother. You have your father in you; perhaps not the fully corrupted version, but he is in you. In the fibers of your genes and in the very cells of your body—in your personality and temperament. And unless you can find a way to forgive him for all the terrible things he did to you, your mother, and sister, those parts of you will always live in the shadows, controlling you, yet invisible to you.

"When I tell you to forgive him, I do not say this for his sake nor because I believe he deserves it. I *implore* you to forgive him for your *own* sake! Because I love you as a father and a friend! Until you can bring that darkness into the light and accept even your father as a part of yourself, it will consume you. He was a powerful, violent man with an irascible temper; *you* are a powerful man, Daniel, with a temper, who is, at times, capable of great acts of violence.

"You are not fully him, though; you have learned to restrain yourself and channel your wrath towards injustice and evil. But he is still with you, a part of who you are...so is your mother, all her love and desire to protect others, her willingness to sacrifice herself and take another's beating. You must accept all these parts of yourself with compassion and grace. You must welcome each of them home as if they were frightened children. If you cannot, they will control you from the shadows. And as the years go by, you will find yourself growing darker, angrier, ever more self-righteous and self-assured, yet simultaneously more abusive and tyrannical. Whatever we cannot accept within ourselves will always have power over us."

Daniel was trying to listen, but his head was swimming. Let his anger go? Forgive his father and accept him as part of himself? It was insane! "How?" Daniel caught himself asking quietly.

The priest looked up, a bit surprised yet with hope and care in his eyes. "It is often too much to ask of the heart, mind, and body to move directly from hatred to love. If you want to stop hating someone, you might have to find compassion or pity for them first. You told Abby those men you killed were pure evil. Do you really believe that?"

The Marine wanted to scream *yes*, but he knew the priest was testing him. "Two of them were followers; they probably just fell in with a bad crowd who led them down a bad path... One evil choice leading to the next until they didn't even know *how* to be honorable men anymore. Compassion and honesty were completely foreign to them. I doubt either of them ever had a decent upbringing to help them seek out a good path or make an unselfish choice."

"Mmm," Paolo mused encouragingly. "That's very gracious of you. And what about the one you dispatched personally, slowly. Their leader. What about him?"

Daniel stared back at the priest; he felt himself closing off again, the iron setting his jaw rigidly. He couldn't—not today; that man *was* evil through and through.

"He reminded you of your father, didn't he?" Paolo pressed gently. "Crafty, wicked, cruel, and unfeeling, crass, and violent. You could almost forgive the others for being mindless, uneducated followers, driven by desperation or poor upbringings. But their leader? He was a monster in your eyes, like your father."

"Father, I—I can't," Daniel stumbled, trying to fight back a sudden swell of emotion. After more than a decade of holding his past in check, he hated how powerless he felt to control his emotions when his biological father was brought up.

The old priest patted the warrior gently on the arm. "Give yourself time, time and grace. God is in no hurry. He plays for the long-game of all our hearts."

Daniel nodded silently. This small, Syrian abbé carried nothing but kindness and patience within. He bore no threats, coercion, and wielded no physical or political power, yet he was able to disarm the strongest person at every encounter.

"And Daniel..." Paolo spoke again. "Don't ever think I speak from a place of naivety or ignorance. In the homeland of my youth, I witnessed evil as you cannot imagine; I watched it raise its hideous head in the forms of famine, disease, chemical warfare, religious persecution, and ethnic genocide. I saw and felt its effects up close. But late in this old sinner's life the Lord Jesus, in His everlasting grace and mercy, has taught this weary pilgrim something."

"What's that, Father?" Daniel asked, still thinking of all the evil he had witnessed in his *own* days. He had to deliberately shift his focus.

"The smallest act of hope and trust will always prevail against the most powerful host of evils. Simple acts of love will ripple through the cosmos and into eternity, melting hearts and tearing down fortresses of darkness. Kindness will echo on through the stars long after greed and power have departed these lands. And Love will pass beyond even Death's door, where neither fear nor hatred can follow."

Daniel doubted he grasped what the priest was saying, but it was a nice sentiment.

"Will you please cut down the bodies, Daniel, and bury them?" the priest asked with tender humility.

Daniel winced as if someone had cold-cocked him from nowhere. He stiffened a little, remembering Jennifer O'Connell and her young children without a father. He thought of the murdered sentry and the fresh mound of soil under which Sadie was now laid to rest. "I will do it for you, Father," he answered reluctantly. "Because you ask."

Paolo bowed his head in reverent gratitude. "I will find someone to help you dig and take no more of your time." The priest turned to leave, and the warrior pensively watched him go. Then he re-ascended the sturdy cottonwood trunk and resumed his tranquil post in the branches.

* * * * *

Some weeks passed; the days and nights continued to grow cooler, blustering into late October. There was joy and excitement in the air again, even a carefree spirit of happiness that made people forget their troubles and angst. This night marked the start of the Harvest Celebrations—three evenings of music, games, dancing, food, laughter, and general revelry. It was a time of being together as neighbors—a time of celebration and thanksgiving for all they had, and for collaboratively surviving another year.

Early on in the life of the settlement, Father Paolo

and the council had decided these days of rest devoted to celebration and gratitude would be vitally important to the collective health and spirits of all in the community. People made their 'secret' recipes: chili, venison and vegetable stews, spiced jerky, and cornbread. There were pies, cobblers, and sweet rolls; home-crafted beers and wines; freshly pressed cider' and no shortage of corn-on-the-cob straight from the stock.

Brother Martinez would play classical guitar; a quiet woman of the community played the Celtic bagpipes; and Raoul had fashioned a deer-skin drum, which he played as a kind of bongo. John, the introverted engineer, could also set people to dancing and clapping with his fiddle. There were many honored solos, duets, and encores to stir hearts and cause people to relax, smile, and give thanks.

The dances which took place were largely folk style, lively and energetic, with simple movements that could be learned easily. Periodically, a couple might make an exhibition of Latin or ballroom styles, which they remembered from the old world. Neighbors would pause to watch these displays of slow, steady patience, partnership, and synchronicity as two spirits moved as one. Their motions full of a grace, beauty, and interdependence, which audiences sometimes mistook for ease. There was a kind of mutual respect in dance not often seen in the world any longer. Everyone would grow still and a little nostalgic in these moments, warm smiles of remembrance passing over their faces.

To the outside observer or citizens of an advanced superpower, much of these simple festivities might have appeared quaint or absurdly antiquated. Yet no one in the community shared such sentiments. There were no electronic devices to blast hip-hop beats through the air or television sets through which to idolize celebrities. Instead, these unpretentious folk knew their neighbors well. They entered into each present moment fully. Contentment, joy, gratitude, hope for a future, and shared laughter and hardship were *their* reality. Simplicity wasn't such a bad thing in this community.

Beth Forsythe lingered at the fringes of all the revelry. People were conversing and laughing boisterously. Music echoed across the glade. Younger children shamelessly freestyled their own definitions of *dance*. The sun had gone down an hour earlier, but the celebration was only just beginning. Lanterns, roaring fires, and standing torches lit up the clearing for everyone to enjoy the food and merriment. It felt so good to see them all smiling and joking again; too many premature deaths had overshadowed the past year and darkened people's spirits.

With no announcement, Captain Daniel Weston suddenly appeared, standing beside her. Beth gave a short start; she had not heard him approach. "Hey!" she greeted with a smile. "You startled me! How are you doing?" They were not particularly close and only knew each other in the friendly, passing-acquaintance sort of way. Still, Beth found it hard not to notice his height, muscular frame, and firm jawline. He had nice eyes too. She knew he was several years older than her, but that didn't keep him from being extremely attractive.

Daniel returned her casual smile. "I'm good, how 'bout yourself? It's nice to see everyone having a good time." It had not escaped his notice that Beth was also very attractive: slender frame, blonde hair, kind spirit, radiant heart, and intelligent. She was his type. Similarly, though, he couldn't remember the last time they had really spoken more than a few sentences to each other outside of self-defense or weapons training. On his end, the attraction was more of a mental note—an objective observation. He had built up strong defenses and a long habit of locking those kinds of feelings down, deep inside.

"I'm good, too!" Beth answered genuinely. "Well, better..."

Daniel nodded and did a quick, visual scan of her face. "I can't even tell you got hit anymore."

The black eye and ugly bruises that had once turned sickly shades of green, purple, and yellow were healed this evening. It had taken a several weeks. Now only a small mark remained beside her right eye where a bad cut had been inflicted by Luther's heavy blow during the attack on the camp. Beth touched the faint scar gently, self-conscious of it.

The warrior shot her an easy-going smile. "Just tell everyone: 'The other guy got it worse'."

"Seriously!" She laughed, but internally reflected soberly. She had only been half-conscious after taking the hard hit, but there were a few flashes, images, and sounds. Abby had filled her in on some things, and she had heard the rumors. The whispers of how Daniel and Jonas had torn those brutes apart, burned their corpses, and strung them up as a warning to other enemies who might come skulking about.

Daniel returned his gaze to the gaggle of revelers before them. Several adults were already intoxicated-with others well on their way. The Marine veteran laughed a little at the sight of Jonas with his face in a water-filled barrel, bobbing for an apple while Ellie cheered him on from close by. He was hamming it up as usual, pretending to be drowning, splashing his daughter to make her squeal.

Beth noticed that tonight the warrior carried no rifle; it was one of the first times she had ever seen him without it at least within an arm's reach. There was a pistol holstered on his right hip, but it was small and subdued. Perhaps even the great Daniel Weston was letting his guard down a little tonight in honor of all the festivities.

The two of them continued loitering on the outskirts, appreciating the sights and sounds of all the hubbub and their neighbors' joy. They talked now and then about small happenings in the community or shared a laugh at someone who was acting–a-fool. They ventured over to greet Raoul who was also sitting near the edge of the firelight, beating his drum whenever it complemented other instruments. After an hour or so, a kind woman who was a bit tipsy on wine asked Beth if she could go fetch a freshly-baked batch of rolls that were cooling in her cabin.

Beth graciously excused herself and left Daniel to stand alone or visit with others. She made her way across the damp grass and found the appropriate cabin. The rains were quickly turning the meadow into a mud pit. She entered the warm abode and wrapped the hot morsels of bread in a plain linen towel to keep them from losing heat. She loaded the batch into a wicker basket sitting beside the stove for just such a purpose, then she headed back out into the night air and closed the door behind her.

It was growing rather chilly away from the fires, and she stopped to bundle her coat and scarf about her. The months had turned mostly wet and overcast so there were no stars to enjoy on her walk back to the firelight and revelry. She smiled slightly, thinking of maybe continuing her conversation with Daniel Weston. She let herself imagine a little. She had lost everyone and everything before practically collapsing in the glade two years earlier. She had lost virtually all hope, ready to give up and end her own life or just sit down on a log and wait for a band of ravagers to claim her.

Beth knew she still carried all that pain and grief somewhere inside, but it didn't keep her from dreaming a little. The thought of having a family one day or just a partner was a pleasant one. She treasured her housemates, but it would be nice to not go to bed alone for the rest of her life.

Half way back across the meadow and to the revelry and lights, Beth's personal thoughts were interrupted. A voice called out from the shadows off to her right, "What's goin' on, babe?"

Beth knew the voice; she stopped and waited for the tall figure to show himself.

Jamal Williams emerged from the darkness. "What's good, girl?" he said with a head toss. He had his usual mischievous grin and egotistical swagger, but tonight the liquor bottle dangling from his fingertips commanded Beth's attention.

"I'm good, Jamal," she responded slightly guarded. "I'm heading back up to the celebration? Have you been there yet? You should come!" she invited.

"Nah, that's not for me, ya know, bunch of awkward

white folks dancin' around like it's a Resonance fair or some shit."

Beth wanted to point out that *she* fell into the group he had just dismissed, but she knew there was no point with Jamal. About a year ago, they had seen each other romantically for a time. It didn't last, and Beth had learned some things about Jamal: one being that, generally speaking, he was not open to alternative ways seeing matters. He tended to be highly self-assured of his own thoughts and opinions, and he did not take corrective feedback well.

The former infantry leader took another step towards her and moved to block her path. She could smell the alcohol on his breath now when he spoke. "How about you and me go have a little party of our own?" he said, starting to slide his fingers across her hips.

Beth took an uncomfortable step backwards to remove herself from his touch. She was still holding the basket of rolls, so she couldn't brush his hands off. "I'm not really interested, Jamal. We ended things, remember? I'm heading back up to the party; you should come join everyone! It'll be a good time," she said, trying to encourage his thoughts away from the two of them being alone together.

The former Army sergeant ignored her redirection and came closer again. Once more he slid his hands onto her waist. This time he leaned forward to kiss her.

"Come on," he pressed. "It'll be like old times. Let's go have some fun; you look like you could use a little stress-relief. I still remember what you like." He grinned flirtatiously.

Beth's skin was crawling now, and she struggled to remove herself from his overbearing presence again. She really did not want to think about their past interactions. Not that it had all been bad at the time, but dating in a small community at the end of the world created some awkward tensions. Besides, she had moved on...completely.

"Jamal, stop!" she pushed back, growing angry and shoving him away.

In his drunken state, Jamal treated her rebuffs as playfulness, but Beth detected a spark of anger in his eyes when she pushed him away. He came towards her once more, this time moving to bite her ear and neck. "Come on," he urged. "You just don't remember how good I can make it feel. I know how to show a girl a good time."

Beth started to panic inside. If he kept pressing or tried to force her, it would be the second time in a month that she had been accosted by a man. She was scared, but becoming livid. How dare he treat her this way! She was still trying to maneuver away from him, but it was time to drop the rolls and fight him or simply run for help.

Then a third voice cut in. "Is there a problem here?"

Beth immediately felt a wave of relief wash over her entire body. Daniel stood about fifteen feet behind Jamal up the slope and to his right. The Marine had assumed a stalwart, unflinching posture; his face was stoic and his jaw set. He knew he was not witnessing an appropriate or appreciated interaction.

Jamal straightened up a little and curled his lip. "Nope," he said without turning. "We're doing just fine. Feel free to get lost."

Daniel did not need a response from Beth; the fear in her eyes told him everything he needed to know. "Beth looks uncomfortable; how about you give her a little space and let her go back to the party. You and I can take a walk; let's get some fresh air."

Jamal finally glanced over his shoulder. "Man, how 'bout you piss off and stop interfering in things that ain't any of your business!"

Daniel's voice took a deadly serious tone. "That wasn't a suggestion, Jamal. Take a step back and let the lady go or so-help-me-God you'll be breathing out of your neck for the next six months."

"Oooh, big, scary MARSOC! That's right, white boy, threaten the black man! You gonna get a posse together and string me up?! In case you forgot, I don't take orders from you!"

"You're the only one making a problem here, Jamal.

And you know I take every person by their actions, not the color of their skin." Daniel shifted his focus for a moment. "Beth, are you all right?"

She nodded slightly, still tense.

"Then walk away now. Go back to the party," he instructed, never taking his eyes off Jamal.

Beth moved quietly away from Jamal's grasp. She could tell he was angry and embarrassed, bristling to do something brash, to flex his muscles and show he was still in control of the situation. To his credit, however, he stayed quiet and let her go.

When she had gone, Jamal slowly turned around to face Daniel. He grinned and gave an exaggerated shrug. "Well, what now, Cap'?"

"How about we take that walk and talk about all this."

"No thanks," Jamal said flatly, narrowing his eyes. "I got nothin' to say to you, the *great Captain* Daniel Weston, guardian of the community and protector of all. I know what you really are, asshole. I've seen your dark side, and I know you've got skeletons you haven't told *nobody* about—not even the priest." Jamal spat. "You're the biggest poser in this place."

He turned to leave, and Daniel called after him, "You know I'm gonna have to tell the council what happened here, don't you, Jamal?"

"What happened here?" The younger man laughed.

He chucked his bottle of bourbon against a boulder, smashing it, and tossing Daniel a middle-finger as he walked away.

Jonas approached from behind. "What was that about?"

Daniel stared after their fellow veteran who had disappeared into the darkened tree-line. "Jamal was getting very handsy and pushy with Beth," he answered. "Wasn't taking no for an answer."

"That's not good," Jonas said gravely.

"No, it isn't. He was drinking, but keep an eye out for him tonight. We'll work this thing out tomorrow. I'm gonna go check on Beth, make sure she's still doing all right."

✸ ✸ ✸ ✸ ✸

Daniel took a long walk and found Beth standing by herself beside one of the roaring bonfires. She was closed off to everyone around her, just staring into the flames. "Hey," he said, handing her a cup of hot cider. "You okay?"

She took the cup gratefully and kept staring at the blaze. She rolled her shoulders out uncomfortably, trying to ease some of the tension in her body.

Daniel took a drag of cider from his own cup and listened to the pleasant melody being picked out on

Fernando's guitar. A woman stood beside the Benedictine brother, playing her flute in a tender duet. "Jonas and I will be having a serious talk with Jamal tomorrow. He doesn't need to be coming around you anymore, not for a long time. Do you want to be a part of that conversation?"

"I'll think about it," Beth said reluctantly. "Let you know."

The once-powerful warrior was racking his brain for something funny to say. He wished he could make her laugh and get her mind off what had just transpired. It was sickening; Jamal had behaved no better than an animal in heat, coercive, without restraint or remorse. Now Daniel was left trying to help pick up the pieces, to cheer her up and get her back to the present moment. "Did I ever tell you I was once kicked out of a yoga class back during the war?" he said at last, cracking grin of pride.

The faintest smirk crept across Beth's lips for just a moment; she took the bait and looked up at him skeptically.

"Seriously!" He laughed, toasting his cup to the fire, his smile intoxicating. "I was dating this girl from San Francisco, kind of a granola-hippie type, but really into fitness. We met at the gym."

Beth rolled her eyes. "Classy," she quipped dryly.

"I know." He winked. "So I went to one of her yoga

classes. Ya know, take interest in something she liked and all that, maybe sweat a little too. I took my shirt off in the studio, but apparently a bunch of limp-wristed, tree-hugging war protesters had shown up for a meditation or some trash. They didn't care for all my Marine Corps tattoos about death, killing, and warrior ethos. So five or six of 'em all lay into me, guys *and* girls! And they all start shrieking about how I'm just some drone of the government and a racist baby-killer; all that shit!"

Beth smiled again for the first time; she even laughed a little, imagining the scene. "What did you do?"

"I told them all they could go to hell! That they wouldn't even be able to survive without warriors like me to keep the peace and maintain our borders."

"I'm sure that went over well."

"Yeah, one of 'em started shaking her finger right in my face, yelling: *'I'm very uncomfortable with a government-sanctioned murderer like you being here in my spiritual sanctuary! It's bad energy! I can't focus with you around; you have to leave now!* Meanwhile the rest of 'em are all screaming obscenities at me. I figured they were gonna start forming a lynch-mob pretty quick, so I chose to take my exit."

Beth burst out laughing. "I'm a little surprised you got run off by a bunch of New Age yogis!" She was beaming now.

The Marine enjoyed another reminiscent laugh. "Yeah, I think two or three of 'em were getting riled up enough to try and fight me. Don't get me wrong, that would have been a *serious* mistake on their part. There wasn't a single body in that place that I couldn't have snapped in half across my knee! But it's like taking on a pack of stray cats and Chihuahuas, you know it's gonna be a royal pain in the ass, and you'll come out the other side covered in scratches and bite marks."

Beth was still smiling, calmer now. "Glad you were able to be the bigger man and not break anyone in half across your knee." She applauded.

"Hey, you like that story, maybe some other night I can tell you about the time I had to gauge a shark's eyes out while surfing with some buddies off Oceanside."

"Come on!" Beth scoffed.

"No, I'm serious! What was I supposed to do? Let the damn thing eat my arm or take my life?"

As the mirth faded, their eyes lingered for just a moment before returning to the fire. "Thanks for being there earlier," she said quietly. "I'm not sure what was going to happen next, but it wouldn't have been good."

"No problem," he replied warmly. "That's what I'm here for. I know you're a fighter though." He winked. "You'd have been able to take his drunk-ass if it had gotten any further."

"Just glad I didn't have too," she exhaled.

The two continued talking for another hour by the fire; Daniel found himself opening up with her, even telling her some of his experiences from the war. She told him about her family, where she had come from, and how she had arrived in the community. It was good conversation, but Daniel eventually excused himself to head to bed. He had to rise early to make his rounds and check in with all the perimeter sentries. Beth said goodnight and gave him a light hug.

The warrior left the fires that night and returned to his cabin feeling something he had not felt in many years: happiness.

CHAPTER SEVEN

Daniel awoke with a start; someone was beating on his cabin door. He glanced up at the window; it was still pitch black outside. The celebrations were not supposed to go later than midnight, but Daniel had left early. He did not know what time it was or how long he had been asleep. Someone pounded loudly on the door again. "Daniel!" It was Jonas. "I need you now! Wake up!"

"Coming!" Daniel called back deliriously. "Give me a minute." He felt around the floor beneath him for pants and socks. The cabin was very quiet, yet another reminder that Sadie was no longer with him. He used to wake up to hear her snoring or stirring in the middle of the night. Sometimes the cabin would stink of noxious gas when she ate something out of the ordinary. He would have gladly accepted a stench back if it meant having his dog again.

In the dark, he pulled on boots and grabbed his rifle, not knowing what this would be about. He threw the cabin door open and found his friend waiting on the doorstep uneasily. "Yes?" Daniel inquired groggily, rubbing an eye.

"You need to come with me," Jonas said gravely. He offered no explanation, but there was an urgency in his voice that concerned the Marine.

The two strode briskly in silence for a full minute, Jonas leading, Daniel following and still trying to wake himself up fully. "What's going on, buddy?" he finally asked.

"You'll see soon enough," Jonas replied, passing between a pair of cabins and rounding a third long one to its entrance.

Daniel shook the mental fog off. "Wait, this is..."

Jonas was nodding as he pushed the door open for his friend to enter.

Daniel crossed the threshold into the lit cabin. He had a knot in his stomach at what he might find. There were three beds in the small, rectangular home. Beth Forsythe, Abby Jenson, and a third unmarried woman lived in this cabin. Daniel tightened his jaw and braced himself for the worst. It was very bad, but still not the worst he could've imagined.

At the far end of the cabin where the glowing lights

emanated from, Beth was sitting up in bed, tears on her face holding her knees against her chest. Her expression was blank, as if in shock. Janae Wells sat beside her on the bed, arms wrapped around the younger woman.

"What happened?" Daniel growled. "And please do not say the name Jamal Williams."

Jonas was nodding grimly. "Beth left the celebration and fires sometime around ten. At some point after she returned to the cabin, Jamal came in and tried to force himself on her... again. This time he was mad. He pinned her to the bed, started kissing her. She tried to fight back, but he overpowered her..."

Daniel had no intention of adding insult to injury here; he was not really surprised by Jonas' report, though. Beth had fought back admirably, but she lacked both the muscle mass and hours of training and experience to beat back a former infantry platoon leader like Jamal. She would have had to score *several* very lucky hits to win that fight.

"Did he..." Daniel asked quietly.

Jonas shook his head. "The other girl, Abby, came in from the fires while he was still on top of her. Beth thinks she had some sort of flashback or psychotic break. She said Abby went berserk, started screaming at the top of her lungs that she was gonna kill Jamal. Then she attacked him with a kind of primal rage—clawing, biting, hair-pulling, everything! She jumped on his back and wouldn't let go, and he planted some *serious* elbows to her face and ribs. She was going completely nuts on him until he finally threw her across the room against the wall. That's when he made a break for it and bolted."

Daniel stared at the floor, taking it all in. He knew they were about to lose one of their best fighting men, during already strained times. "Has anyone seen him since?" the Marine asked.

Jonas shook his head.

"Get some men together and wake up Ava and Raoul. You know what this means."

Jonas nodded gravely. "I do."

"It's an exileable offense. I'll start waking the council members."

"Wait!" a female voice called out. "Stop."

Jonas and Daniel halted, both caught off guard by the unexpected outburst. It was Beth at the far end of the cabin, still in bed. She had overheard the tail-end of their conversation. The two war veterans looked in her direction and waited.

Beth swallowed hard, closed her eyes for a moment and took a breath before speaking again. "I request a Restoration Circle."

Daniel and Jonas just stared in disbelief for a long moment. They exchanged looks; still no words.

"Do I have the right to request a Restoration

Circle?!" Beth demanded, a fresh tear stinging her right eye. She brushed it aside quickly and resumed a strong demeanor. In an even tone she said, "I request the right to face my attacker and demand an explanation for his actions, for how he could treat me with such disdain, as subhuman! I want him to have to look me in the eyes, admit what he tried to do, and make it right in front of the entire community!"

Daniel and Jonas listened intently and then glanced at each other again. Daniel finally spoke slowly, his words measured: "You do have that right, Beth, if that is what you want. I respect your courage to face him, but let me be clear. You know that by entering a Restoration Circle you turn the entire outcome over to the judgment of the council? If Jamal complies with all they demand of him in recompense and amends, he will be allowed to stay...here...in the community."

Beth nodded, hot tears burning her cheek.

"And you can accept this? After he tried...after he tried to rape you practically twice in one night. I'm not telling you what to do one way or the other, but you have to be absolutely certain this is what you want. You are the victim here, and the council will side with you no matter what."

Beth swallowed again and gritted her teeth. "Yes. Exile is a death sentence; everyone knows that. And I won't have anyone die on account of me, even someone who attacked me."

Janae squeezed Beth from the side and kissed her forehead.

"Then you'll have your Restoration Circle tomorrow morning," Daniel promised.

Beth did not respond. The glazed look had returned to her eyes.

Daniel turned to Jonas and spoke in a low, steely voice. "Find him."

✶ ✶ ✶ ✶ ✶

Warm sunlight shone down on the clearing from a barren autumn sky. The mid-morning air was chilly and moist, and low fog still clung to the wooded tree-line that encircled the settled glade. The seven council members had been summoned, and all seven were now present and starting to take their seats at a long, half-moon table of finished cedar. There was a tense anticipation in the air to see what would ensue. The meadow was quiet; only a few council members conferred privately with one another. No one from the throng of assembled witnesses spoke.

Daniel had heaved and lugged a large, finished seat carved from a cedar stump to the gathering. He set it upright to the right of the council's bench and the wide circle of stones, which marked the Restoration Circle.

He did not feel the desire to stand for the entire length of proceedings this morning. His rifle had returned to public view and rested peacefully across his thighs. Jonas stood close by with a semi-automatic pistol holstered on his hip.

Meanwhile, Beth stood alone, tall and resilient, in the center of the large circle of stones. Everyone was waiting... waiting to see if Jamal would show up. No one had seen a trace of him since the night before. He had vanished into the night without a trail or sign. Still, if he was anywhere near the camp, he had to know the entire community was searching for him. Would he venture from hiding to present himself? Would he face his neighbors' ire and answer for his despicable, violent actions from the night before? Would he face the judgment of the council?

Janae waited in the crowd of witnesses and held her daughter close, her arms clasped protectively in front of Ellie. Ava and Abby were present, as was Dr. Ellenson; even Muhsen and his family had turned out. Everyone had come, save a few on perimeter watch. Raoul and Father Paolo were taking their seats at the table for council members, along with Fernando Martinez, a woman in her mid-fifties named Mary Waynewright, and three others.

The seated elders surveyed the audience and noted that Beth still stood unaccompanied in the circle.

Ellie looked up at her mother, wondering aloud: "What's gonna happen, Mommy?"

Janae quieted her daughter, but she herself did not know. Her heart swelled with compassion for Beth standing bravely out there alone and under everyone's gaze, feeling terribly vulnerable and exposed. Janae wanted to cross the line of stones and go wrap the younger woman in a tight hug.

A few low whispers crept through the gathering as emotional tensions continued to rise. Father Paolo felt they had waited long enough. Mercifully, he gestured to Jonas and said, "Please radio the tower to ring the bell."

The heavy, copper bell which hung in the top of the community's lookout tower had been placed there (with great difficulty) to raise the alarm in the event of attack or emergency. If the bell was rung, it signaled all community members to return to the camp and assemble for defense or to seek shelter. To ring the bell on this morning would be a final call for Jamal to come forward. If he did not present himself after it was rung, the council would have no choice but to banish him without hearing. He had been afforded every opportunity to voluntarily offer explanation for his actions. The council would not wait any longer nor waste any more of the people's time.

If Jamal chose to return at a later date or time, he would be escorted under armed-guard to the border in the woods and commanded to leave. If he desired to come back after six months of exile and appeal his case before the council, he would be afforded that opportunity. If he tried to return before his six months of exile had passed, however, the perimeter guards would be instructed to treat him as a hostile and authorized to shoot him on-sight if he refused to depart willingly.

Jonas pulled a two-way radio off his belt and spoke into it. "Watchtower, this is Pathfinder, over." Before he could finish, someone in the assembly pointed and called out, "Look!"

Marching up the soggy slope towards the gathered community was Sergeant Jamal Williams. He was dressed in his wartime battle fatigues; his uniform was neat and his combat boots laced snugly. He wore a camouflaged flak jacket, and the straps of a heavy pack were secured firmly across his shoulders. In his right hand hung his M-4 rifle, which he carried by the pistol-grip. He trudged ominously up the marshy hill, his boots making squishing noises as they trod the muddy grass underfoot. He strode aggressively towards the large circle of stones but made no eye contact with Beth, who still stood in the center by herself.

She looked both bewildered and nervous. The gathered witnesses suddenly grew quieter and very uneasy. No one was sure what this was about or if Jamal might suddenly turn and open fire on them. A hush fell over the crowd and all murmurs died.

Daniel maintained a steady, cool demeanor but rested his firing hand lightly on his own rifle. He did not think Jamal was here to shoot anyone; if he had wanted blood, he could have started a sniper's spree from the cover of the tree-line. No, this was different; he was angry about something. This was all for show; he was here to make everyone listen, to speak his piece.

The former infantry sergeant dropped his heavy rucksack to the wet ground with a thud. He scowled at the gawking audience and then turned to glower at the seated elders. He still had yet to acknowledge Beth's presence in the circle.

Father Paolo was the first to speak. Using both hands, he raised himself up from behind the table; with an undaunted firmness, he stared down the younger man. "Why have you come before us in this manner, Jamal? This is a place to lay weapons down—a place for vulnerability, repentance, and being reconciled to one's neighbors. Why do you come before us dressed for battle?"

Jamal narrowed his eyes and locked his gaze on the frail priest. "Shut your mouth, old man," he snarled. "I didn't come here to be lectured by you *or* any of your churchy minions!" He glanced around, surveying with belligerent disdain his captive audience. His bristling defiance rippled through the crowd like a shockwave or the fragments of a hand grenade.

The people had mentally prepared themselves for Jamal to not show up, or for him to come submissive and remorseful. No one had foreseen indignant hatred.

"What do you want, Jamal?" Jonas asked. Beside him, Daniel still sat quietly.

"What do I want?! I want this place to open its eyes! We should be ruling this place, Jonas! All those marauders we've killed in the past two years, none of them were equipped to take this place, but they did have the right idea. The strong rule, the weak serve! That's how it works from here on! It's the end of the world, assholes, and you've all been trying to live some fairytale! Well, maybe it's time for a *new* sheriff in this town."

Jonas' right hand slowly drifted to his holstered pistol. Daniel saw his friend's silent motion; he made eye contact and shook his head.

Jamal was finally looking at Beth now, no apology in his eyes though, only arrogant contempt. "You should be bowing to your lords right now. If you had any idea what we're capable of you'd be on your knees ready to serve your masters in any way we desired and without us even asking."

Beth, Daniel, Jonas, and everyone else who heard Jamal's words were immediately aghast. Dr. Ellenson nearly lost her mind with disgusted outrage, yet Jamal continued on.

"That goes for ALL of you!" he shouted at the crowd. "We give you protection and in return you give us devotion and service! That's how it works from now on; unless you'd prefer to roll the dice and see how far you make it out there in the wilds...on your own." He pointed to the trees and horizon of untamed, hill country.

At last, Father Paolo, who was still standing, cut in. He had heard enough. "Jamal Williams! You have shown blatant disregard for all life! You attacked one of your sisters in violence and have demonstrated pure contempt for every one of your neighbors in this community! You have no place among us anymore, and you are banished from this settlement. Leave! Now! In peace, while you still can!"

Without warning, Jamal raised his rifle and pointed it at the priest's head. "Old man, I told you to be quiet!"

Jonas reacted abruptly and drew his sidearm, leveling his sights on Jamal's face. Daniel *still* remained motionless and calm.

Jamal glanced over at Jonas, a look of hurt and sadness in his eyes for a moment, before the anger returned. "You take his side against me, Jonas?!" Jamal demanded, nodding towards Daniel. "You'd take the white man's side against a brother?! What's wrong with you?!"

"What's wrong with me?!" Jonas snapped. "What's wrong with you?! Look at where you're standing, Jamal! What are you doing, forcing us to choose sides?! You're talking about making people into slaves! YOU, of all people! I have a family, man, a daughter! Which side do you *think* I'm gonna choose?! You've gone and lost your *damn* mind! You let something take hold and poison you! These are good people and you've been just as much a part of this place as anyone! Don't play the victim like you're some kind of outsider here! Has anyone EVER treated you unfairly here?! Have they?!"

It was then that the former Marine captain finally spoke. "Your version of reality will never happen here, Jamal. Do you think because we're warriors we deserve to rule as kings and be served like dictators? There are already enough outlaw gangs out there who live like that; feel free to go join one. I bet life among a band of thugs isn't as appealing as you might think.

"You're right though, this *is* the end of the world, and that is *exactly* why we, the powerful, have to be magnanimous now more than ever. We protect the weak and empower the defenseless—not for some reward or to be served, but because *that's* our calling. It's who we are, and our only path to redemption for all the blood we've spilt in the name of God, country, or freedom."

Jamal swiveled from the waist and pointed his M-4 directly at Daniel.

Jonas winced and prepared to fire. He did not want to, but he would if the infantry sergeant forced his hand.

Daniel maintained his placid demeanor, though internally he was nervous. At this point, Jamal did not like him, at all. In fact, he probably hated him, and he might just shoot Daniel here in front of everyone.

Jamal grinned. "That's right, folks, there he is, the GREAT *Captain* Daniel Weston!" Jamal lowered his weapon and let it hang from his chest by the sling. Suddenly he began to clap. Applauding loudly, he beat his gloved hands together, laughing and grinning simultaneously.

"Mmm, that's good," he said taking a step towards the MARSOC Raider. "That's real good. That's him, isn't it, folks? The Marine! The man, the myth, the legend—your fearless leader and savior!" Jamal craned his neck sideways. "Or maybe I should even say, Messiah? Yeah! That's it, your white messiah! White Jesus! The one who's always been there to make the hard call and protect everyone. Am I right? Come on, let's give him a hand!"

Jamal resumed his applause. The majority in the crowd of witnesses were too stunned to know what to do. Amusingly, a few actually joined in and started clapping.

Jonas did not know where this was going, but he didn't like it. His sights were still fixed on Jamal, and he wasn't planning to move them. The younger veteran's behavior was so erratic, no one could predict what he might do next.

"That's right! That's right!" Jamal encouraged them. "But see, here's the deal, folks…" He began to sober. "You've made this man into an idol. And come on, before you deny it, just think about it; you really do worship him!" He paused here to let his point sink in. "But hey, I get it! I really do. What's not to like, right? He's strong, brave, courageous—a man's man! Wooooooo, MARSOC! Come on! You know those were some hard-ass sons-of-bitches! And here he is, probably the last of his kind, right here with us, like an angel sent down from heaven…am I right? Can I get an "Amen"? Somebody, please, testify!"

The grin started to fade. "But you know, you don't really know this guy! Well, not his *true* self. Has anyone here ever wondered *why* Mr. Weston never talks about his past? I do! But I know some dirty little secrets that *Daniel* hasn't wanted any of you to know about!" He looked back at his fellow warrior, grinning again, triumphant, smug, and certain his victory was near.

No one from the assembly objected or came to Daniel's defense. They all just waited silently for Jamal to make his revelation and enlighten them.

Daniel could not be certain what Jamal was about to share, but he knew it wouldn't be good. He mentally braced himself for the worst and remained quiet.

"See the truth is, *Captain* Weston is a deserter! A traitor to his own country. And not only did he desert his country in its hour of need, he also abandoned his *own* men on the frontlines!"

There was look of shock on everyone's faces. They weren't sure if they could believe a word coming out of Jamal's mouth, but it was disturbing to hear nonetheless.

"That's right, folks, a deserter! He ran away from the war in South America and left *NO ONE* to look after the men under his charge!"

Daniel finally spoke up in his own defense. "You know nothing of the things you speak, Jamal. And I'm not the one on trial here today."

"Oh really?" the infantry sergeant retorted. "Well, maybe you should be! Do you deny it? Go ahead, *captain*, go ahead and tell all the good people how you *didn't* do it. Tell 'em I'm wrong! Tell them you didn't run away from the war and leave your men to die on the frontlines without a leader, without you their commanding officer. Tell the people you *weren't* a coward who ran away from a combat zone, who only thought of his *own* damn self!"

Daniel did not respond, but his expression had grown dark and his iron gaze locked on Jamal.

After another long moment, the Army veteran continued. "I know it's sad. I know it's hard to accept—

I really do. But it *IS* the truth! And I'll even tell you how I know all of this. See, at the tail-end of the war just about the time Mech-Tech took over the military and started beating back all our enemies with its crazy-ass machines, my unit got pulled from the frontlines. We were given some well-deserved furlough and reassigned to guard a P.O.W. camp.

"Now most of our prisoners in that camp were the enemy, captured Russian and Chinese soldiers. But there was a smaller part of the camp designated for some of our own, for traitors and defectors. One day I'm standing there on guard duty, and who should I see sitting down there in the mud looking all depressed behind the wire fence?! That's right, folks, Captain Daniel Weston, U.S. Marine Corps…"

Once more, those gathered were rendered speechless. No one wanted to believe it, but murmurs began to trickle.

Daniel, in the meantime, had passed into a kind of trance, staring off into space and remembering…

Jamal was still going on and on, but the accused had ceased to hear any of it. All external noise faded to incoherent babble like the mindless chatter of chickens clucking in their coop.

Images started to flicker, and long forgotten sounds and smells reawakened from the murky depths of his subconscious. *Daniel sat shivering in stinking mud, his clothes soaked and mildewed as rain fell on him in an open pen. There was no cover or shelter to seek. He felt the grime on his skin; his face was bearded; he had been unable to shave for many weeks. He coughed violently, sick with bronchitis or pneumonia...half-delirious. He looked up and saw one of the armed soldiers through the steel mesh wire. He recognized Jamal's dark face; he was younger then but it was him. Daniel felt a tremendous wash of sadness break over him like a tidal wave; he felt despair, like the earth itself might open up to swallow him into bottomless darkness.*

Then it was gone—everything changed and more memories flooded his mind. *He was marched down a poorly lit corridor and questioned by C.I.A. and military interrogators. He heard the scraping of rusty hinges and the thunderous BOOM of a heavy, steel door slamming behind him.* Then another set of images began: *He was escorted by armed guards to a set of beautiful, mahogany doors. As they parted before him, he saw a collection of colonels and generals sitting and talking behind a judge's bench, waiting to commence a tribunal. It was his court martial...*

Gradually, the scenes faded away. Daniel's vision returned, and his consciousness drifted back into focus. Everyone was staring at him. Even Beth was watching with an expression of helpless confusion in her eyes. They were all wondering the same thing.

Jonas looked down at his friend and asked quietly, "Is it true, Dan?"

The Marine captain looked off to the right, into the distance and sighed. "There's a lot people don't know about me, Jonas; a lot that happened...just...know I had my reasons."

"That's right." Jamal preened. "Just give the white man a free pass. Rationalize it away. But now you know you've allowed a deserter to mislead you. You gave him a position of authority, put him in charge of protecting you all. But can you really trust a traitor who would abandon his own men on the battlefield? Should he really be in charge of protecting anyone?!"

Jamal and Daniel glared at each other, but Father Paolo was the next to speak. "Whatever Daniel's reasons for keeping this from us, I have faith they are legitimate and his own. This is not the time for an inquisition into Daniel's military career and personal history. Jamal, *YOU* were summoned here today to answer for committing a despicable act of violence against your neighbor and sister. You have revealed a savage disrespect for this entire community, and I do not believe you are capable of repentance in this hour. I think it is time you left. You have no place among us anymore. You may return in six months if you find any remorse in your heart for your shameful acts and words. Go now, and may God Almighty watch over and protect you."

Jamal raised his rifle once more. "Old man, I could shoot you right here and now; who do you think you are, giving me orders?!"

The second Jamal raised his weapon against the priest, something finally snapped in Daniel. He sprang to his feet, rifle at the ready and yelled, "Drop it, Jamal! Leave now, or I swear to God I'll blow you away right where you stand!"

Jamal turned his M-4 on Daniel and shouted, "YOU WANNA GO?! YOU WANNA DO THIS?! WE CAN END THIS RIGHT HERE! RIGHT NOW!"

A slough of shouting, yelling, and barking out orders and threats erupted. Jonas and Ava joined in on the screaming match. Even Dr. Ellenson entered into the verbal fray, still bristling with outrage at some of Jamal's deplorable remarks from ten minutes earlier.

Finally, the uproar hit a crescendo and then everyone quieted down. Miraculously, no one had fired a shot, just flung loads of accusations.

Jamal grinned, still peering through the scope on his rifle. "See, there's the *real* Dan Weston. Good to see him come out from behind that mask of Zen maturity. I kinda like the real Daniel Weston, or at least I can respect him as someone not to mess with..." Jamal lowered his M-4, still smirking.

"Folks!" he declared. "It's time for me to hit the

road. It's been a real ride, but it's time to go. Y'all enjoy your little fairytale dreamland here, 'cause it ain't gonna last. This place is gonna burn before the end; it's only a matter of time. And I choose not waste another second of my life up in this bitch. Time to wake up!"

He turned to face Beth who was still standing in the circle of stones. She had waited bravely through the entire morning for her chance at vindication. Jamal gave a short chuckle and shook his head. Grinning, he shrugged. "Beth, I really don't care..."

The crowd was dumbstruck by his audacity and calloused lack of remorse, but Jamal only paused for a moment. "Good luck to ya! You're gonna need it before the end-when this whole bitch comes crashing down around you. All y'all will."

With that, the former infantry leader picked up his rucksack, heaved it back over his shoulders, and walked away, enjoying the birds and morning sunlight as he went.

CHAPTER EIGHT

Autumn wore on, blustering into colder months. December came and so did the snows. Christmas Day arrived to find some meager celebration and acknowledgement by the community. Then it was gone, replaced by a long, bleak, and merciless winter. January and February came with knee-deep snows. Wild game grew scarce, and hunts were evermore fruitless. Often the only reward for those who ventured out was taking in the beauty of the stillness—the frozen wood, glistening and buried beneath blankets of white powder. Any who did hunt enjoyed the serene quiet, watching the mists pass over those lonely hills.

As conditions grew harsher, the task of sentry duty became increasingly miserable. Those on perimeter watch suffered the greatest, standing out in the elements for hours on end, shielding their faces from biting winds. Daniel mercifully shortened the watches to two-hour shifts. And whenever he made his rounds, he always carried a thermos of hot coffee or cider to share with the lookouts. The only positive aspect to the unforgiving conditions was that no one else wanted to be outdoors either, including lawless bands of killers. Individuals on perimeter watch during the winter months seldom encountered a stranger and even fewer who were looking for trouble.

When there was no snow on the ground, there was freezing rain or a damp, muddy chill which penetrated to the bone. The community weathered most of these long days and nights in the warmth of their cabins, passing the time huddled near wood-stoves and draped in wool blankets. Had it not been for the community's foresight and planning during the earlier, kinder months, starvation would have ravaged the settlement. By spring, only a sad collection of deserted shacks would have remained with curtains rippling in the wind like ghosts, telling an ominous tale of misfortune.

But spring did come to that hidden glade, slowly but surely. And it brought with it revitalized visions of hope, which only those who live dependent on the earth can fully comprehend. Spring showers gathered over the hills, beckoning new life and abundant growth back to that meadow and woods. The chill thawed and gave way to sunlit mornings once again. Song birds returned and summoned with them further sounds of life and vigor in the trees.

It had been another long winter. Jane Ellenson and her medical team had remained busy throughout the entire season, treating flu, coughs, fever, and other ailments brought on by the unyielding elements and confined quarters. But now it had passed, and the members of the community had begun to emerge from their winter dens. Gradually, at first, people began spending longer hours outdoors, returning to their work. Beginning anew to survey neglected gardens and other outside projects halted by miserable conditions. There was a freshness in the air once more—the sweet scent of blossoming honeysuckle and the roll of distant thunder sweeping across plains to the east.

One morning a few weeks after people had begun returning to their labors, there was an unexpected knock at the door of Paolo's cabin. When the slight and grizzled priest gently pushed the door open to greet his unanticipated caller, he found the warrior standing there on his stoop. "Daniel!" he exclaimed, beaming in radiant delight.

"Hello, Father," Daniel replied with a genuine smile. "It's been a while—thought I might stop by and see how you're doing. How'd you fair through the winter?"

"Fine, fine," Paolo rasped; his years had truly begun

to show in his voice. "By the grace of our Lord, I have survived another year! I wish I could say the same for most of my plants!" The priest lamented with amusement, he nodded toward a muddy plot where his garden had once been. "But I live to plant a new harvest!" he concluded with a hopeful smile.

"May I come in?" Daniel asked politely, noting the fresh mud clinging to the base of his boots.

"Of course! Of course!" Paolo said, beckoning his guest across the threshold. He shooed a dark, long-haired cat who was purring loudly atop one of the wooden chairs. The creature was a rescue from the winter months. It was nothing short of miraculous that the feline had found the community and not been torn limb from limb by coyotes. Since the priest lived alone and was advanced in years, it had been decided that he should care for the creature and keep her for company. The children in the camp had promptly dubbed the cat "Mittens," though she bore not a single distinguishing feature that merited the name.

Mittens crankily protested the disturbance of her nap as she was ousted from her throne. Father Paolo held the door open for another moment so she could saunter outside and combat the local rodent population. She meandered lazily towards the door, taking her time, careful to visibly communicate her indignant dissatisfaction over the situation. Once outside, she immediately plopped down on the stoop to sulk.

"How's the company?" Daniel grinned, taking the empty chair.

"Oh, she's enjoyable to have around most days; though I might have threatened to turn her into a stew more than once during the winter." The priest chuckled lightly. "She gets into especially foul moods now and then for no good reason."

"Sounds like a typical cat," the Marine said dryly.

It had been a very long winter. After the day Jamal was exiled, the last day anyone in the camp had seen him, a few community members had come forward to voice concerns regarding the accusations leveled against Daniel and his past. Father Paolo had assuaged the people's worries, assuring them that he would speak to Daniel about the matter when the time was right. Five months had passed since that day, though, and the conversation had yet to take place.

Nevertheless, the people trusted Paolo's word, and for the most part they still trusted Daniel. Despite what outlandish claims had been lobbied against him, for the community, Daniel had proven himself to be steady, reliable, and faithful in the face of endless adversity. Most folks reassured themselves that if any stains *did* exist in his past, they must have been for a just cause. Still, a few worried quietly. Whispers and rumors crept up privately now and then between close neighbors.

Daniel paid no heed to these, and Father Paolo had yet to press the issue with him. Perhaps he did not fully realize that the priest was waiting for *him*; waiting to see if Daniel would volunteer the tale by his own volition.

Paolo gently eased himself down onto the other wooden chair. He seemed more fragile today, perhaps the harsh winter had punished his aged body more severely than in years previous. The priest waited patiently for Daniel to begin; he was curious what had brought him by on this day. When the Marine captain remained silent, Paolo smiled warmly and finally broke the quiet. "To what do I owe the pleasure of this visit?"

The warrior was mulling something over but seemed unready to share what he was chewing on. His host offered to make him some tea, but he politely declined it.

After another spell of silence, the priest said, "Daniel, you know you can say anything to me, don't you? Whatever is on your mind, there is no shame here in this place."

Daniel shifted in his seat, resting an ankle atop his left knee. "Yeah, I know," he replied noncommittally. He glanced around the room uneasily, taking a moment to gaze up at the window. At long last he asked, "Do you think I could give a confession? You know, like a *real* confession, not like last time where I told my whole life story."

Somewhat surprised and wanting to be sure he understood correctly, Paolo inquired, "You mean a moral confession? You wish to confess your sins?"

"Yes," Daniel replied simply. "You do that with the others, don't you?"

The Franciscan touched the stubble on his chin lightly. "Yes, I do," he answered, still uncertain where this was leading.

"So I want to confess something."

Father Paolo bowed slightly and gestured in acquiescence. "Go on."

The Marine let out a breath slowly. He was clearly feeling uncomfortable, out of his element and fairly vulnerable. He wondered if this was a mistake. "I live alone," he began.

"Yes."

"I'm not married; I don't have a partner. Hell, it's been over five years since I even dated anyone."

The priest smirked, entertained that the warrior could not keep from swearing, even while giving confession. There was a lull, so Paolo encouraged him to continue.

"I—how do I say this right to a priest? Some nights when I'm lying there alone in my cabin, I burn with lust..."

"You have a desire for physical intimacy and passion," the priest reflected back.

"Something like that." Daniel exhaled. He looked away to ease some discomfort. "Anyway, some nights I…"

There was another catch here. Paolo pressed, "You?"

Daniel was visibly uncomfortable. "Gratify myself," he admitted, instantly feeling embarrassed and like a complete fool. He inwardly chastised himself: Why had he come here? He should have kept personal stuff like this to himself. It was one thing to make an off-color joke when hanging around Jonas, but to have a serious talk with the priest? He wasn't sure what he had expected coming here, but now he just felt like an idiot, exposed and not in control.

Paolo chuckled mercifully. "So you are a man who struggles to manage his lusts and sexuality—not a particularly *original* story."

Daniel felt a little relief. The priest's sense of humor diffused a weight of awkward tension. "That's probably true," he allowed, meeting the Syrian elder's gaze. "But it's not something I've ever really talked seriously about. It's always been part of just-bein'-a-guy, ya know? Believe me, Father, none of the guys in the Corps ever took lust or sex seriously. *Maybe* some of the married guys, but not always even them; sex was just a biological craving, an endless urge. In that environment of warriors, sex got blended up with bravado-conquest or bragging rights most of the time."

Paolo listened intently, not a trace of judgment or concern in his demeanor. "Why do you think this part of your life has begun to trouble you so?" he said, his instincts leading him now. "You say you have been alone for many years; why should *lust* only recently start to bother you?"

There was a long silence as Daniel searched for an answer. Finally he exhaled a little. "Probably because of Jamal. It's been a few months since his exile, but when it's cold outside, you spend most of your days indoors and have a lot of time to think about stuff. I got to thinking about how he was at the end there; he just wanted to take without any regard for whoever he took from. It got me thinking about my own private thoughts. Even if they're only in my mind, I began to wonder if that same moral darkness that took Jamal over might also reside in me..."

The priest smiled graciously. "Daniel, your humble and honest questioning is inspiring, and your conscientiousness gives me hope for mankind. Let me say this once and for all: you are not Jamal...It is true that, as humans, we are all capable of falling prey to similar kinds of vices. We are all subject to many of the same temptations: self-importance, greed, and envy; a desire to take without empathy. But Jamal did not arrive at the place of malice and violence we last saw him at-overnight. My guess is, for a variety of sad and complex reasons, he made a long series of small decisions to harden his heart over the course of many years..."

Paolo paused here for a moment; his voice was full of compassion and tenderness. "I hear your fear, Daniel. You fear what you might become. You fear becoming not only like Jamal but also like your father...a man so broken and wicked that he abandoned all decency and self-control; a man whose *lusts* destroyed everyone closest to him."

Daniel stiffened, silent for a moment. "Maybe so," he admitted at last.

In that moment, Paolo chose to shift the focus of the conversation. For Daniel to simply come to an awareness of these things was enough for the time. The priest knew that revelation could be a powerful yet fragile thing; it often required space and time to be accepted *and* useful. Sometimes a lighter touch served better than delving deeply into the muck of a man's life and psyche. He smiled warmly. "The Scriptures encourage that a man or woman who burns with passion should seek a spouse. Have you ever considered finding a wife here in our community?"

There was a very long pause before Daniel answered, "No, Father, that's not possible."

"You are attracted to other men?" the priest inquired.

"What?! No!" Daniel burst out laughing.

The Syrian chuckled, amused; the warrior appeared

less impressed. Silence returned.

The Franciscan was curious why Daniel resisted the thought of seeking a mate, but he chose self-restraint for the moment and left the matter alone. "In my earlier years of youth and zeal," the priest resumed, "I might have been tempted to give you a lengthy lecture about the perils of sinful thought and carnal action. Today, though, the grace of Jesus has tempered me. Your own conscience has already punished you far more harshly than any admonishment I could give.

"God has given you a body, Daniel, so you must care for your body. If you surrender your heart, mind, and spirit unto Christ, whatever you do in body-it will not be sin. For the body must follow wherever the heart, mind, and soul lead it."

Daniel looked at his friend; then he said simply, "Bless me, Father, for I have sinned."

The priest smiled. "What is sin, but being disconnected from yourself, your neighbor, and your Heavenly Father? Your disconnection is forgiven you, Daniel."

"Thank you, Father," The warrior responded gratefully; he returned the warm smile.

"A final thought," the priest added.

Daniel waited.

"It occurs to me that in the desperate circumstances of your youth, your mother was probably not able to attune to your emotional needs during some of the most important years."

"I'd say that's an understatement," Daniel replied quietly.

"In this conversation of sexuality and who you are becoming, I wonder what a mother's voice might say to you…" The priest paused. "Do you know Mary Waynewright?"

"Yes," Daniel answered. Mary Waynewright was a kind, industrious, middle-aged woman with a jubilant laugh. She had served as an elder on the council for the last year and a half, and was one of the most respected women in the community. It would have been impossible for the Marine to not know who she was.

"I understand she raised five sons of her own before the war. I would like you to go and visit her tomorrow—spend some time working in her garden with her." Paolo smiled. "I will tell her to expect you."

The former captain nodded and thanked the priest again. He rose from his seat, saying he needed to check in on some things around the glade.

The priest arose also, slower; he spoke as Daniel reached for the cabin door. "One final thing, Daniel; it would be good for us to discuss more of your past soon, especially as it relates to the war and the end of your military career. My intuition tells me those are not things the entire community needs to be informed of but *someone* should know. And I did give them my word that I would look into it."

Daniel nodded and stared down at the plank floor, his left hand resting inside his pants pocket. "We will," he promised. "Soon." He said farewell and pushed the door open, careful not to step on the tail of a sleeping Mittens on his way out.

❈ ❈ ❈ ❈ ❈

Captain Daniel Weston, United States Marine Corps, stood tall before the panel of field-grade officers and one brigadier general. Their decades of service were reflected not only in their rank but also in the stacks of ribbons pinned to their uniforms.

It was gone; it was all gone. The only thing left to do was take the punishment for his men and find death when it was all over. He'd eat a bullet when this was finished, and that would be the end of it.

Death, it was such a peaceful thought now. He had fought it for so long, always trying to delay or avoid it, always fighting to survive and win. Here at last, he had finally come full circle, to the place where he could welcome death as a friend. No more pain, no more hidden tears. He'd get a hold of a pistol when this was all over; he'd slide that muzzle inside his mouth and slowly squeeze the trigger...

It would be quick and merciful. Sad that this was where life had led him, but what had life been anyway? One devastating blow after another. God, if there was God, was a sadist...a cosmic, omnipresent monster who delighted in tormenting him, seeing how far He could push him before he broke. Well, they had finally found that place.

"General, gentlemen," he spoke calmly, addressing the panel before him. His face was cleanly shaven for the trial. "I ask that you commit all sentences for my men onto me. I alone chose to act in defiance of our mission. I ordered my men to follow me and fed them false intelligence. I told them what we were doing was a sanctioned mission. Whatever punishment needs to be meted out here today, let if fall to me. I'll sign whatever confession you put in front of me, and this will all be over. These are good Marines; there's no reason to punish them or destroy anyone else's career on account of my actions."

Daniel's entire team was present in the courtroom, several of them awaiting their own courts-martial. His faithful second-in-command and enlisted advisor, Master Sergeant Miles Davis, looked over at him and shook his head in disgust. He knew it was all a farce and a filthy lie, but neither was he surprised. He knew Dan Weston; they'd served together under fire for years, all over the world. This was exactly the kind of thing the captain would do—the only thing he would ever think to do. He was saving their asses, and they would thank him for it by keeping their mouths shut and watching him burn. Someone had to take the fall for everything, and Dan Weston was that kind of leader.

The captain did not even make eye contact with his second-in-command; he faced forward and kept his gaze steadily toward the judges.

The oldest man—a brigadier general—reclined in his leather armchair, studying Daniel carefully. A colonel, also seated behind the bench, leaned over to confer and whispered something in the general's ear. "I appreciate that, Captain Weston," the one-star finally responded, leaning forward over the bench and clasping his hands together. "Your willingness to take full responsibility is at least commendable; we will take it under advisement when the time comes for the trials of your men."

There was a long pause and the general scanned a sheet of paper before him. "Your charges are very serious, Dan, and given your long and decorated record of service to our nation, I'm guessing you already understand that-because you committed these offences during a desperate time of war we could give you the death penalty for everything you did; despite whatever moral justification you think you had."

Daniel blinked. Like a veil of heavy mist being lifted, the memory was gone, vanishing away into the dark abyss of his unconscious. He was staring at a gurgling stream a half mile from the camp, seated on a damp, moss-covered log, his rifle resting across his lap. "I can hear you," he called out, sensing a presence close by. "I know it's you, Raoul."

The Lakota man approached light-footed from behind. He grinned. "It is good to see you, Daniel."

The former Marine nodded in acknowledgement and respect for his friend. "You're the only one in the community who can move that quietly."

"I must be losing my touch, though," Raoul replied soberly. "Did I rustle a fern?"

"No," Daniel answered, staring at the woods across the stream. "But I can feel your presence. I can feel when someone's watching me, and when it's *that* quiet, I know it has to be you. Jonas can get close, but he always announces himself. At least with friends, his personality gets the best of any desire to be stealthy."

"Mmm," the Sioux elder mused and let the quiet settle once more. He took a seat next to Daniel on the fallen tree, gazing at all the lush green across the flowing creek bed. Spring was bursting forth with wild vibrance in the wood. He closed his eyes and breathed it in—all the moisture, the new growth, the cool, fresh air. "Every year about this time I am reminded I have been given another chance to live," Raoul remarked.

Daniel did not respond, but he, too, felt the truth of

his friend's words.

"What is it that brings a man out into the forest to sit alone by a stream?" Raoul mused with an inquisitive smirk.

Daniel patted the rifle lying across his knees. "I'm hunting; can't you tell?"

"I'm sure that's all it is." There was a pause. "I saw Beth this afternoon. She told me you stopped by to say hello earlier in the day."

"Yep," Daniel answered.

Silence fell again. "You two seem to have formed a strong friendship since last fall."

"Yep."

Silence.

"Game has grown short around here," Raoul observed. "It is dangerous, but we may have to start sending out scout parties to scavenge supplies again soon. Our food stores are nearly spent; it was a long winter."

"How long do we have?" Daniel inquired, bothered by this report.

"Two months, if we are careful. We're basically down to those bulk bags of flour, rice, and beans. A pair of raccoons got into the henhouse last night and killed all but two of our chickens."

Daniel exhaled slowly, keeping his eyes on the woods. No more chickens meant no more eggs. "Yep," he said.

"That's a real problem we're gonna have to address. How many vehicles do we have right now?"

"Running?" Raoul smirked. "One, and we're low on fuel as well. I don't know how long we'll be able to keep the generators and freezer running."

"Well, there's always something to do..." Daniel said glibly. "At least we won't be bored for the next month or so."

There was a long pause. "Daniel," Raoul said "is something troubling you? You seem...quieter than usual."

The Marine grinned. "What, you don't like me changing the roles up on you? You like being the quiet one all the time?"

"It does help keep things simple," Raoul replied, catching the humor. "How else will I know which part I am supposed to play?"

The stillness returned once more except for the churning brook and the breeze whispering through tree branches above. "You ever think of leaving this place?" Daniel asked soberly. "You know, going to look for your people, see if any of your tribe are still out there?"

Raoul was quiet for a time. He stood up, pressing one end of his bow into the cool, dark mud of the creek's bank. He leaned on his weapon as if it were a staff. "Sometimes," he said at last, "but then I remember that my tribe is right here. There's not much out there anymore, Daniel. What's not controlled by Unity has been turned to a burnt and ravaged wasteland."

"Mech-Tech," Daniel uttered the other infamous superpower's name.

"I cannot imagine many Sioux or other tribes have survived in that land. Where else would I have to look? Across the oceans? No, my people are gone. Or they have found small pockets of life like this one to live out their days in. I feel a great sadness, more than there are words to express, yet I know the Great Spirit led me here for a reason.

"When my family perished, I became lost, delusional you would say. The Great Spirit reached out to me and sent signs in the forms of animals or provisions along the way. It led me on the long walk, a great journey; if it had not been for the Great Spirit, I would never have come here. I would have returned to the earth and gone down to sleep with my ancestors.

"I do not know what purpose I was spared for, nor do I fully understand why the Great Spirit carried me here like the wind, but I know that this is my home now. It is as much a home as I am likely to ever find again. So I must tend to this tribe which I have been given, though it is full of people very different from my own."

Another long pause. "I will see my family again, one day," Raoul said assuredly. "My wife, my brothers, my sons, and my granddaughter. I will find them in the wide open plains of the next world-where the Great Spirit will watch over my people and keep the peace. Where the sky is blue and the horizon unending. I will find my people gathered there, riding bareback on the wild mustangs once more, with the great bison herds roaming free and untroubled.

"Perhaps I will go and seek the wandering tribes one day, but I am sure when that time comes, I will know it. And it has not come yet."

Still drinking in all of the bursting life around them, Daniel asked, "What was it like, when your people were together? When you were with your family, before the war?"

Raoul was quiet as he pondered and remembered. "Many of my people had lost their way. They lived in poverty, subjected to crippling hardships. Drugs came to the reservation lands, and with them came crime, violence, gangs, and madness."

"Was any of it good?" Daniel asked.

"Of course there was good!" Raoul said abruptly, slightly offended. The quiet had to settle again before Raoul continued. "The Lakota are one part of the great Sioux Nation, but at times, all the confederated tribes would come together for *wacipi*. It is what a white-man would call *powwow*. Dance, music, food, remembering the old ways and the old stories. The clans and tribes would wear traditional garb—some bright, colorful, and beaded. When I was young and we would go, my grandmother would make the best flatbread and berry *wojapi*. And she would scold me for being greedy and eating too much of it." Raoul's grin had returned as he reminisced about better times and his own youth.

"It sounds good," Daniel affirmed genuinely. "Better than anything I had growing up...Sorry for offending your culture."

"We are friends, Daniel; offences can be forgiven."

"I am thankful for that," Marine said to Lakota.

The stillness of the woods returned, and the two men sat together in silence. They watched the rippling of the water and heard the chirping birds in the trees. They drank in the gurgling of the stream and the rustle of breeze-blown leaves above. At last Daniel spoke. "Do you think things will ever get better than this? Better than trying to survive one winter, day, or month at a time?"

"I think..." Raoul considered "...that many ills have come from men who could not live one day at a time. I do not know how long our community as it is now will endure. But what *better* can there be for a tribe than to enjoy the good things Mother Earth offers freely and to have peace with one's neighbor? What better is there than to wake in the morning with strength in your body and gratitude in your heart to the Great Spirit?"

"Amen," Daniel agreed quietly.

* * * * *

The next day, the warrior found himself leaning against the handle of a shovel. He soaked in the mid-morning chill as doves cooed softly in the misty tree-line. He watched his gracious host carefully push away the cool, damp earth with her bare hands, the dark soil coating her fingertips. The sky above was clear, but the sun was not yet high enough to warm them with its rays. At this time of year, the cascading hills and surrounding forest cast long shadows across the glade until late morning. Everything lay wet from a light shower the night before and covered in dew from the new dawn.

It was a time for planting, and that was exactly what Mary Waynewright was tending to. Daniel had already helped her dig out several plant rows, scooping away excess mud that the winter rains had washed in.

"You know," the middle-aged woman mused, "planting seeds is a lot like faith in some ways." She plucked a few of the squash seeds she had saved from last year's garden and dropped them into a fresh hole. Then she crushed lumpy mounds of soil with her right hand and brushed the result over the top of the seeds. She gently smoothed the surface for good measure, smiling to herself as she did. "Every year, people put seeds in the earth, trusting that the rains will come, the sun will shine, and the seasons will do their work. And you know what? Most of the time that's exactly what happens. Kind of funny, though, the little seeds don't really do any of the work; they come already made with everything they'll need for the journey. The rest is just time and process...whether that little seed wants to or not, it's going to grow and change. Even if it tried to resist, the rains will still pour and the sun will still heat the soil.

"Time and the seasons seem to get us all where we need to be. I suppose it's really just a matter of how we choose to spend the days. Will we pass the time railing against the seasons, against the heavy rains and the dry times, or do we have faith that it's all going somewhere? Can we hold onto hope and gratitude and not become bitter and resentful?"

Daniel spoke up. "I thought you were going to say that seeds are like faith because we plant them not knowing if we'll live to see the harvest. It's a kind of delayed gratification; you hope it pays out."

Mary looked up at him and smiled. "I guess you could look at it that way too. I'm not much of an *only-one-right-answer* kind of woman anymore."

Bright beams of brilliant sunlight were breaking across the treetops as they worked. A few fell on Mary's dark hair to reveal glittering strands of silver. Daniel thought she looked rather regal, even kneeling there in the dirt. He remembered his own mother and his heart swelled with pain for all she had suffered. There were no tears, but he instinctively rubbed his right eye. He would try valiantly not to expose any of that part of his past today.

Mary moved down the row two feet and began to dig in the dark earth again. "Father Paolo tells me you've been *laboring under some heavy burdens* lately," she said non-threateningly.

There was a lull before Daniel asked, "Did he say anything else?"

"No," she replied. "He simply said that you endured many painful things growing up." There was something very soothing in Mary's voice. Her way and speech were gentle, full of grace and genuine care. "He said you could probably use a mother-figure in your life right now." She continued. "I wouldn't pretend to know exactly what that means or what you need, Daniel, but is it true?" She asked, glancing up at him.

"Which part?" Daniel laughed morbidly. "The terrible things?"

"Sure."

"Yes, that part's true," he admitted.

"Hmm." Mary acknowledged his response but was quiet for a while. She was pondering something or just absorbing his answer and reflecting on it.

"May I ask a question?" Daniel requested.

"Certainly."

"Father Paolo said you raised five sons; where are they now?"

Mrs. Waynewright stopped working for a moment. She gave a short smile, yet there was sadness in her eyes. "Two of them are here in the community, the oldest and the youngest. My oldest has a wife and children. This place is small, I'm sure you know Will and Ryan."

Daniel did know both men, but he had not made the mental connection that they were her sons. Will was in his late thirties and had served as a fighter pilot during the Last War. Ryan, the younger, was twenty-seven, a quieter soul until the Harvest Celebrations came around.

"All of my sons went off to fight in the war or were drafted," Mary explained. "Will, my oldest, was always a natural-born leader. The other three were good, strong boys; they made perfect soldiers. Ryan was my sensitive one, but when he was growing up with all his brothers, he used to be the entertainer of the group. He could talk his way out of *any* situation and stole the spotlight every chance he got!"

"What happened?" Daniel asked carefully.

"The *war* happened, hunny. My three middle boys never came home. One of them left a wife and little boy behind. The other two had fiancés waiting. Ryan, my baby, came home, but he was never the same. All that death and killing, all the maiming and ugliness...whatever he saw, it took the spark right out of his eyes. It stole his joy and laughter. In a way, I buried Ryan along with my other three boys. He never really came home, not the young man who went off to serve his country anyway."

"None of us did," Daniel commiserated.

A silence settled between them, and Mary resumed working with her seeds and the earth.

Daniel looked off at the trees. He heard the nesting finches chirping and singing again.

"I don't know what you're wrestling with, Daniel," Mrs. Waynewright continued. "But I've seen how you take care of people around here, and I know you're a good man. I hope my sons had leaders like you looking out for them during the war and in their last moments..."

Daniel was silent. There were no words, no words for this kind of suffering, for the crushing pain of this woman's losses. For the empty chairs at the dinner table and family gatherings.

"I know that if one of my boys were hear now struggling with something, I'd tousle his hair and give him a big hug. I'd squeeze him tight and tell him I loved him. I'd tell him nothing he could ever do would make me love him less. I'd tell him not to let any *one* part of his life define how he sees himself. I'd tell him to find a way to give to others and be a blessing to those around him. If we over-focus on a single issue in our lives, a character flaw, a regret, a mistake, we only enslave ourselves more to shame.

"I'd pray for my boy-so hard! And I'd tell him I was praying. I prayed for all of my sons to find loving partners when they were younger and unmarried. And I prayed for them during the war."

"Did it work?" Daniel asked.

Mary was quiet for a moment. "In a way, though not as completely as I would have liked. He brought me my Will and Ryan home, and I know I'll see my other boys again one day." She wiped a misting tear from her eye, then stood up and brushed her hands off on her apron. "Oh my, I didn't realize today was going to be one of those emotional ones!" She laughed, trying to compose herself.

Daniel felt guilty for pressing into such a delicate place. He should have steered the conversation away from such raw pain.

"We all have a part to play, Daniel," Mary said, looking up into his light eyes. "That's the only reason I'm here today, I'm sure of it; even if my purpose is just to give a little encouragement to someone else along the way. Whatever's got you down right now, don't let it keep you down. It's just a season. And one day, like everything, like us, it'll have to pass on to make room for something new."

The Marine listened intently, staring down at the freshly turned earth. He'd been carrying so much for *years* now...

He was carrying more secrets inside than seemed possible for one life. It was so overwhelming, so crushingly burdensome and endless. He did not even know where to begin nor how to sort through it all.

When he looked up, he saw Mrs. Waynewright's flowing tears and brokenness. He wrapped her up in a tight embrace, and she sobbed for her fallen sons. They had all lost people to that God-awful war.

"Thank you," she cried softly, tears streaming down her face. It was a simple gesture, but it meant something in that moment; she thanked him again.

After another moment, she gave him a final squeeze and withdrew from the hug. Dabbing her eyes, she tried to apologize. "Oh my, sorry about that, and here I was thinking today would be about you!"

"It's fine," Daniel assured her. "Really, it's fine; please don't apologize. You have helped me, more than you know."

"Okay." Mary relented; she smiled again, pressing through mild embarrassment. She thanked him one last time before laying the matter to rest. "Care to help me plant some carrots?"

"Sure," Daniel replied. "I'd be happy to-"

BONG... BONG... BONG... BONG... BONG...
BONG... BONG...

They both turned in the direction of the long, resounding clangs, each stroke lingering eerily into the next...

Daniel's heart sank into the pit of his stomach.

The watchman in the lookout tower was ringing the heavy, copper bell hanging from the rafters. In the two years the warrior had lived in the glade, that bell had only ever been rung on two occasions. Both instances had been devastating and left more than twenty dead. They were raising the alarm to warn everyone; the camp was under siege.

CHAPTER NINE

The bell was still ringing when Daniel reached the foot of the watchtower. "What's going on?" he called up. "What do you see?"

The lookout, forty feet above, pointed to the horizon; he leaned over the tower rail and called back down, "A dozen armored vehicles just rolled up. They've halted out on the hard-ball; they're blocking the gravel drive. The trucks are white, Dan."

"Unity," he muttered.

Other community members had begun to gather at the base of the tower, all wondering aloud what was happening.

Daniel reverted to an old, authoritative voice rarely used anymore and addressed them. "Listen up, everybody! Unity has found us and they mean business.

Get to the armory, load your weapons, and move into defensive positions. Put the children and anyone else who can't fight in the bomb shelters. If Unity wants a fight, that's exactly what we'll give them. We don't know how many of them there are yet, or how well they have us surrounded. As soon as there's a break in their lines, take it and get out! We're evacuating; everyone should run for the nearest rendezvous point just like we practiced.

"Don't wait for anyone to tell you what to do. Trust your instincts and training; you already know what to do so just do it. The next thirty minutes will be a fight for survival. Expect chaos; you will feel afraid. Defend yourselves and show no hesitation to kill; we'll receive no mercy. You're fighting for your families and children now. Go! And pass the word along!"

Daniel knew they were terrified; the dread showed all over their faces, yet they heeded his call-to-arms without question and dispersed quickly. The crowd of men and women spread out across the camp to locate and hide their children. They sprinted to retrieve weapons and warn neighbors. Even amid previous attacks by lawless marauders no one had felt such an intense urgency. It was their worst nightmare come true.

Out of nowhere, there was a sudden, deafening and ugly roar and whine of engines. Two of Unity's monstrous aerial transports bellowed across the sky above the settlement. They did not stop or even slow, though. Their engines rumbled as they passed over the hillside, the base of which the community nestled against.

"Where are you going?" Daniel growled, watching the vessels slip away over the crest of the hill; they left only swaying cedars as evidence of their trail. Daniel rushed to his cabin to grab body armor. His flak jacket was resting beside his cot, fully stocked with loaded magazines and two grenades leftover from the war. He dragged a dusty seabag full of explosives out from under the cot, and tossing the bag over his shoulder he seized several spare firearms.

At the door, he breathed an honest prayer. "I know we don't talk much; I know we don't have the kind of consistent relationship that you and the priest do. And I know I still hate you for a lot of things...but if you're up there, if you're really here, in this place, right now, and if you *EVER* gave a shit about any of these people, you have to help us today! Or there won't be one of us left alive by nightfall."

The warrior slammed the cabin door shut behind him for what would be the last time. He sprinted back toward the watchtower, radioing Jonas on the way to meet him there. He pushed himself harder and harder for speed; old images and sounds began to slice into his mind. The whirring helicopter blades, the blaring alarms, one of his sergeants shouting, the flaming city below. He felt that old, familiar pain but pushed it away. The past could not distract him right now! He stopped running and struck himself in the face several times to make the images stop. He had to focus. He forced the sounds and feelings down. He had to be present, here, in this moment! Not back there in the past! His people, his...family...was counting on him now.

He reached the base of the watchtower and found Jonas, Janae, Ava, and Raoul all present. They were armed and clad for battle. Father Paolo, Brother Martinez, and Mary were also there, with no weapons to be seen.

"Father, Fernando, where are your weapons?!" Daniel demanded indignantly. "Here, take one of these." The former MARSOC captain tried to force one of his extra rifles into the priest's hands.

But Paolo recoiled from the firearm as did Ava's brother. Even Mrs. Waynewright politely declined to take one.

"What's the matter with you?" Daniel demanded. "Do you not see we're under attack?! Death is on our doorstep and you won't fight?!"

Father Paolo sighed, gathering all the patience he could muster before speaking. "Daniel, you must deal with this crisis as the Lord has called and enabled you to, but I took a vow never to raise my hand against another human. I will not take up arms against my fellow man, even if they be deceived and manipulated toward evil ends. Even if they are here to do violence to me or kill me, I will not slay another made in God's Image, who bears His divine mark of dignity and worth."

"Father, they are not going to give of us any quarter! They are going to KILL ALL OF US! Do you not understand that? They will kill *everyone* here, even the children if they have to. ANYONE not willing to surrender and become one of their brainwashed, slave citizens!"

The priest maintained his air of serenity. "I will help Dr. Ellenson care for the wounded and dying. I am certain there will be many before the day is over."

Brother Martinez nodded in agreement, stating that he would do likewise.

Daniel turned to Mrs. Waynewright. "Mary? Your sons died for the belief that people should live in freedom and safety."

The matronly woman drew in a deep breath and replied, "Yes, Daniel, they did. And I would give anything to have them back here with me. *And*, we all have to do what we're each here to do. Ellie and the other children hiding in that shelter will be terrified; I've agreed to watch over them to my last breath."

Janae held her hand out to the Marine. "I'm here to

fight, give me a rifle."

Daniel looked to Jonas for confirmation.

"Don't look at my husband," Janae snapped. "Believe me, he's already tried to talk me out of this, but I know you're gonna need every gun you can get to hold that line. I'd rather be with my daughter, but if we don't stop them in the woods, it won't matter where I am. Ellie will wind up in one of those nightmare Reeducation Camps."

"I married a strong woman," Jonas said, shaking his head.

Janae slid a semi-automatic .45 caliber pistol into the holster on her hip. "I guess we're both stubborn that way," she granted, kissing her husband. "Love you too, baby."

Jonas' radio crackled to life. It was one of the scouts at the peak of the hill behind them. "Pathfinder?"

The Ranger lifted the radio. "Go ahead."

"Those two transports set down in the next ravine over, on the other side of the hill. They're debarking now."

"How many?"

"At least one hundred strong. Easily..."

Daniel and Jonas exchanged grim glances. "Give 'em hell on their way up to you," Jonas responded. "Use the high ground to your advantage while you have it. Pick off as many of them as you can; then you get the hell out of there and fall back when the time comes."

"Solid copy, Hill-Crest out."

"A hundred-plus from the hill and a dozen trucks on the road means at least another hundred; plus whatever they've got closing in on us from the woods." Daniel was doing the mental math.

"They're gonna hit us from every side and try to crush us in a vice," Jonas said gravely. "It doesn't look good, Dan. They've got us out-manned and out-gunned three-to-one, and that's just the ones we know about."

"That's how Unity works," Daniel responded. "Leave nothing to chance; crush all resistance with overwhelming force of numbers, then write a story in their media about putting down 'violent rebels.' We're Special Forces, Jonas, when have the numbers ever been stacked in our favor?"

The Ranger cracked a grin. "You're right about that, but these ain't no ragtag Submission fighters or guerrillas from South America, man. *TWO HUNDRED* battle-hardened Pacification shock troops! You know that's where Unity puts all its sociopaths—in suits of white armor or running its Reeducation Centers!"

"No shit," Daniel shot back, aware of the precious seconds slipping away. "Good thing I brought extra ammo. We're wasting time here; let's move."

✷ ✷ ✷ ✷ ✷

The five defenders dashed through the woods, darting between trees until they reached the rows of staggered fighting positions, which had been dug out over the past few years for just such an instance. They jumped inside the five foot deep trench holes and checked weapons. Daniel glanced to the left. They were about seventy-five meters from the gravel access drive leading down to the lonely, country road. They were about 250 meters from the asphalt where a convoy of Unity's finest Pacification troops were gathered around armored vehicles.

"How'd they find us?" Jonas hissed.

"It was only a matter of time; we knew this day would come, eventually," Daniel responded. He peered through binoculars past the line of unfurled concertina wire. He focused his attention on the gathered hostile forces down on the road. He had spent years getting the people and community grounds ready for an assault like this. He would soon see if any of it had paid off.

A handful of Unity officers clad in gray uniforms were congregated near the front of the lead armored vehicle. Pacification Enforcers had pushed up a few yards off the pavement to create a perimeter. Still, none of them were advancing yet.

Jonas spoke quietly into his radio. "All defenders, this is Pathfinder, hold your fire. I say again, do not engage hostile forces or give away your position unless you are under immediate threat. Stay in your defensive positions and prepare to unleash hell on my mark."

Daniel studied the small group of officers intently. They seemed to be strategizing, conferring with other units or their command via satellite comms. Daniel panned right, surveying the Enforcers, their faces all concealed behind helmet masks. He felt an intense urge to grab his rifle and start dispatching them, to drill them through their visors. He restrained himself though; he knew it would begin soon, and he'd kill more than his fair share.

A female officer of Unity suddenly picked up a crowd control loudspeaker off the hood of the lead vehicle. She took a few paces off the asphalt and up the gravel drive, not so brave as to pass the dispersed line of Enforcers, though. Her clean and dully shined black boots seemed out of place for what was about to take place. She raised the loudspeaker and blasted the woods with proclamation.

"Attention outlaw fugitives: you are trespassing illegally on territory belonging to the Sovereign Republic of Unity. You have five minutes to disarm yourselves and surrender. If you willingly submit and cooperate with all Unity Pacification agents, you will not be harmed. You will be transported to the nearest legitimate settlement where you can then be processed by Unity agents for legal citizenship. We welcome all; for those willing to abide by our laws, there is no discrimination within our borders. Please send out an emissary who can negotiate a peaceful surrender and transition for your people."

She lowered her voice cannon for a moment. A long silence ensued, and several Enforcers, with rifles raised, looked at one another. Finally the officer spoke again. "Anyone who refuses to relinquish weapons or who is unwilling to comply with lawful orders by Unity agents-will be considered an enemy of peace and tolerance, will be treated as a hostile, and subject to summary judgment and liquidation."

"All those fancy words." Jonas shook head.

"She means they'll execute us." Daniel smirked glibly.

"I know that, jackass."

Unity's harbinger of doom was still pontificating. "Unity does not harm children! If there are any minors hidden within the compound we will find you! You have nothing to fear from Unity; we are here to liberate you! You will be cared for and transported to a safe location where you can be evaluated for psychological abuse and reoriented for productive service as young citizens of peace and tolerance." Another long pause. "Illegal settlement, you have three minutes to comply. Send out your emissary."

Jonas leaned his back against the dirt wall of the

fighting hole. He grinned, glancing over at Daniel who was still scoping out the enemy force. "Three whole minutes! Man, if I'd have known they were gonna give us so much time, I would've brought a pillow and caught a nap!"

Daniel smirked. He caught the humor, but nothing was going to make him take his eyes off that road.

"Booby traps set and ready to go?" Jonas checked.

"We're in a world of shit if they're not," Daniel said warily. He patted his canvas bag loaded with explosives and detonation devices.

There was another lull, then Daniel's mouth fell open. "Holy shit…"

"What?!" Jonas demanded, standing up and facing toward the road.

"See for yourself," Daniel said, passing off the binoculars. "Standing on the far side of that lead vehicle in an officer's uniform."

Jonas scanned for a moment before slowly uttering, "Son of a bitch…is that?"

Daniel nodded but double-checked through his rifle scope to be sure. "Looks like it."

"Well, that would explain how they found us." Jonas spat. "What an absolute piece of shit!"

On the far side of the first armored vehicle stood former Army Sergeant Jamal Williams. Based on his current gray uniform, he was apparently now a lieutenant in the ranks of Unity's Pacification Forces.

"Should I shoot him?" Jonas inquired.

"As much as I'd like that, and it wouldn't be a bad way to kick this fight off, it would give away our position. Don't get emotional; we'll end him before the day is done."

The female officer strode back to the front vehicle. She scowled at Jamal and huffed. "If your friends are still here, it doesn't look like they're coming out."

"Oh, they're here," Jamal assured her, glancing around at the trees. "They're probably watching us right now."

"Aerial thermal scans confirmed it," the major responded.

"They're stubborn like that," Jamal remarked.

"You mean fools," the major admonished.

"That too."

"Well, there's an answer for that too. Unity does not stand for these kinds of hate-mongers." She turned to her subordinate officers. "Kill anyone holding a weapon; I want everyone else in restraints and loaded for transport by nightfall." She looked at the Enforcer commander. "Tell your troops to lock and load. I want this band of criminals exterminated and their camp burned to the ground."

"You got it, ma'am," the commander responded in a dark, metallic voice. Using tactical hand motions, he directed his troopers along the line. The Enforcers, who had been hunkered down and kneeling, rose and started to advance on-line into the trees. Then the commander turned to the first armored vehicle and motioned to the driver. "Let's go, move it out!"

The column of trucks rumbled to life. Because Unity was so sensitive to carbon emissions, pollution, or any other form of industrial waste or mining, the vehicles were powered by a sophisticated, renewable charge coil—one which had *not yet* been proven harmful to the environment, though proper disposal of these was still under heated debate.

The enormous wheels began to turn, and the first two behemoth trucks made the left-hand turn off the asphalt, starting up the gravel drive.

"Here we go," Jonas said; his grin had vanished.

Daniel pulled at the radio on the collar of his flak vest. "All defenders, all defenders, this is Defender One, prepare to engage enemy targets at will. This is it, folks. Good luck and God-speed to you. Defender One out."

"Seems like a good day to die," Jonas said blithely.

"Don't even joke like that," Daniel rebuked him. "You've got a kid, man; Ellie needs you."

"I made my peace with death a long time ago, Dan; you and I both had to…"

The MARSOC captain knew it was true. It was something he and every warrior had come to terms with early on. It was necessary to functioning effectively under fire. "Just bring me some of those sons-of-bitches," Daniel growled, assuming a steely mindset. "I promise to drop at least four dozen before I start thinking of dying myself."

"Respectable goal," Jonas grinned. "I'll see your four and raise you a fifth. Make it an even sixty!"

The Raider glanced over at the Ranger. "You're on," he said, fist-bumping gloved knuckles with the Army staff sergeant.

Daniel looked down the line at the other fighting positions. He made eye contact with Raoul and nodded to Ava and Janae in the next one over. It was a tense moment, but they were all ready.

Jonas had sighted in on his first cluster of targets. Daniel peered through his scope and flicked his weapon's safety off. Time to pay the bills.

"You ready?" Jonas checked.

"Hell yeah, brother, see you on the other side."

A cacophony of gunfire erupted from every defender and fighting hole. The Enforcer ranks instantly thinned by twenty as their comrades were riddled with bullets and blasted to the ground. The sheer ferocity of the counterattack stunned and overwhelmed many of Unity's troops, most of whom had never been engaged by an organized oppositional force. The sniper and small-arms fire seemed to spray from behind every rock, tree, and fallen log, and their comrades were falling decimated in the barrage.

In lieu of the shock and heavy resistance, several Enforcers lost their footing and stumbled into fern-ridden ditches and brush. A few even felt the unbridled urge to turn and flee—to regroup and fashion a better plan of attack before attempting another push. They all knew this was impossible, however; if they tried to turn back now, their officers would activate their Blue Chips and *compel* them to advance. They stood a better chance of surviving the hail of bullets in full control of their faculties.

The troopers doubled down and pressed forward into the fray, deeper into the woods, taking ground slowly, one step at a time. They moved together and reformed the firing-line. With all of their rifles raised in unison, the Pacification units opened a mass, return-fire barrage. The suppressive bombardment tore through the forest, disintegrating leaf and stock, shredding trees and turning bark to wooden bits of ricocheting shrapnel.

The community defenders dove for cover, tucking themselves low and tightly hugging the earthen walls of their holes. As the rounds poured forth and decimated all life above their heads, Raoul suddenly rose up with a razor tipped arrow notched on his bowstring. He let it fly and dived back to the dirt. The arrow blitzed between trees and found its mark in the neck of a

Pacification Enforcer just between the shoulder plate and helmet.

The Enforcer crumpled, dropping his weapon and clutching at the foreign object lodged in his throat. One of his squad mates stopped to aid him while the others pressed forward.

Daniel pulled the two frag grenades from pouches on his flak jacket. The enemy had closed the distance quickly; they were roughly 125 meters out now. "Cover me!" he shouted to Jonas.

Jonas stood up with his SCAR rifle raised and hollered to anyone in earshot. "Covering fire!" He blasted away at the oncoming horde, dropping three almost immediately, drilling them through the facemask between the eyes. Janae and Ava were also up. They fired valiantly, hoping to slow or drive back the onslaught or simply to kill as many Enforcers as possible before they reached the concertina line.

Daniel stood up and hurled his grenades, which served as good disruptions. The explosions knocked several troopers off their feet and halted their companions who tried to assist them. One blast killed at least four Enforcers while crippling and disorienting three others. The second grenade landed short and only blew shrapnel into the faces and torsos of two.

"KILL THEM!" Daniel bellowed, raising his own assault rifle and blasting more of the enemy. "KILL AS

MANY AS YOU CAN!"

Even amid the chaos and noise, Janae and Ava were slightly alarmed by their friend's ferociousness in the next fighting hole. Daniel had always been so subdued in front of them. Today they were bearing witness to the inner beast set loose. With heavy adrenaline and fear pulsing through them, their surprise dissipated almost as quickly as it registered.

Out of nowhere, Janae's body contorted sideways, and she slammed back against the dirt wall of the fighting hole. Ava turned to look. A spiked enemy round had struck Janae in the left shoulder, ripping through muscle and chipping bone.

Jonas, who was still engaging the enemy horde, caught sight of his wife out of the corner of his eye. She was gritting her teeth and clutching the wound in pain. Jonas ceased firing and reacted without hesitation. He seized the ledge of the fighting hole and scrambled to hoist himself out so he could crawl to his wife.

But as Jonas was heaving himself up, Ava saw and shouted, "No! Stay where you are! I've got her!"

Daniel, also seeing the danger at hand, grabbed his friend from behind and pulled him back down. A volley of rounds, which resembled spiked musket balls, peppered the entire area and tore up the earth around them.

"She's all right!" Daniel hollered over the noise.

"Ava's got her; she'll be all right!"

Regrettably, the short seconds that passed during this incident gave their advancing force several moments with four fewer guns firing on them. A war cry went up from Unity's host as a final act of intimidation and they surged forward with refueled aggression. They would break through the lines and overwhelm this pathetic band of terrorist insurgents, then slaughter the rabble down to the last one.

As Daniel prepared to stand back up and reengage the oncoming wave of shock troops, he caught sight of the fate of several of his neighbors. An Enforcer sheltering behind a tree near the concertina line fired a large weapon at one of the fighting positions down the line. A spring-loaded, steel mesh net launched through the air. The second it made contact with one of the defenders, it engulfed and snapped shut around him via a magnetic field. Then the net emitted an electrified hum as it charged and surged its hostage with coursing volts of energy.

Daniel could hear the man's electrocuted screams from fifty meters up the line, but he could do nothing for him. The defender's companions who were in the hole with him struggled furiously to free their friend from the cruel device that was rapidly frying him alive. The would-be rescuers' efforts fell in vain, however, as the charged net shocked and burnt them badly whenever they touched or tried to cut the steel mesh.

By now, a hole had been cut in the concertina wire and a larger, heavily armored Pacification trooper stomped toward the crippled defensive position. His armor glinted a chrome silver different from the standard Enforcer white. He did not hesitate for a moment but unleashed an enormous flamethrower on the remaining, distracted defenders. He doused the fighters in a hellish inferno, then watched through darkened goggles as they burned and flailed, screaming in agony.

Ava and Janae barraged the heavy trooper with rifle fire, but his armor was thick and deflected the small rounds. He seemed more machine than man. Daniel raised a high-powered sniper rifle, which he had brought from his cabin. In a flurry of motion, he chambered a .50 caliber round and took aim on the behemoth fighter. He squeezed the trigger and blasted the armored bruiser through the side.

The giant buckled to one knee, emitting a strange, mortally wounded, metallic groan. Daniel racked the rifle's bolt and chambered a second round. He took aim again, targeting the heavy Enforcer's inferno cannon, then fired. Upon impact of the massive round-the weapon exploded into flames, swallowing up its master in a storm of fire.

A shower of rifle fire sent Daniel diving for cover

again. He had only narrowly been missed. An enemy round had shredded the sleeve of his camouflage utility blouse, scraping and scorching his forearm in a close graze.

Jonas was also huddled down in their fighting hole and yelled over to him, "You ready to blow the charges and take out that line yet?!"

Daniel shook his head. "No! Not yet! We'll give it another minute—get as many on that line as possible!"

"Don't wait too long!" Jonas shouted back. "We might not be alive!"

Daniel grinned. "Nah, man. This ain't nothin', they've just got us pinned down and outgunned! It ain't bad yet!"

The Ranger shot him a look, noting the rounds spitting and zinging just above their heads. "I'd hate to see what *bad* looks like to you!"

"Wait long enough and you just might!" Daniel hollered back over the ruckus.

Just then, a silver stick with a black head fell down on top of the two warriors. It made a bleeping sound and had a blinking red light at its top.

Jonas recoiled in a start. "What the?!"

Daniel seized the device and hurled it back out of their hole. A high-pitched whine pierced their eardrums, followed by a commotion of panicked Enforcer shouts and a deafening blast mixed with the clatter of simultaneous thuds and crunching noises.

"What the hell was that?" Jonas demanded.

"Let's not to dwell on the past!" Daniel responded, sneaking a peek over the brim of their fighting hole.

Unity's forces had all but reached the concertina line. A few Enforcers were fighting their way through it while others brought out large, steel cutters to remove the obstacle.

Two holes down, Raoul nailed another Enforcer between the armor plates with an arrow, killing him instantly. Ava fired her pistol with both hands over the top of her hole; one of her bullets struck a Pacification trooper square in the facemask. The round tore through his helmet, penetrating his skull through the forehead. The trooper fell over backwards from the blunt-force impact and hit the ground with a thud.

A third Enforcer flung another beeping stick at a pair of defenders down the line. They were not so fortunate to notice and send it back in time. The device detonated like a reverse grenade. A concussive implosion ripped all solid matter apart at the core of its blast, but the weapon was engineered with a kind of powerful, gravitational vacuum. Rather than blowing shrapnel and debris in all directions, it sucked all carbon matter into its nucleus with devastating results.

The Gravity Grenade imploded, instantly and violently sucking all dirt, bark, rocks, weapons, tree limbs, and humans into itself. The gruesome outcome occurred in the blink of an eye, leaving gore and limbs split open, mangled, stuffed inside one another, and twisted in knots with stones, mud, and branches. The black barrels of firearms protruded from the bloody, dripping mass like rebar rods from a puncture wound.

When Janae saw her neighbors turned inside out and mashed together in the grisly blend of bone, organ, and nature, the horror overwhelmed her. Her stomach churned at the ghastly sight, and she retched into the bottom of her own fighting hole, then began to shake and cry uncontrollably.

During the Last War, Ava had witnessed her fair share of post-explosion dismemberments and abdominal injuries with intestines spilling out. The first couple of times the horror had overcome her, but after a while she no longer reacted. She felt the pain of loss and sickness inside, but she had found that dark, hardened place which allowed her to take in all the ugly without flinching anymore. Over time, she just met it all with a vacant, unblinking stare and stone face. The moment was desperate though; while still firing her rifle, Ava cried out to her disoriented friend. "Janae! Janae, you have to get up! You have to get up and keep fighting! Fire your weapon or we are all going to die here!"

In the next hole over, Jonas and Daniel were blasting Enforcers on the fence line left and right. A rocket exploded close by, showering them with dust and branches; the blast sent Jonas, who was in the middle of a magazine change, to duck for cover. Daniel was still upright firing on the advancing horde of adversaries. "Now?" Jonas shouted up at the Marine.

Daniel's teeth were gritted as he fired twice then pivoted forty-five degrees and fired again. Under a heavy barrage, he ducked down as well. "Yeah, now seems like a good time!" He rummaged through his bag of explosives and fished out the specific detonator he was searching for. He lifted the plastic cap that guarded the safety switch, then flipped the chrome switch to the "off" position. He cupped one hand over his right ear and yelled to his companion, "Hold on to something!"

A few Enforcers had breached the concertina line and rushed up on the warriors' hole at that very moment. In a frantic flurry, Jonas gunned them down through the chest. Even as their bodies fell down on top of the veterans, Daniel hit the detonation button and a thunderous, deafening BOOM erupted. It felt to Jonas as if someone had taken a power-drill and bored holes through his eardrums. The whole earth quacked and rocked as all along the concertina line-charges of explosives blew in unison.

Accompanying the shower of rocks and melon-sized dirt clods, dozens of Enforcer bodies, helmets, limbs, armor pieces, and weapons rained down through the wooded canopy. After Daniel and Jonas shoved two armored corpses off themselves, they dared to peer over the brink of their hole. The sparse remaining teams of Pacification troops had begun retreating back through the tall grass towards the road. All along the line, Enforcer squad-mates lay maimed, crippled, dazed, and mortally wounded. "Fall back, fall back!" one of the troopers was shouting to his comrades. "Fall back and regroup!"

Even as he watched the armored shock troops fleeing through the trees, Daniel did not dare celebrate prematurely. Down the line to the left and across the gravel drive, pockets of defenders and Pacification troops were still locked in vicious skirmishes. But this was not what concerned the Marine.

As if on cue, the lead armored truck, which had idled slowly up the drive, swiveled its turret in the direction of Daniel and his companions. The weapon was entirely enclosed in a case of steel atop the vehicle's roof, and it appeared automated. There was no exposed gunner for the defenders to target or neutralize.

The weapon made a charging noise as if winding up. Then a steady and powerful beam of focused laser blasted from the turret. The weapon sliced side to side, cutting through solid tree trunks like a hot knife through butter. Instantly, birch, firs, and cottonwoods were knocked down to the forest floor. Even the largest and oldest trees cracked and crashed down on top of the already battered and injured defenders. The laser barely slowed as it slashed sideways, left and right, felling old-growth oaks and cedars in the blink of an eye.

Entire trees crashed down right on top of the defenders and their fighting holes, crushing some while trapping or pinning others. John, the engineer, was struck on the head by a careening pine and killed instantly. A few defenders attempted to flee their holes in retreat. Those who weren't flattened by collapsing trees were sliced in half or straight up the middle by the steady, pulsing beam.

Between the screams of the injured and the crashing timber, the din was overpowering. In addition, whenever the weapon's beam came in contact with the earth, the ground virtually exploded around the blast of concentrated energy. A massive tree came smashing down on top of Daniel and Jonas' hole. Both of them ducked for cover and barely missed having their skulls caved in. The branches were also a serious threat, and Jonas only narrowly avoided being impaled by one. He received an ugly laceration across his right bicep as a parting gift.

After shaking off the disorientation, Daniel slid his head through branches and foliage to peer out of his buried fighting position. He choked and coughed on the dust and debris in the air, but managed to yell to the others, "Stay down! Everybody stay in your holes!"

"Is it bad yet, Dan?" Jonas asked morbidly. He drew in a sharp breath' the cut on his arm was nasty.

"Yeah, buddy," the Marine answered. "It's getting there." He peeked over the ledge and brush again, carefully noting where the turret was directing its fury. "I don't know how many of us are left," Daniel lamented, "but we won't last long against that thing." He ducked back into the hole and rummaged through his explosives bag, retrieving an old-world, anti-tank mine.

"Dan..." Jonas looked at his brother. "Dan, you go out there and that thing will dice you to pieces."

"Yeah? Well, there are more trucks right behind that one; if we can't stop them here, we're finished. They'll cut us to pieces, mop up the survivors, and we'll all be in Reeducation Camps by nightfall. Give me whatever cover you can for as long as you can."

At that moment, out on the road, the female officer seized a radio and began screaming into it. "Tell your gunners to clean up their shooting. Stop being so sloppy! You're destroying plant life and damaging the environment! I said slaughter the insurgents, not cut down half the forest!" Furious, the major flung the radio away. "Idiots!" she fumed. "I have to write a report for every tree they knocked down! Unity protects the Earth! We aren't *savages* like those Mech-Tech corporate elites!"

Immediately, the rate of destruction by the beam weapons of the first two trucks decreased, and their firing shifted to precision bursts at identified defenders.

Daniel noted the change in aggression and looked back at Jonas. "It's now or never, brother; see you in the next life."

"Dan!" the Ranger shouted after his friend, but it was too late. With his rifle and the anti-tank mine, Daniel broke from cover. At full speed, he sprinted toward the white armored trucks, which were posted up single-column on the narrow, gravel drive.

From inside the first vehicle, a Pacification gunner observed the bold outlaw charging toward his truck from the left flank. He swiveled the turret directly at the fool and grinned behind the weapon's control console. "Where you goin', bitch? You coming to see me?" Malevolence dripped from his smile. "All right, baby, I'll give you something special—carve you up nice and pretty." The gunner aimed the cannon at Daniel's shins. He intended to slice the warrior's legs clean off below the knees; then he'd take his time dicing up this radical, one piece at a time.

The Marine knew his time had run out. He was still fifty meters away when he heard the weapon charging. This was it; he wouldn't make it and there was nowhere to hide. At least he'd tried to save his friends. He pushed himself harder, bounding over fallen logs towards the armored truck. He waited to be sliced in half; any second now he would be lying on his back, a cripple before his inevitable death.

Then, all at once, from the left and further up the sloped, drive came a dramatic cry, "Allahu Akbar!"

Daniel looked just in time to see Muhsen racing down the gravel road straight at the first truck. The Jordanian dropped to one knee and fired a rocket launcher retrieved from one of the community's hidden weapon caches. The blowback nearly knocked him over backwards, but the rocket found its mark, slamming into the lead vehicle's weapon turret.

Daniel did not even have time to dive for cover; he turned away from the blast and shielded his eyes from flying, metal fragments and wreckage. The rocket alone would have destroyed the turret, but because the energy weapon was charged, it fueled and amplified the blast enormously. The resulting explosion liquefied three-inch-thick, solid steel armor and caught the entire truck on fire from the inside out.

The driver and team leader in the cab were instantly vaporized. And Daniel felt the scorching heat of the massive eruption; he paused for only a moment before realizing he still had a mission to complete. He bolted toward the fiery coffin and decimated vehicle, leaping over fallen trees and dodging charred craters as he went.

"Go, Daniel!" Muhsen shouted. "Go, my friend!"

Every remaining community defender now opened fire from their fighting positions. They were attempting to save Daniel by drawing as much fire on themselves as possible. The second vehicle sitting behind the flaming shell of the first was still very much active and sending resistance fighters to their Maker.

"Knock that wreck off the road!" the commander of the second vehicle barked at his driver. "They're trying to box us in and block the path into their compound."

The driver complied and started the truck forward, accelerating straight for the hellish skeleton of their comrades' vehicle.

Daniel made one final dash for the second truck. The turret gunner spotted this mad charge but he was too late to cut the veteran down. As Daniel rushed the vehicle, he dived face-first into the gravel, tearing the flesh off his forearms. He was unwilling to even notice the pain and blood at that moment. He dragged himself in front of the moving truck and pulled the safety pin from the anti-tank mine; it was now armed for motion activation. The Marine rolled out the far side of the truck and was nearly crushed by one of its massive, rear tires. Then he dove into the bushes to protect himself from the impending explosion.

As the armored vehicle continued forward, the gunner sensed something was wrong and screamed down to the truck commander. "Sir! Stop the-" But it was too late. The mine beneath the vehicle detonated and blasted a superheated, copper plate straight up through the belly of the beast. The centrifugal force of the spinning disk turned everything in the vehicle inside out and then exploded against the ceiling.

The truck's armored doors and reinforced windows blew out as the vehicle erupted in flames. Fire poured forth from every opening, and the truck's burning driver fell out of the front door. Everything inside had turned to molten or human soup.

A triumphant roar went up from the remaining, tattered defenders who had witnessed the bold counterstrike. Only a madman would have attempted the fool's errand, but Daniel had pulled it off. Somewhere inside him, the MARSOC hero of the Last War still lived. Jonas threw a fist in the air and gave a victor's shout for his brother and the halt of their enemy's advance.

With two armored trucks in flaming wreckage and immobilized on the access drive, they had effectively, albeit temporarily, crippled Unity's siege. The only vehicle-friendly gateway into the glade was now blocked. If the Pacification convoy tried to force its way up the canalized path, they would encounter fierce resistance and only incur greater losses.

Daniel did not waste any time surveying his exploits.

He raced back to the fighting hole and jumped in for cover, checking the ammunition in his magazine.

Jonas was in the middle of whooping and hollering when his radio crackled to life. The voice on the other end was frantic. "Defender One, Defender One, this is Hill-Crest, over!"

Jonas looked up at his friend who was still catching his breath and assessing his shredded forearms. Jonas tossed him the radio.

"Defender One here—go ahead."

"We held as long as we could, Dan, killed maybe a dozen of them before they had us pinned down and swept up the backside of the hill. We're falling back, Cap. They've taken the ridge; I say again, Unity forces have taken the over-watch position!"

"Get out of there, Hill-Crest; you did all you could. Fall back to the camp; we'll try to halt them at the base." Daniel dropped the radio and stared off through the trees toward the road.

"Whatcha thinkin', Dan?" Jonas asked.

"I'm thinking this was a nice place, but there's no way we win this fight and come out alive. Even if we beat them here today, they'll just come back and finish us off. They underestimated our defenses and resolve today, but next time they'll completely wipe us out or bomb us into oblivion."

"I know," Jonas acknowledged solemnly.

Daniel glanced to his right, down the line of fighting holes. "Raoul!" he called. "I need you to lead these people. I'll take a few of our shooters to the base of the hill and try to hold back the tide. You rally everyone here and move on the road. Press our advantage while we still have one. They're regrouping for the moment, trying to figure out how to beat us. Pick off as many of them as you can from the cover of the trees; make it impossibly miserable for them to hold that road. If you can kill some of their vehicle crews, the drivers and gunners, we might be able to neutralize a few of those trucks."

Raoul gave a short nod. Daniel pulled two detonators from his canvas bag and secured them in a magazine pouch on his flak vest. Then he set the bag of remaining explosives on the debris-covered ground. "Take these, you might be able to use some of them."

Jonas climbed out of their hole to help his wife. He triaged her gunshot wound. It was messy and needed cleaning and packing soon. Janae had lost a lot of blood; she groaned in discomfort and appeared dazed. Still, she expressed a desire to go with Jonas and Daniel to the base of the hill.

Jonas shook his head. "No. I'm putting my foot down on this one. You're injured; you need to get help. Take your gun and go see Dr. Ellenson, then get to the shelter. If we don't make it, at least you'll be left to kill off the Enforcers who come for our daughter. Ellie ain't growin' up without her mama." Jonas' eyes misted for a second.

Fatigued and in significant pain, Janae relented. "Ellie's not growing up without her daddy neither, Jonas; so you come back to us, hear?" She kissed her husband. "I love you, baby."

"Love you too," Jonas said earnestly. He wrapped his arms around her tightly. He didn't want to let her go, but he'd been doing the hard thing all his life. He knew when he had a duty to perform, and that time was now.

"We've gotta move," Daniel said, interrupting the moment.

Jonas let his wife go; he checked his rifle chamber and magazine. He was ready.

Daniel hung his assault rifle by its sling and hoisted the heavier sniper rifle over his shoulders. Nodding to Janae, he called to Ava. "Help her to the shelter then regroup with Raoul. The people need you now."

Ava nodded back. Even under dire circumstances, she appreciated Daniel's respect for her. He treated her with endless trust and honor, highly regarding her skill as a warrior and leader. She felt a swell of love for the captain. She hoped they would meet again—that they might *all* live to see another sunrise together. She hefted Janae up with her shoulder, guiding her steadily up the slope, between trees, and back towards the clearing.

Jonas and Daniel were already gone, running straight into one final fray.

CHAPTER TEN

The warriors reached the base of the steep, wooded incline behind the infirmary. They were quickly joined by five other defenders, two retreating from enemy potshots on the hilltop above and three others from the southeast border of the forest beyond the modest grove of apple trees. Immediately, the small band fell under fire from Unity's second wave, which now descended from above.

The team sought shelter behind a large pile of split firewood. As enemy rounds tore at the barricade, spitting and ricocheting overhead, Jonas grumbled, "Didn't we just kick their asses?!"

"Don't worry," Daniel assured him. "We'll have the advantage this time."

Jonas noted the treacherous angle keeping them

pinned down under a volley of fire. "I hope so!" he shouted back. None of the defenders dared to raise their heads above the five-foot, protective barrier. Chunks and bits of firewood were splitting and flying wildly as the onslaught from above gathered momentum.

"Seven against a hundred?!" Jonas laughed over the racket. "Yeah, that's a fair fight!"

"Could be worse!" one of the lookouts shot back. "It *was* a 120 to start with; we whittled a few down during their climb up the backside!"

"Thanks!" Jonas hollered sarcastically. "I really notice the difference!"

Nearly 500 meters up the sharp, wooded slope, the Enforcers had staked a wholesale monopoly on fire superiority. Unity's troops would reach the meadow in minutes if Daniel's next play shorted out. The MARSOC warrior did not waste any time; he pulled out the two detonators he had brought with him from the fighting holes and prepared for the next phase of this battle.

From the top of the forested peak, the second Pacification wave traversed down the rough terrain. Enforcers moved methodically, careful not to trip and tumble down the steep incline. They were so focused on their footwork and laying suppressive fire on the few, pitiful renegades below that they neglected to observe several key, subdued features.

They did not notice the massive rock heaps or stacks of logs covered in musty, worn tarps. They did not heed the sublimely placed planks propping these up from collapse nor consider the potential and catastrophic avalanche looming if such supports were somehow neutralized.

Two years earlier, for weeks on end, Daniel had led the community in a concerted effort to fortify the camp. Part of this had involved digging fighting positions and stretching out spools of concertina wire. Some of it had been chopping fallen trees into workable lengths and then hauling these and medium-sized boulders to the precipice of the hill.

Portions of the labor had been grueling and even dangerous, requiring every able-bodied member of the community to lend their strength and ingenuity to hoist the backbreaking loads to the near-summit. But Daniel had assured the council that these "defensive countermeasures" were necessary, even vital, to the survival of the camp in the event of a full-fledged assault upon the glade. At last, a day had come for all their sweat and toil to be repaid.

Daniel cupped a hand over his ear and shouted to the others, "Watch your heads; it's about to get a little crazy!" The Marine Raider hit the detonator's button, and far above, the charges blew.

The shockwaves knocked several Pacification

troopers right off their feet and sent them face-first into the dirt or careening end-over-end down the abrupt slope. A handful standing near the piles of boulders and stacks of logs were killed instantly in the explosions when the plank supports were blown free.

From the glade below, a series of enormous BOOMs were heard. Then there was a low cracking and rumble as rocks and twelve-foot logs broke loose and began crashing down the steep hillside. Simultaneously, a commotion of frantic shouts arose from wooded crest as Unity's shock troops tried desperately to get clear of the violent avalanche. Enforcers cried out in alarm and terror as cascading boulders smashed them, shattering skulls, crushing limbs, and flattening armored bodies under hundreds of pounds of force.

The line broke quickly as Enforcers sprinted and dove, mostly in vain, to get out of the path of falling payloads. But the logs kept rolling, the boulders kept tumbling, and the rocks continued to fly. Troopers collided with one another amid hysteric efforts to save themselves from being crushed, decapitated, and utterly pulverized. Their commander, still standing at the hillcrest, was dumbstruck. He watched powerlessly as his men were flattened and annihilated by the unstoppable slide.

Daniel chose this moment to rise up from cover and return some precision fire. He peered through his scope picking off stray Enforcers who had evaded the avalanche by fleeing to the flanks or who were making frenzied dashes to shield themselves behind sturdy cedar trunks. The Marine's companions took their cue from him and also rose up. When Daniel's magazine ran dry in his assault rifle, he laid it aside on the wood pile and reached for the sniper rifle.

Logs and boulders were spilling down the hillside straight towards them. Daniel knew the seconds were precious before he and his comrades would also need to run for cover from the landslide. He located the Enforcer commander at the summit of the hill; the trooper was still shouting orders to his subordinates and trying to regain control of the situation.

The commander was waving an arm vehemently and screaming directives when Daniel squeezed the high-powered rifle's trigger. One second the trooper was trying to restore order to his Enforcers, the next his head was blown completely off. From the power of the massive .50 caliber round, a portion of the commander's upper torso was also ripped off along with his head. "Tell your Presiding Council the U.S. Marine Corps says hello," Daniel taunted.

"Dan, we gotta move!" Jonas hollered, seizing his friend by the flak jacket.

Daniel, who had fallen victim to a mild case of tunnel vision glanced up suddenly to see boulders and logs smashing right for him. He grabbed his assault rifle off the wood stack and sprinted away from the barricade just in time. The avalanche of logs and rock slammed into the pile of firewood, toppling and burying it without a trace.

The defenders raced for shelter as boulders crashed across the glade, smashing cabins, fences, and any livestock that got in their path. After dodging tumbling logs, the band came to rest at a safe distance-near the place where Father Paolo convened his weekly contemplative hour gatherings. Grinning and laughing nervously at their narrow escape, the team began to pick themselves up and catch their collective breaths. Jonas gave a victory whoop.

Far above, the twenty remaining Enforcers had clambered back up the hillside to regroup. They had just suffered a humiliating and epic defeat. With their headless leader at the summit and eighty-five percent of their unit lying pancaked on the forest floor, their contingencies were limited. After taking a beating like that, none of them bore the will to assault back down into the camp again, not without reinforcements. They scrambled over immobilized logs and boulders towards the peak. A dozen troops would remain behind to hold the ridge, the rest would rush back to their shuttlecrafts and report the disastrous rout.

✳ ✳ ✳ ✳ ✳

A stillness had begun to settle over the glade again with only distant intermittent explosions and sporadic rifle fire. Jonas' radio buzzed and Ava's voice filled the receiver. "Pathfinder, this is Echo-Four-Mike, how copy, over?"

"Read you loud and clear, Echo-Four-Mike," Jonas responded, happy to hear her voice. "Glad you're still with us; what's your sitrep, over?"

"We're all right down here at the road; we lost a few more but pressed them as instructed." There was a momentary pause. "Jonas, Unity pulled out."

Daniel looked up in surprise, and Jonas responded in utter dismay, "Say again your last, over?"

"They're gone, Jonas. We were able to kill a few more Enforcers, then, out of the blue, they all just piled into their trucks, turned around, and drove off! They fought for about ten minutes and had us pretty well pinned down with those truck turrets. Then they just left…"

Jonas looked to Daniel. The Marine was shaking his head gravely. "I don't like it."

"We took two prisoners," Ava's voice broke through again.

"Bring them to us," Jonas ordered sternly; he was deeply vexed and knew this could not be good. "Get everyone ready to evacuate."

"Solid copy. Echo-Four-Mike, out."

Daniel was ruminating on the news as well; a dark expression furrowed across his face. "They could've held us off for *hours,* Jonas, maybe even days! They still had at least ten trucks down on that road with enough firepower to cut down half the forest and level any counterstrike we could've thrown at them! All they had to do was wait us out, hold on long enough for another wave of reinforcements to show up! WHY?! Why retreat?"

"I don't like it either," Jonas agreed. "The second their hillside assault fails, they just pull out?"

"We've gotta move now," Daniel said grimly. "You get everyone from the shelter; I'll round up the doc and her team. We'll link up with the last of Ava and Raoul's defenders and get the hell out of—"

"What's that noise?!" Jonas cut in, looking to the wooded skyline.

Daniel caught the short whisk of something cutting rapidly through the air, then the first rocket hit the meadow. The powerful concussion blew Daniel in one direction and Jonas in another. The glade rocked and trembled as five more rockets slammed into the community grounds; it felt as if the world were ending. Twenty more rockets followed, heralding mass devastation to the cabins, sloping landscape, and groves of fruit trees.

Alone, surrounded by fiery explosions and black smoke, Daniel held his hands over his ears and strained to crawl towards a smoldering crater. Yearning for protection from a second blast, he willed himself forward on all fours. At the brink of the blackened hole, he tucked himself into a ball and rolled to the bottom, hoping the rain of fire would end soon.

For the first time since the start of the battle, he prayed for his friends again, for their safety and survival. He did not know how many would survive this reckoning. His bleary thoughts drifted to Mary and Janae huddled with Ellie and all the other children inside the bomb shelter. Would it hold? Would it be enough to shield them from the blasts and flying rubble?

He knew if a rocket struck the shelter directly, it would pass right through that steel hatch and kill everyone inside. He shuddered to imagine pulling the charred and mangled corpses of children from the caved-in hole. Pushing the thought away, he prayed harder. Had he brought this madness on the people by slaughtering the Enforcer squads at the hill? Had he forced Unity's hand? He should have forced everyone to evacuate when they'd halted the roadside assault.

The airstrike lasted several minutes, persisting until there was virtually nothing left of the community's structures nor the years of labor they'd put into cultivating the land. As the heavy wreckage and smoke began to settle, only a thick haze of dust and debris lingered. At last, Daniel dared to raise himself up and survey the destruction. What he took in was pure and utter desolation.

Everything was gone-demolished-from the cabins and gardens to the communal tables and outdoor benches. The few animals not obliterated in the volley of rockets had fled into the woods. There was nothing left, nothing from the years of honest work by steady hands and hope-filled hearts.

In actuality, not *everything* was lost. As gentle breezes began to clear some of the hanging, white smoke and haze, Daniel witnessed several miracles. The first was his seemingly untouched assault rifle lying several yards away in the blackened and upturned soil. Second, he saw Jonas sprinting across the charred desolation straight for the bomb shelter. It lay close to where the henhouses had formerly stood, near the now-burnt apple grove. Third, he saw Dr. Ellenson's infirmary still standing unbelievably intact. Finally, from a distance, Daniel watched Jonas tear open the steel door to the shelter and Janae fall into his arms, both weeping tears of panicked relief.

The Marine walked soberly across the scorched earth and picked up his rifle, dusting it off and cradling it against his chest. He continued to survey the devastation while moving in the direction of the ragged tree-line. Ava and several other bedraggled survivors had begun to stagger out from the smoldering woods to behold their obliterated home. Some sank to their knees at what lay before them-others cried softly on the shoulder of a spouse or neighbor.

As he approached, Daniel could hear the quiet sobs of several people. All their hopes and dreams, all their struggle to survive and come back from the edge of annihilation after the Last War-it was all gone. In a matter of minutes, years of their lives had gone up in flame.

As his friends ventured out onto the charred earth, Daniel moved to give Ava a hug and he clasped Raoul's hand firmly. They had made it; they had all survived. He nodded to Beth and Abby further down the line. Both women were dressed for battle and carrying rifles of their own. The side of Abby's head was bloodied by an ugly gash.

"Good to see you made it," he told Ava.

"Likewise," she replied soberly, still taking in the desolation before her eyes. "I wasn't sure anyone in the glade survived."

"Where are the prisoners?" the Marine questioned.

Ava hesitated for a moment, then picked up her rifle and said, "This way." She guided Daniel behind the row of weary mourners and directed him to the base of a tree trunk. There sat a female Enforcer, armored, hands tied behind her back, yet no helmet to hide her face. Dr. Ellenson was already on scene tending to and triaging the young woman; she used a flashlight to check her pupils for tracking and light sensitivity.

As the warrior drew near, he was slightly startled to see the unknown woman's right eye emitting a steady blue glow. Her pacification chip was active. Jane Ellenson was asking her if she could feel various touches and pressures. Then the doctor asked the question she had been waiting years to: "Do you want that thing out of you?" She pointed to the glowing eye, referring to the chip behind it.

At that moment, the young Enforcer seized up as if something inside were electrocuting her or causing significant pain. She tried to speak, but only a few incoherent groans escaped her lips. Daniel watched Jane patiently and compassionately probe the prisoner. "It's okay," the physician reassured. "You're safe here. Does it hurt? Is it hurting you?"

The young soldier of Unity was barely able to grunt this time; a paralysis had apparently claimed her, and she convulsed. As the doctor observed her carefully, a single tear trickled down the young soldier's face. She was more a slave and hostage to Unity than the community's tattered remnant.

Jane called out for one of her medical aids. "Help

me carry her to the infirmary and prep for surgery; we're getting that chip out of her."

It was then that Daniel interjected. "Doc, let me ask her some questions first; she's a captured Pacification soldier for God's sake! Twenty minutes ago she was shooting at us and probably killed someone you know! We have no idea where her friends are or when they're coming back. Let me ask her some questions before you put her under for brain surgery!"

"No, Daniel!" Jane snapped. "You're a Marine door-kicker; I get that-but I'm a doctor. Let me do my job! Before I escaped, I spent six months being tortured by Reeducation Center monitors! I'm saving this girl and that's the end of it! Besides, do you really think you're gonna get any answers out of her right now? Her superiors activated her chip for a reason, probably when they realized they'd left her behind! Assholes."

The former MARSOC operator wanted to protest; did this girl even want to be saved?! He doubted there was even time to liberate the young woman's mind. He stayed quiet, though, recognizing that in the prisoner's current state any interrogation bore little chance of success. He did admire Jane's resolve and compassion. How many times had the priest quoted the words of Jesus: "Love your enemies! Do good to those who persecute and mistreat you! Bless those who curse you! Bless, and do not curse them back or seek revenge!"

Dr. Ellenson and a former Army medic had begun to lift the young Enforcer off the ground when another distressed voice broke in. "Please, please help us!"

Daniel turned to see Muhsen staggering across the barren soil; the Jordanian man carried the limp body of one of his twin daughters. Quintessa hung unconscious in her father's trembling arms; she was bleeding from the head, and one of her arms was jaggedly splayed open. Muhsen's lip quivered and his eyes brimmed with tears as fear and desperation to help his child tore at his heart.

One of the rockets had damaged the rear corner of the shelter. The beautiful girl had been huddled closest to the wall when the explosion blasted several holes through the roof of the buried structure. Quintessa had taken several pieces of shrapnel to her vulnerable body. In the wake of shock and blood-loss, the girl had lost consciousness shortly thereafter.

Dr. Ellenson cursed under her breath, heartbroken and enraged at the sight of the injured child hanging almost lifeless in her father's shaking arms. "Help me!" Jane shouted to worn bystanders. She now had two surgeries to initiate, both urgent, but one time constrained and life threatening.

Daniel was no surgeon, but he had training and years of experience in stabilizing traumatic bleeding and other battlefield injuries. He was about to jump in and offer assistance when he caught sight of a distant figure emerging through the haze of lingering smoke that still draped over the meadow. The frail figure appeared to be struggling with a heavy load.

From behind Daniel, a sudden, gut-wrenching wail went up. Ava cried out and bolted across the scorched field. She had recognized the figure first; it was Father Paolo, injured, bleeding from his side. He was dragging someone's body on a wide board behind him.

"Oh no," Daniel lamented "God no…"

Fernando Martinez's lifeless arm draped over the ledge of the makeshift stretcher that the old priest was heaving. The Benedictine brother's fingers brushed along the blackened earth; an innocent man killed in a fight he had never asked for. Ava reached her brother and fell into the dirt sobbing. She pressed her tanned face against his and wept his name. "No, no, Fernando!"

Wounded, weary, and struggling to breathe, Paolo turned to the devastated sister and tried to comfort her. "He did not suffer, Ava. He was crushed by a cabin wall during one of the blasts. The force killed him before he ever touched the ground."

Ava was silent for a moment, absorbing the news; then she began beating her brother's lifeless chest and screaming her rage. "Why?! Why, God?! Why did you not protect my brother?! He was a holy man of peace! He devoted his entire life to you! And this is how you repay him?! Why didn't you kill me?! You should have taken me!"

"Ava. Ava," the priest interceded. "Fernando is with the Lord now; no pain or sickness can ever touch him again. I know you are hurting, but God did not harm your brother. It was the evil actions of other men. Your Father has carried him home forever. He rests now in his true home and place of belonging."

Ava's face hardened with bitterness as she stared through tears at her brother's corpse. He was so handsome, so tranquil; if not for the blood, he could have been sleeping. Ava stood up, a grim expression spreading across her stricken face. She gazed down on her last remaining blood relative. "I'll kill them for this, Father," she said darkly. "I'll kill all of them."

"You know your brother would not have wanted that, Ava. That is not how he would want to be remembered-with further acts of killing and bloodshed, violence and hatred! He would want you to live a long and peaceful life, in quiet, gratitude, and joy."

"My brother's dead, Father," Ava replied gravely. "And soon I will be too." She slung her assault rifle over her shoulder and leaned down to lift Fernando's resting body. She kissed him on the forehead gently; then, hoisting him up in her arms, she started back towards the tree-line and battered remnant of the community. What hope for peace or joy in her life had just died with her brother.

Dr. Ellenson's medical team and volunteers passed by Ava, carrying the captured Enforcer and the critically wounded child across the burnt field to the infirmary. Daniel took all this in with a deep weariness in his soul. He no longer felt the pain he once had, but he had wrongly assumed this scale of suffering was behind him at the end of the war.

"I'm so sorry, Ava." He spoke softly. "Fernando was a good man, one of the most decent I ever met."

Ava Martinez stoically lowered her brother to the ground; she tenderly leaned his broken body against a tree. In a kind of absent daze, she responded flatly, "Would you like to see the other prisoner, Daniel?"

The Marine was immediately uneasy and wary. His friend was clearly in a state of shock, but he did want to see the other prisoner and question them.

Ava did not wait for a response. She stepped past the tree-line and wandered deeper into the devastated wood. Though she was in a near-trance, her path was not aimless. After thirty seconds of walking in silence, she stopped and pointed to another tree where Raoul and Jonas already stood vigilant. Light filtered down through the smoke and burnt foliage; at the base of the pockmarked cottonwood sat Jamal Williams, bound.

"There he is." Ava said vacantly. "There's the man who did this to us-the man who killed my brother."

Given her current state, Daniel did not really trust letting Ava too close to Jamal. There was a very high probability she might snap, and strangle the betrayer to death. He caught sight of Beth back at the woodland border; he motioned to her, and when she arrived, he politely asked her to take Ava back to the glade. "Maybe help find her some water," he suggested. He knew the soldier was exhausted and dehydrated from battle. Beth graciously took charge of Ava and carefully guided the weary veteran back in the direction of the meadow.

An unintended scowl had crept across Daniel's face. He turned and strode directly towards the subdued, second prisoner. As the warrior stalked up to the defeated man, dressed in a Unity officer's uniform, his guards tensed. Jonas and Raoul saw the fire in their friend's eyes-the darkness in his appearance. Daniel did not hesitate or bother to mince words. He kicked Jamal full force in the chest, knocking him over backwards; then he drew his pistol and leveled it at the defector's face.

"Give me one good reason why I shouldn't blow you away right here, Jamal," he snarled.

"One of you gonna do something?" Jamal demanded from the ground. "Or you actually gonna let this racist pig do me execution style?!" He glowered back at Daniel, spitting blood between his teeth.

Raoul remained silent, his visage indifferent. Jonas,

on the other hand, clutched his SCAR rifle and shouted back, "Shut your mouth, you pathetic piece of shit! You realize how many people you killed today?! My wife was shot in a firefight by your Unity pals! Don't even think of cryin' to me; you're gonna get exactly you deserve today! I'm so sick of hearing your shit! Daniel has been more a brother to me than you ever were! So, no, I guess not; maybe I will just let him shoot you right here and now!"

Daniel crouched down and addressed the traitor in a low tone. "So tell us, Jamal, did you go straight to Unity when we exiled you? You were pissed about being kicked out so you figured you'd hang us all out to dry?!"

"Not exactly," Jamal answered, glaring back. "It's not like you gave me a lot of options for survival. I made it a couple months on my own, even joined up with an outlaw crew for a while. When that didn't work out-I was back on my own again... Unity started hunting me; they tracked me for two days straight. It all ended one night in the middle of a thunderstorm; there I was alone, soaked to the bone, freezing to death, and out of ammunition. I killed half a dozen of them, but that night they finally surrounded and overpowered me. After they disarmed me, they beat me good and put me in shacks, then flew me to the nearest internment camp."

"And then you gave us up?" Daniel pressed.

"Not at first," Jamal retorted. "But yeah, rotting in

319

the cell of a Reeducation Center one night, getting tortured and interrogated by day, pushed to take their chip. I asked myself 'Why should I suffer for all you assholes back here who threw me out?' So I cut a deal to save myself."

"Did you take the Blue Chip?" Daniel asked.

"Nope! That was part of the deal for selling y'all out. In exchange for leading them back here, they gave me a commission in the Pacification Forces, and I got to keep my free will! See, Cap', you just gotta know how to negotiate."

Filled with rage, Daniel mentally snapped. He backhanded Jamal across the mouth with all his might, thinking of the community's dead and injured: Ava's brother, Muhsen's daughter lying on an operating table, barely clinging to life. The Marine took a step back and pointed his sidearm at Jamal's head once more. "You should have taken it like a man and died in that concentration camp." The MARSOC captain glowered. "But don't worry, I'll finish the job for them, you piece of shit!"

He had already begun to squeeze the trigger when a raspy voice interrupted loudly. "Do not do it, Daniel! Do not let yourself be consumed with darkness and hate! You do not have to be like him! You do not have to be like your father! The Lord says *He* will deliver justice, and we are NOT to take vengeance into our own hands!"

Daniel looked back at the wounded priest leaning on a staff just to keep himself upright. "What do you want me to do, Father, let him go?! Release him so he can go back to Unity and bring them down on us all over again?! He deserves to die! We banished him for attempted rape, and he came back with our enemies to destroy us!"

"Let the council decide his fate." Paolo reasoned. "It is not your place to be judge and executioner of a defeated foe and disarmed prisoner."

Daniel stared angrily at Jamal; he saw the smug look of satisfaction in his eyes. The traitor knew he was going to get away with it all. Daniel cast his gaze downward to the smoking earth. "I'm sorry, Father," he said quietly. "I'm not as good a man as you might have hoped." He raised his eyes once more, saw the look of terrified shock on Jamal's face; then he squeezed the trigger and blew him away.

CHAPTER ELEVEN

The priest cried out in dismay, but it was too late. The bullet struck Jamal between the eyes and passed through his skull just above the nose. The former infantryman slumped over backwards as blood leaked out his penetrated brain cavity and pooled on the earth around his head.

Had Father Paolo not been present, Daniel would likely have emptied the rest of his clip into Jamal's lifeless body. He hated him, hated him for everything he had done and all he had put the community through. It had begun with Beth and ended in today's massacre.

Strangely, at that moment, a soft, blue light began to pulse softly behind Jamal's right, glazed eye-finally transitioning to a steady glow.

"I guess Unity didn't tell you the whole truth, Jamal."

Daniel gibed morbidly.

Jonas and Raoul were silent, both slightly stunned that Daniel had actually shot the traitor. Janae and Mary arrived on scene. The sound of the gunshot had drawn some attention from the clearing; Ava had also returned and saw Jamal's corpse.

"Daniel!" the priest fumed. It was one of the few times the Marine had ever seen Paolo visibly angry and certainly the first time his ire had ever been directed towards him.

"What, Father?" the warrior answered unremorsefully. He was too weary to make any half-hearted attempts at apologies or contrived guilt. In his mind, his actions were completely justified. He had eliminated a threat to the community, one who had been banished yet returned in hostility.

The priest was so furious he could barely form words, yet speak he did. "You have committed an egregious sin in a senseless act of violence! You have committed murder against your brother, no matter how deluded or corrupt he had become! Have you no remorse for slaying another of God's children?!"

Daniel stared coldly back at the Franciscan. "No, not for him; you call it what you want, Father, but I just saved lives and gave Jamal what he had coming. Remember exiling him? He would have been shot if he'd returned to us early or in aggression. Leading an army of

Unity Enforcers on a siege against us seems pretty hostile to me!

"Jonas and I could have shot him before the battle even started, but we didn't; so what's the difference between killing him now versus shooting him when he was standing next to an armored vehicle?! There are no courts out here, Father; there's no law and order, no judges, no rules of engagement! It's us against the world, and I will do *whatever* is necessary to protect the people closest to me!"

The Syrian shook his head in frustrated disgust. "There are *many* ways in which it *differs*, Daniel, but I choose to focus on your soul—what shooting a bound and disarmed man says about the hardness that has grown in your heart!" There was a long silence as the two men locked eyes sternly at each other; then the abbé spoke again. "Tell us the truth. Tell us what happened all those years ago, before you came here, before you ever found the community. Something has been eating and festering the core of your being since the day you came to us. Now tell us, tell us where you came from and what happened to you, in those last days of the war."

"You really wanna do this now, Father?" Daniel laughed. "With Unity probably heading back here this very second to finish us off?"

"Tell us the truth!" the priest commanded. "I have

been patient, and we have ALL waited long enough."

Daniel's eyes locked in a silent glare, his face a bitter grimace, but he heard that hum. He heard those familiar propellers starting to buzz once more. They rose from that dark pit in his mind, that place he had tried so hard to forget and bury forever...

✳ ✳ ✳ ✳ ✳

The MARSOC captain stood atop a hot tarmac on a steamy South American airbase. He was every bit the battle-hardened warrior that his attire reinforced; the rugged toughness in his face revealed years of leading Marines under fire in the worst hells on Earth. Beside him stood the team's chief, Master Sergeant Miles Davis. A C-17 military cargo-transport plane sat primed behind the pair, turboprops already winding up in preparation for takeoff. Before them stood their dozen Raiders-the finest Marines the Corps had to offer, all sturdy men and warriors, all tested and proven in the fires of war.

Captain Weston addressed them loudly and directly over the noise of the cargo vessel. "Gentlemen, I will not bullshit you here today. What I am asking of you will be very difficult; the Corps will consider it desertion, abandoning our post and mission in Columbia. Should you choose to join myself and Master Sergeant Davis, you all need to be very clear about the potential, even likely, consequences that our actions may carry."

The younger, authoritative Daniel fixed each of his Marines with steely eyes. As commanding officer he was responsible for their lives, well-being, and mission-success; he would not mislead them in any way about what he was proposing. "No doubt some of you have felt ambivalence about our mission here in South America the past few months. Though I have done my best to only show it to Master Sergeant Davis and battalion H.Q., let me assure you that I have also felt the same frustration and disillusionment. I have felt it all the more when one of our brothers gets killed and I find myself writing another letter home to his parents or wife.

"The tipping point for me came last week and was two-fold. When that C.I.A. spook showed up and ordered us to burn an entire village with women and children in it, I drew a line and told you all to stand down. That's not what we're about. That's not why I signed up to be a Marine or a Raider, and there's enough of that shit going on around the world right now. We're not a bunch of Submission radicals, you hear me? So I told that ghost she could pack sand; I don't care what's in the ground under that village or who the government is accusing them of aiding. I don't butcher unarmed women, children, and old people!

"*Increasingly, the master sergeant and I have become aware that we seem to be getting sent into harm's way not to save lives or stop the slaughter of innocents anymore, but to protect the drilling and mining interests of Mech-Tech corporates back home. One day you wake up and realize that a lot of the so-called bad guys we're being set loose on are just regular schmoes trying to defend their lands.*

"*And while we fight in this mean bush supposedly for freedom and to protect the future of America and our families back home, I received word three days ago that taking all of Europe wasn't enough for those Winter Steel sons-of-bitches. They have crossed the Atlantic and pushed our forces back to successfully establish a beachhead, on our own soil! The Russians have cut off several, major East Coast cities and are bombing like crazy back home. We were assured this would never happen while we were doing our jobs, but it seems, just as our government failed at its promise to keep Imperial State from taking the West Coast, they have failed us once again. They have failed to take care of their own military service members and our families.*

"*What this has driven home for the master sergeant and myself is an apparent lack of priorities back in Washington. We're down here fighting a no-man's war for 'peace and stability' while politicians and fat-cat corporate heads in the capital can't be bothered to* ensure the defense of our own borders against the Russians and Chinese. And don't even get me started on *Submission's* reign of rape and terror, sweeping its way across northern Africa and south Asia!"

Daniel was finally coming to the heart his message; he paused to let his words and obvious disgust sink in. "Gents, my wife, Kate, is seven months pregnant with our first child. As I stand here speaking to you, she is currently trapped behind enemy lines in Baltimore. Winter Steel's forces have taken the city and surrounding countryside in a shock-and-awe bombing campaign. Master Sergeant Davis and I have decided to abandon the fight hear in South America. We're going home to rescue our families and get them to safety. We know this will likely be the end of our respective military careers, but at this point we're choosing family over unquestioned loyalty to a dissolving government.

"You each have to decide what you're going to do; master sergeant and I can't order you to come with us, and we wouldn't ever try to. But we are getting on that bird in five minutes. It's flying to Lackland Air Force Base, Texas, where I have some pilot friends willing to take us the rest of the way by chopper.

"I won't ask you to abandon your posts and shitcan your careers for me and my family, but I promise that any man who does set foot on that plane with us will be my family forever. And after we rescue my wife from

Baltimore, we'll help any of you make sure your own families are safe and secure. Our government has turned its back on us, this brotherhood right here is all we have left—each other. We've already been to hell and back together a hundred times over. There's not a man here I'd trade; you are all the very best America and the Marine Corps have to offer."

The captain paused for a moment of sobriety. "Gents, I pray for American families back home right now. It's times like these we feel the burden of every American warrior heading straight into the eye of the storm. We pray for our Army brothers and all the battered reserve units being called back up for another ugly fight on our soil..."

There was another lull, and Master Sergeant Davis took this as his cue to address the team. He was a thick, stocky man, originally from the hills of Indiana. His body was pockmarked with old scars from previous missions and bar brawls, and his voice was like crushed gravel. "Let me reemphasize, gentlemen; this is NOT a command-sanctioned mission. We will be operating on our own behind enemy lines, on our own soil. When our actions are discovered, the Marine Corps will almost certainly brand us as deserters and mutineers. Think hard about your choice; it is yours alone to make. No man here will be thought less-of should he choose to stay behind here in Bogota. We only ask that you give *us twenty-four hours before you report our disappearance to command.*

"We've added ourselves to the flight manifest for transport, so they won't question us once we're onboard; however, this also means that once battalion realizes we've gone, they'll have a trail to follow. Any of you who are with us, we'll see you on the bird. Good luck and God be with you all. It has been the highest honor of my own and Captain Weston's careers to lead you these past years. God-speed to those who choose to remain behind; maybe we'll meet again one day in another life or after this God-awful war is over…"

Having spoken their pieces, the captain and master sergeant shook each Raider's hand firmly. Then they donned their Kevlar helmets and strode toward the open ramp at the rear of the cargo plane.

✡ ✡ ✡ ✡ ✡

Captain Weston clutched tightly to the frame of the helicopter's open bay door. Powerful winds gusted against his face and legs hanging over the ledge. He watched all the smoke and smoldering wreckage blur past as the choppers roared towards the city center. This was the America he had fought for; this was the state of his homeland and nation, after all the fighting, all the killing, all the buried friends, and all their sacrifices...

"*Thirty seconds!*" the pilot called over the closed radio channel.

The captain's heart raced and pounded within him; sweat beaded on his brow under his operator's helmet, but his jaw was set and his gaze iron. He had passed his rifle off to one of his Marines; he wanted to have free hands to help his pregnant wife climb aboard when they touched down. The last contact he'd had with Kate was twenty hours ago by satellite phone when the team was still in Columbia. She had agreed to meet him at the park for emergency extraction, along with the survivors who were sheltering her.

Leaning further out of the open helicopter bay to improve his view, he spotted the throng of refugees. The choppers were coming in fast, still several hundred meters out, but he was certain he could see her. Daniel's heart thudded so fast he thought it might explode out of his chest. It had been six months since he'd last seen Kate in person or held her. He was also very aware of the great danger they were all currently in. They had to pick up the survivors hastily and then exfil as fast as possible. They could not risk being spotted by any Winter Steel forces or aircraft.

Suddenly there was a sound like clapping thunder; the captain's gaze snapped up and he saw two dozen rockets break the skyline and descend on the city. His worst nightmare had been realized. Time slowed to a crawl; his stomach flip-flopped with his heart, and his throat closed off. He could hardly breathe. He watched helplessly as several of the rockets struck burning business towers already on the verge of collapse. At least four others slammed directly into the park and engulfed the entire lake and group of survivors in an enormous fireball.

The concussive flames blasted out and the searing heat burned against his face. Daniel screamed for his wife—a guttural, primal agony seized him. His arm was still outstretched, still reaching for her, even as the explosions' residual blaze scorched him. The shockwaves rocked the helicopter hard, nearly knocking the aircraft out of the sky. One of Daniel's sergeants reached out to grab the team leader by the flak jacket to keep him from being ejected out the bay door.

Winter Steel jets rocketed across the skyline, firebombing the remaining city blocks below. As alarms blared around his head from the cockpit, Daniel fell back onto the steel deck of the helicopter. Reeling from utter shock, the once-impervious captain began to shake and weep uncontrollably.

"Get us the hell out of here!" one of his brawny sergeants barked to the pilots. The Marine looked down at his emotionally compromised team leader. It was startling, even jarring to see Captain Weston in this state. All over the planet, he had always been an absolute pillar under pressure, even in the worst gunfights and ambushes they had walked into. Now he was a broken man. The sergeant shook his C.O., trying to snap him out of it. "Sir, we have gotta get out of here now or we are all going to die! She's gone, sir! They're all dead down there; there's nobody left alive!"

The choppers banked steeply upward and careened sideways to change directions and escape the destruction below. The pilots feared being targeted by enemy fighters or anti-aircraft missiles at any moment. Daniel watched out the open bay as the blazing city flew past; all he could hear was the whirring of helicopter blades. Then, as tears streamed down his face, a strong arm wrapped around Daniel from behind. Master Sergeant Davis held his friend and brother tightly, trying to console him. All he could say was, "She's gone, Dan; she's gone." He repeated it over and over. "She's gone, buddy; she's gone. I'm sorry—I'm so, so sorry."

In a literal flash of light, his beautiful, beloved wife had been taken from him, along with their unborn daughter. He watched the world burning outside. It was the world's ending...but his world was already gone. He would forever live with the knowledge that had he left South America sooner, he might have saved her. He could have saved them both...

✶ ✶ ✶ ✶ ✶

Daniel stared darkly at the burnt soil, having finally recounted the story and relived it one more time. He looked up at the priest, and continued in a low tone, "Shortly after our failed attempt to save my wife and daughter, my team and I were surrounded and arrested by military police while refueling a helicopter. We made the choice not to shoot our way out of it; we could've escaped, but we weren't willing to kill other American soldiers to do it. Sadly, most of the team's families did not fare much better than my own. We had waited too long to act, and that will always be on us—trusting our families to a government that had grown bloated and corrupt.

"For six months we rotted in the mud of a detainee camp set up for captured enemy soldiers. We were interrogated by the C.I.A. and other military intelligence groups. They treated us like spies and double agents, like we hadn't spent the last ten years fighting for America and peace.

"Finally, when they convened our court martial hearings, I took full responsibility, hoping they'd lay the brunt of everything on me. Failure to comply with lawful orders, abandoning one's post, desertion in a time of war, grand larceny and misuse of government property, conspiracy to commit mutiny, and conduct unbecoming of an officer—those were my charges. Per my request, the presiding general sentenced me the hardest: eighteen years in a military prison, stripped of all rank, and a dishonorable discharge upon my release. That was my punishment."

"Yet here you stand, not in prison," Paolo observed.

"While my team and I were wasting away in that detainee camp, Mech-Tech finally assumed a complete and total takeover of the U.S. military in a final effort to stop the fighting and bring an end to the war. With their high-tech machines and advanced weaponry, they turned the tide and pushed our enemies back into the sea. This led to an eventual ceasefire until everyone could carve out their new, respective territories.

"The Last War literally ended the morning after my trial; word came down from the top that all deserters or draft dodgers were to be granted amnesty and pardoned. The brass had no choice but to release me; they discharged me as quickly as possible.

"Mech-Tech disbanded all U.S. military branches shortly thereafter and opted to form its own private security army. God-knows the liberals and hippies who flocked to Unity didn't want an aggressive, fighting force of elite warriors anymore. The old world had effectively been swept away; Unity and Mech-Tech were setting up mass defenses to guard their new borders. In spite of all the years of hardship and bloodshed, that was the end of the America we had all fought and died to protect."

Daniel fixed the priest with a cold stare. "You wanted the truth, Father? Here's the truth: my wife and daughter died...they burned to death in a Winter Steel rocket strike, and every night I watch them die over and over and over and over again. There's your truth." The veteran spat.

"And what does she say?" Paolo asked, unabated.

"What?!" the Marine growled.

"What does she say to you, Daniel, your wife? You know the moment I refer to, the one in the smoke and glow of flames, the one you relive every night, where you can see her speaking to you—what does she say?"

"I told you before, I don't know," Daniel responded flatly. "I can't ever hear, I just see her lips moving."

"What does she say?"

"I just told you I don't know!" Daniel shouted.

"Stop lying and tell the truth!" the priest commanded. "You can hear her; you've just refused to for all these years! Go to it now—that place in your heart and mind. You know the one I speak of, Daniel. Return to your pain. Return to that pain so great and deep that you fear it might swallow you up. That pain you fear you will not be able to control. Go back to that place and hear her at last. Let go and listen to your beloved wife; what does she say?"

Daniel felt haunted; frozen in time, standing there in

the tattered woods, sunlight filtering down through the shroud and remaining trees. Yet at the priest's direction, he saw her.

The smoke and flames swirled around him once more. He had returned to that world of shadowed veil...one last time...

She was waiting for him, his partner and best friend, his confidant and lover, his life-companion, beautiful wife, and mate, Kate. There she stood bearing their child in her womb. He gazed on her fearfully, expecting accusation, a harsh reproach or blame. After all, it was what he deserved for not being there when it had really counted, for not saving her in time...

But, to his astonishment, she smiled back at him lovingly. The unexpected kindness struck him like a powerful blow, weakening his knees. Still, he tried to speak to her through the haze. Tears brimmed at his eyes and started to flow down his soot-covered face. "I'm sorry, babe; I'm so sorry. I tried to get to you, to save you. I tried so hard...I left the battlefield, my unit, everything, but I was too late...I'm so sorry." He had begun to shake with grief now.

"I love you, Daniel," she said tenderly, warmly, genuinely, her eyes filled with the purest affection. "I know you did everything you could. You were always my hero, and I always believed in you. I knew you were coming for me, for us...When I saw the choppers I knew

it was you, that you'd come for me. And I knew you'd have come alone, through hell if you had to."

Daniel sank to his knees, ash billowing around him; he gritted his teeth and wept bitterly, his shoulders quaking uncontrollably. "I miss you; I miss you so much...I lost everything that day; I even lost my way."

Kate smiled through tears of her own. "That's not possible for my Daniel. The way has always been in front of you, one step in front of the other. You are not lost, Daniel, my love; you're exactly where you're supposed to be. But you have to let me go now, baby; you have to let me go."

"I don't know how." The warrior wept bitterly; his chest burned and ached from the anguish. "It wasn't fair. How could He take you from me? How could He take our child?! He took everyone from me!"

All at once she was there standing close to him. He pressed his tear-stained face against her thigh and shook with the crushing weight of loss. His tears wetted the leg of her jeans. "I know," she consoled. "It wasn't fair, but I want you to know I'm safe—we're both safe. And we'll see each other again. I can't wait." Kate smiled and laughed through the tears. "It'll be all right, you'll see." Her hope and warmth were intoxicating and unwavering.

"I don't know how to keep going," Daniel uttered in defeat. "I'm so tired, babe, so tired..."

"I know, but you have people who need you right now and people who will continue to need you along your journey. Don't be afraid." There was a pause, and she caressed his head lovingly. Then she inhaled deeply, resting one hand on her pregnant belly. "Now, Daniel, you have to let us go; you have to go back. We'll always be with you. I promise."

In the dim light of the cloaked and glowing flames, Daniel picked himself up and wrapped his wife up in his arms.

"Mmm," she cooed, melting into his embrace. "I've missed you so much! Missed these arms."

She gazed up at him, her eyes sparkling like the glitter of sapphire in the midnight sky. "I love you, Daniel." She leaned up to kiss him gently.

The moment her lips touched his, it was as if a million shared moments and precious memories surged through his senses. They were slow dancing on their wedding night, cuddling on a radiant beach in the South Pacific, he was tickling and playfully pinning her to the bed. There were laughs and smiles, slow kisses, contented sighs, and quiet conversations. Their breaths synched in rhythmic harmony under the stars as they held hands. He saw her adoring eyes staring up at him. She knew she was safe and loved with him, cherished beyond measure. He saw the night they found out she was pregnant, and he watched himself tenderly kiss her stomach as she rested on the couch, her fingers in his hair.

And then she was gone and all he was left with was the fading whisper of her voice in his ears. "I love you, my Daniel; don't be afraid."

There in the forest, surrounded by his closest friends, the seemingly invulnerable warrior had finally come to the end of himself; he had faced his ghosts. His knees pressed into the soft dirt, and he shook and wept inconsolably.

From nowhere, Father Paolo laid his hands upon the Marine's shoulders and breathed quietly. "Daniel Weston, I bless you in the name of the Lord Jesus Christ. You are kind and compassionate, bold and courageous, a guide and protector to your people. May God in Heaven cause you to forget the agony, shame, suffering, and humiliation of your past. May He cause you to be fruitful moving forward into the future He has for you. You are my beloved son, and in you I take great delight."

The warrior only cried more heavily at these words. He had finally released the floodgates, and all the years of his bottled regrets and pain were pouring forth. As he cleansed his soul there in the woods, it was as if he were surrounded by guardian angels: Paolo, Raoul, Jonas and Janae, Ava, Mary, and even Beth had each quietly arrived to bear witness to the veteran's anguish and his first tears of healing.

All those who had walked with and beside him for the past two and a half years, challenging him, loving him, forgiving him, laughing with him, learning from him, trusting and valuing him, relying upon him—they were his family now, and their presence had combined to serve as something even greater: a catalyst for his restoration...

CHAPTER TWELVE

The final members of the community climbed a distant hill with their once-peaceful home behind them. Daniel, Jonas, Janae, Raoul, Father Paolo, Muhsen, Ava, Beth, and Abby had all chosen to remain behind the main flight of refugees. They had opted to stay with and guard Dr. Ellenson while she completed surgeries on the young Enforcer and Quintessa Ali. Now the beleaguered remnant helped to carry the two unconscious patients up the mount on stretchers.

As they struggled up the rough terrain, a colossal blast of radiant energy poured down from the heavens. The brilliant pulsing pillar of violet measured fifty meters across and disappeared up into the clouds above. The weapon consumed and vaporized all life in the once-settled glade, turning everything in the meadow below to molten glass. The weary sojourners felt the blast of heat on their backs as they fought their way up the steep slope. No one had the heart to turn back and witness the awesome destruction of their once-tranquil home.

Unity had employed one of its massive energy weapons in orbit above the Earth's atmosphere to unleash this final act of devastation. With no true war to fight any longer, it reserved the use of such fury for its most despised adversaries—those who defied the will of the Presiding Council and the Blue Chip. The community had earned this unfettered hatred and wrath; their resistance had bruised the superpower's boundless ego, so they would be destroyed, completely and utterly. Not even a trace would be left of the peasant rabble who had dared to fight back, if only for a few short hours. Unity's sovereign reign of absolute dominion and power would spread, and no one who challenged her would ever live to tell of it.

The stretcher bearers guided the line of beaten and homeless defenders upward, with Daniel and Father Paolo bringing up the rear. They would rendezvous with the rest of the community's remnant by nightfall, and from there determine their next move. The task of scouting a new home lay before them. They had to find a hidden sanctuary to rest a safe distance from the burning glade behind them. It might require walking a hundred miles by foot in the coming days. One thing was certain, though, Unity patrols and aircraft would be sweeping the surrounding hill country for weeks to come, scanning for any trace of the escaped criminals.

Dr. Ellenson had managed to clean and dress Father Paolo's wounds before they hurriedly fled their destroyed settlement. He was still feeling the sharp, burning pain but slowly continued to ascend the steep hillside with the others. During a momentary break he caught his breath and glanced up at Daniel. "I think it is time; this is a good place."

Daniel said nothing in response, but he and the priest exchanged a knowing look that the others did not understand. The weary band had halted to rest for a moment, waiting for their injured elder.

"Time for what?" Jonas asked abruptly. He did not care for being kept out of the loop nor Paolo's current demeanor.

A long quiet fell over the bruised and drained party. The priest took one more look at the Marine who had become like a son to him. A burdensome sigh escaped his lips before he turned to address the others. His eyes revealed both sadness and resolve. "Daniel will not be coming with us to our new home. He will not be continuing on with us."

Immediate shock and disbelief broke over every face. "Dan, what's he talking about?!" Jonas demanded heatedly. "You're comin' with us! Why wouldn't you?!"

Daniel glanced up at his friend; their eyes met and Jonas realized there was no mistake or practical joke here.

"Dan, You're coming with us!" the Ranger announced stubbornly. "That's not up for debate!"

"Jonas," Daniel began quietly, a twinge of lament in his voice. "I killed a man in cold-blood. And I was not honest about my past. I lied...I broke the rules and trust of the community, and there's a cost to everything."

"Nah, nah, nah," Jonas said, pushing back. "So what! What, you talkin' about? Jamal?! He got what he had coming, Dan! You and I both know that! That son of a bitch got exactly what he deserved! So what, so you messed up, we forgive you. The father here will pardon you, isn't that how it works? God forgives and we forgive too!"

Daniel was shaking his head. "That's not how it's gonna be this time, Jonas. I crossed a line, and I have to own the consequences. If I stay, I undermine the very fabric of the community, everything we've worked to build. There can't be a double standard for me; I won't tear the people apart in a divide."

"Well then I'm coming with you!" Jonas asserted. "You're not going out there alone! What, you gonna go out there by yourself to die or get captured? Not on my watch!"

The former captain stared sadly at his friend. "No, Jonas, you have a family, and you have to stay here. Protect the others; they will need you now more than ever. They will need a Ranger."

Jonas was starting to shake he was so furious.

Father Paolo spoke next. "Daniel will not be going alone. Raoul has decided to also venture out from our fold and journey with him. He intends to search the lonely lands for his people who may still remain."

It was here that Abby Jenson cut in as well. "I'm coming with you," she stated resolutely. Daniel was about to flatly refuse, but the eighteen-year-old continued, "You saved my life once; I won't let you go out there and die alone. A life for a life; you can't stop me. I'll follow you no matter what you say."

Daniel did not approve of this idea, even if the girl had admittedly come a long way since the day roving thugs abducted her. She bore the look of a fighter now; there was a fire in her eyes and a fierceness in her jaw. Nevertheless, Daniel feared for her safety if she roamed out into the wilds with him and Raoul. She would be an immediate target from *many* threats.

"So this is it then?" Jonas asked. "You're really leaving us. Can he ever come back?" the Ranger asked Paolo. "How long does he have to stay out there?"

The priest met Jonas' irritated gaze. "We do not set a time limit on his exile. I have told Daniel that he can return only when he is able to see God's Divine Image and priceless mark in all people, even those who behave spitefully towards him. For Daniel to complete his task, he will have to travel to the lands of all the superpowers and their enslaved territories. He must witness the depths humanity has fallen to-in even the most inhospitable corners of the earth, and he must find compassion, pity, and love in his soul for all of them. Only then can he return to us."

Jonas had to turn away; he was so exasperated by the lunacy of it all, the sheer insanity of such a vague and abstract proposal. He was on the verge of laughing out loud or outright lambasting the priest.

"Jonas," Paolo remarked gently. "I am old and now injured. How many more winters do you suppose I have left with you all? And now Fernando is gone. The community will need a leader one day, and Daniel is not ready for the task. He may be able to physically protect people, but that is only one small part of being a shepherd and spiritual guide to people. He must be made ready, and he is not yet. I trust that if the Lord should bring him back to us, he will be a different man and perhaps ready to lead when I and others have gone."

Jonas shook his head in frustration. "What do you mean he's not ready to lead? In case you forgot, Dan led Spec-Ops Marines during the ugliest war in human history! And how's he supposed to find us again,

Father?! You really think he's gonna come back to us? You're sending him on a suicide mission! This is insane! You're insane!"

The priest did not react to the Ranger's insult and defensiveness. "I understand that Daniel is an excellent tracker, Jonas. I am certain when the time comes, he will be able to find his way back home."

"Jonas," Daniel intervened, watching his friend struggle. "It's okay; it'll all be all right. I borrowed time in a good place; I don't mind paying for it. Stay with the people. They will need you."

Janae was the first to accept the reality of what was going to happen. She came forward and hugged Daniel, tears in her eyes. She held the Marine tightly. "Be safe out there, Daniel, you hear? Ellie will expect to see her uncle again." The black woman smiled warmly, kissed him lightly on the cheek, and then backed away.

Ava approached next and embraced the man who had grown to be a mentor, friend, and brother. "Take care of yourself," she whispered, her eyes full of a grit and resolve but also fear for him. "I won't be far behind you," she told him quietly. "You're not the only one whose time has run out here."

Daniel looked at her with mounting concern; in his heart he knew what she was planning. The Latina woman and former soldier had the look of someone headed out on a path to war, and nothing would stop her. She was going for blood and she would find it; God-knew Daniel wouldn't try to dissuade her from it.

Jonas was the last to bid his brother farewell. He was not skilled at goodbyes and labored valiantly to put his emotions in check. Daniel came to him instead; he pulled his friend into a tight embrace, and they firmly clapped each other on the shoulder several times. Both felt the overpowering surge of sentiment but were unwilling to cry in front of the other.

"I always knew you Rangers were a weepy bunch," Daniel jabbed.

"Shut your mouth, jarhead!" Jonas shoved him, trying to wipe away the misty evidence.

"I love you, man," Daniel said earnestly. "I'll never forget you; never forget all the kindness you and Janae showed me."

The Ranger was losing control over his emotions. "I love you too, brother," he echoed, not able to make full eye contact. "You take care of yourself out there, promise?"

Daniel nodded; he extended a sturdy handshake and the Ranger took it. "I respect the hell out of you, Jonas, and I always will."

The former Army staff sergeant met the Marine's gaze. "Dito, if there was ever a man I'd want standing next to me at the end of the world, it'd be Captain Dan Weston. Who'd have thought, right? Who'd have thought…" The two hugged forcefully one last time, then there was nothing left but to take the first step.

Father Paolo walked with Daniel a short distance away from the others. "You are my son, Daniel, and you always will be," the priest affirmed with sober conviction. "May God go with you and protect you. May He send friends and allies, brothers and sisters, to watch over and rescue you when you fall into danger. Come back to us when your time is finished. I would like to see you again before I die; I would like to meet the man He shapes you into."

Daniel nodded quietly and stared at the uneven ground. The priest patted him lightly on the shoulder, and the Marine looked back up to smile. "Goodbye, Father, I hope you find safe harbor. Thank you for everything; sorry I was such a headache for you the past two years."

"I will only ever think of our times and talks with the utmost fondness," the old priest assured him.

Daniel nodded solemnly. Abby had slung her rifle and pulled the hood of a dark cloak up over her head; Raoul was ready to depart as well. The Marine embraced the priest gently then turned to leave. They would descend back down the summit they had just climbed, but in a direction pointed safely away from the smoldering crater where home had once rested.

Daniel looked back at his friends one last time and

caught Beth's gaze. No words were spoken, but there was a shared look of forlorn resignation. The expression held both yearning and restrained desire. It was a look that lamented: *"I'm sorry; maybe in another life..."* Then the warrior and his two companions departed back down to the valley and beyond.

And his friends were left to watch the trio vanish into the forest below and remember happier times...

EPILOGUE

The Marine warrior, the Native elder and hunter, and their younger companion all stood upon the brow of a grassy knoll. They remained close to the cover and concealment of the dark trees behind them. It was dusk, and the gray sky was dimming rapidly as they surveyed the wide open plains before them. In the distance, they could see the soft glow of twinkling lights in a Unity city. The settlement appeared so peaceful from their quiet vantage point across the miles of open country.

"How do you intend to start this journey?" Raoul inquired with a stoic yet legitimate curiosity.

"I'm still figuring that out," Daniel admitted. "But I know we'll have to head that way sooner or later."

* * * * *

Later that night, Raoul and Daniel sat cross-legged and reclined beside a humble campfire to warm themselves. Abby had already fallen asleep, curled up on her unfurled bedroll, her loaded rifle lying immediately beside her.

"What was that thing Paolo used to say when we'd all watch the stars in the evening?" the warrior inquired, a pipe smoking between his lips. He looked to Raoul, watching the shadows dance on the Lakota's face.

Raoul turned his gaze upward to take in the stars, which had finally revealed themselves in the night sky above. He drew in a deep inhale, then lowered his eyes back to the flames. "I believe it was a quote." He observed solemnly.

"Do you remember it?" Daniel prodded.

The Sioux man continued to stare into the elegant dance of fire, ember, and radiant coals. "How do you measure a life? In only what good they did? In only what evils they committed? In only what love they held, or in what love cherished them? In possessions or power? In influence or renown? In skill and strength, or weakness and frailty? In courage, bravery, and sacrifice, or in cowardice and fear? In generosity and kindness, or acts of violence and hate? In what was known of them, or what was hidden? In only triumphs, or in efforts too? In successes alone, or also intention?

"We will all fall naked in the presence of pure love and goodness one day, laid bare by our own imperfections, selfishness, wasted time, and petty grudges...

"We will all weep at our desperate need for an eternal love, expansive enough to reach across the cosmos and save us from ourselves. And we will weep at the blanket of undeserved acceptance which the light extends and wraps us in.

"So let us be slow to pass judgment and quick to give mercy. Let us pray for mercy, both for ourselves and for others. Turn from selfishness and vengeance; forgive and do good in the land where you have been placed. We are all children of one loving Maker, and one day we will all return to the source—the place from which we came—that place we must all return. So be ready; make yourself ready. Purify yourselves and fill your minds with joy and gratitude. Fill your hearts with courage and strength—endurance for the road of hardships ahead. Give thanks for those most precious to you and for all the true gifts the Maker offers each day."

ACKNOWLEDGEMENTS

Special thanks to:

Richard Rohr, W.P. Young, Donald Miller, and Henri Nouwen for their own inspirational works and thoughts towards a transformative view of the human race and gospel.

To Seth Elliott, Zach Elliott, and Sean Flannery for hundreds of profound conversations towards an ever-expanding vision of real life, love, and community. The good work of the Hillside Inn Ministry will forever remain an influence on my life.

To my dear friends Bekkah, Sheila, and Sarah, who believed in my writing, and voluntarily gave up precious hours to provide helpful feedback for this book.

And to God who is ever present, even in times of darkness, turmoil, and silence. You are the very essence of hope, courage, and enduring love.

ABOUT THE AUTHOR

A native of the Pacific Northwest, Brennan Silver is a combat veteran of Iraq and Afghanistan who served as a sergeant in the United States Marine Corps. He returned home from overseas conflicts in late 2010 to find himself forever changed. Today, Brennan works in the field of mental health and counseling and holds a deep passion to see fellow warriors find peace and purpose in their lives after war.

For more information, please visit:
www.BrennanSilver.com